A HOSPITAL

in the

CLOUDS

Mhairead
MacLeod

For Seonaid Ellen
child of the rainforest

AUTHOR'S NOTE

A Hospital in the Clouds takes place in the 1920s in tropical Australia and was inspired by two women, one of whom remains anonymous to this day. She was a suffragette in Edinburgh, Scotland, who made a daring stand against the male-dominated bastions of that time. The other was a nurse who established one of the first private hospitals in the frontier town of Cairns. The story covers true events in Australia, particularly the Far North.

PREFACE

Out here I call myself Anna, a name similar to my own but not so much that it provides a clue that could arouse suspicion. Writing about everything that happened is difficult. This is partly because I come from a family that has made an artform of being circumspect. But it is much more because I've had to keep secrets for so long. In any case, I'll try to be as honest as possible in setting the record straight. After all, the pursuit of peace is everything to me now.

PART ONE

1918 – 1920

1

When I saw Tom Austen that March morning of 1918, I knew there was something about him I recognised, something shared. It was in his expression as he let me dress his foot, rotten and black around stumps of cartilage where his toes had been surgically removed. He held in the pain, hissing through clenched teeth.

I drew the screen and squeezed a fresh cloth into a warm basin of water. 'Here, Lieutenant Austen, I'll help you off with your things.'

His shirt was damp with sweat, his pants soaked with urine.

'Do you need to use the bedpan?'

'Too late.'

As I pulled off his pyjamas his hand went to cover his crotch.

'You should be used to this by now,' I said, handing him a towel.

I wiped his face, the fair chin stubble uneven from alopecia, then massaged the washer gently down his chest, across red shrapnel scars and under his arms.

'I was quite a hairy bugger until the war,' he said.

'Why didn't you stay in England until your recovery?'

'Must have been homesick. And Australian nurses are much prettier.'

We'd heard that old line from the soldiers many times, as if they were determined to assure us they were still virile men inside those broken bodies. We nurses usually played along – it was our job to heal, after all. But it was more than a job, more than just providing moral support and sympathy. We were part of their new family, we sisters who cared for them day and night. But the men we tended in the Injured Veterans' Ward of the Cairns District Hospital were only a few of the hundreds who'd been shipped up to regional centres. It made room down south for the newly-arrived from Passchendaele, Pozières, Villers-Brettoneux, Lagnicourt – exotic names these men had no trouble pronouncing.

'How lucky am I, eh? Shelled with phosgene. Didn't realise what was happening. Thought I'd landed back home in a vat of newly picked corn – that's what it smelt like. Didn't feel it at first, then couldn't breathe for the life of me. Crawled around, found my gas mask. Got patched up and sent back. Took another hiding from Fritz. Now this bloody trench foot.'

He made his butchering sound like a jaunty boy's adventure, but I knew the truth. One night when the other men were asleep, I had found him, drawn back into that dark underworld, his body curled into a tight ball, his shoulders shaking.

A fly crawled over the bed, attracted by the rot that even disinfectant swabs couldn't wash out. I flicked it away. 'Your lungs are healing, Lieutenant. Our tropical weather will help. And you *will* get better, you hear?' There was a liver-coloured wound at his neck, fading into scar tissue. At first, I suspected shrapnel damage, but when I looked closer, it resembled the more rounded scar of a bullet. 'How did you get that?'

He propped himself up on one elbow and looked at me. 'I can see what you're thinking. So, don't say it.'

'Say what?'

'That I'm really quite a *lucky* chap.'

'I wasn't going to.'

'Then you'd be the first. That's the platitude they come up with.' He coughed, and the pain from his burned lungs made him slump back as he squeezed his eyes tight, shutting everything out. 'Bloody carbolic floors,' he said.

It was supposed to be a quick wipe down before I changed the basin and cloths for the next patient, but I slowed the process a little, the water wringing and splashing, sponging and soothing the pale landscape of violence. I patted dry the tattooed profile on his bicep. 'She's a pretty one. With her dark blue hair flying around.'

'On leave with the battalion when I had that done. Got myself blotto. Didn't have a girl to write home to, so I thought I'd carry one in my arms.' He gave a chuckle then coughed again. 'It's just not the sort of thing… an *officer* is supposed to do. Is it, nurse?'

I guessed a warning about STDs would embarrass him, especially from someone his own age, and he'd probably have heard the standard lecture many times. Instead, I said with a smile, 'You'd know how to set a good example, then.'

'I'm the least qualified in the world to do that.'

'Sounds like false modesty to me.'

'No. Hard to explain – and if I tried, it would probably be bulldust.'

'What's with all the chit chat?' The Sergeant, as they called him, just a shadow on the bed behind the calico screen, had been dismembered by shellfire – his left leg torn off and his right arm amputated at the elbow. The weight of tissue and bone was now replaced with leaden discontent. He had a nose for weakness and thought he sensed this in Austen, who even here remained his military superior.

'I'll be with you soon, sergeant.'

Austen ignored him. 'You don't usually do this, the washing, do you?'

'Some junior nurses are down with something.'

'Anyway, you're my favourite Scottish nurse.'

'Is it that obvious? Well, I consider myself Australian now, just like you, serving the glorious British Empire.' I immediately regretted the sarcasm, but he didn't react. 'Matron Chalmers will give it to me if we keep talking.'

'*Charmers*, we call her in this ward.'

'That's a bit sarcastic.'

'Obvious reasons, don't you think?'

But he'd obviously charmed *her*. On the shelf behind his bed were photos of the Bastille and a roughly drawn portrait of a young girl. Pictures, or anything else which might encourage clutter and germs were not usually allowed.

'Nurse Anna, isn't it?' he asked.

'You can call me Sister Sinclair.'

I was one of the newly certified junior sisters. At Brisbane city's General Hospital, I'd been a pupil nurse, staff, and charge nurse. I'd done my rota in surgical as the 'dirty' nurse, cleaning blood off the walls and floor in the operating theatre, counting used swabs and gloves, brushing out the tracheostomy tubes with a feather, sterilising the forceps, clamps, saws and scissors in spitting, boiling water. The hospital culture was one that suited me – the busyness of it gave me a sense of belonging, of community; the work was therapeutic, even addictive.

'Well, you can call me Tom,' he said.

After the patients were washed and changed and The Sergeant's underarm rash treated with salve, I went back to Tom, and took him out to the veranda in the wicker wheelchair. In the breezeless air, the humidity stuck to my skin like a fever.

'It's sure as hell getting dark out here.' He pointed to the sky clouding over the sea.

The Sergeant craned over his crutch: 'A storm must be coming. Look at those boats.'

Yachts and smaller vessels pitched over the agitated waves as they made towards the river inlet and the protection of the mangrove trees.

'With a bit of luck, it'll blow all the officers away,' I said.

Tom responded, clutching his chest. 'Aw. That went right through me.' There was no weeping in daylight.

I went back to the ward and helped Sybil turn the beds and retrieve the bedpans.

'Well, well! Look who's flirting with you,' she said as we changed the sheets. 'But you can't have him,' she said, laughing. 'The lieutenant is mine!'

'He's just bunging it on. He doesn't mean anything by it.'

'He's been asking questions about you.'

'I hope you didn't tell him too much.'

'Nah. Only that you're a widow and from Edinburgh.'

Three years and it still felt strange, being called 'widow'. I should be surrounded by lace doilies, cats, and grandchildren. Sometimes, rolling a patient over, when that familiar twinge in my lower spine came, I felt like one. I'd counted the number of times in a typical shift that I'd have to do this – about fifty – twice my age.

We were interrupted by Matron running from her office. 'Get the patients inside and windows blocked. Now! Telegraph's come. It's confirmed. Cyclone's going to hit.'

The sky, the sea, the wind had all been so calm that it took us by surprise.

'Matron, may I use the telephone?'

'No – it's not for personal calls, Sister Sinclair. Get that cart down to the laundry.' She was the old breed; dedicated to and intent on keeping the respectability hard-earned by Nightingale. Thick-waisted and solid, Matron Alice Chalmers would forge through the hospital, her quick arms thrusting a path before her, as if her critical guidance was required everywhere at once. We were her substitute family – she, assisted by Deputy Matron Verity Timms who had returned from the Front, was the mother; the Medical Superintendent the father; the staff nurses and sisters her daughters. Even the hospital motto could have been distilled from her essence: Honor et Servitas.

Downstairs, the entrance was being latched and blocked. There was nowhere for a building full of sick people to hide. The sea began to swell and simmer; trees on the esplanade tossed their leaves like great grey creatures shaking off water, dropping branches onto the sand. People had deserted the shore. Papers, odd objects were flicked up and skittered down the street. In upstairs wards, the orderlies and patients who were mobile helped take everything in from the veranda and block the windows with stripped beds and mattresses.

'Don't you worry,' I reassured a soldier with bandaged eyes. 'This building isn't going anywhere. It's solid brick.' I did not mention the hospital in Townsville. In the last cyclone it had been blown into a pile of rubble.

The storm stripped roofs and felled large trees, hosing the evening blues out of the sea and sky, smashing the ocean against the foreshore. It crashed into everyone's lives, pushing hard rain through doors which shook on their hinges. Our non-infectious patients were forced into two crowded rooms – women, children and veterans ordered to their beds while we waited for the scream and roar of that black evening to stop.

'Bloody hell!' someone shouted. 'We're going to lose the roof.'

Evie, almost four, would be huddled and confused in our rented room on the esplanade with Dorrie, our landlady. They'd be terrified, the walls sucked in by the pressure. So much of this town was temporary, sheet-iron houses collapsing into clay, as if it still hadn't the nerve to put down foundations.

As I walked downstairs, I saw Deputy Matron Timms on her knees and pressed up against the front door, her hand frozen on the handle. Her expression was fixed, terrified.

'Deputy Matron… Verity… it's all right. Leave it.' I took her hand away.

She snatched it back. 'We all have to get out now!'

I held her firmly. 'This will blow over. You're having a panic attack. Remember to breathe. I'm with you.'

When she had calmed, she said, 'It's like the gunfire. That was so silly of me. I've never done that before. Please don't tell Matron.'

'Of course not.'

When we returned to the wards, the sound of timber squealed against the corrugated roof. Tom crawled under his bed. He and Timms were still fighting the same war.

I knelt on the floor. 'You're safe in here, Lieutenant Austen. Nothing will get you.' I wished I fully believed it.

'He's a sodding coward,' The Sergeant said. 'Officers got off lightly,' he pronounced within earshot of Tom.

'It's just a touch of nerves,' I replied. It was clear that Tom shouldn't have been transferred from the city where there was some form of treatment for shell shock, even if only experimental at this stage.

'Can't you give the bugger something to shut him up? Between him and this bloody wind, I'm going crazy myself.'

I lay on the floor and began a lullaby I used to sing to Evie – the lyrics nonsensical – until Tom settled into a sob.

It was too much for The Sergeant. 'The British army would put a bullet in his head if they got hold of him.'

I massaged Tom's neck, my cuff catching in his hair. 'We'll look after you.'

He bit the fabric of my sleeve as if trying to swallow a scream.

There was a bottle of *P. Opii* pills in the dispensary. Just one would be all that was needed. I thought about dashing down to get it while it was unguarded, with everyone fixed to their allotted places by the storm. I could risk giving him a dose without prescription and I knew where 'Major Matron' kept the key.

Instead, I whispered, 'Shh. You're safe now. You're with friends. You are a *man*, a *brave* man.'

Tom Austen, and countless other brave men, like Andy, my husband. Did he cry when he was sliced in half by Ottoman fire? Did he feel that terror? They said it was quick – but they always do. When his ship pulled away from the wharf, the waving soldiers packed together, the horn blasting with pride, I couldn't feel it, I couldn't register the words around me: 'so *brave*,' and, 'it won't be long before your husband is back.' I knew this war was a disastrous, foolish thing, and I wasn't the only one.

Anger was my defence. It had never really left. I'd read about the votes against conscription, the anti-war rallies, and I joined the Women's Peace Army, with its paradoxical name. We were condemned for being a Marxist confederacy of weaklings and traitors; even our own soldiers tormented us. But I needed that sense of release, I needed to regain that feeling that I could change everything. I marched under the purple, green and white flag and handed out pamphlets in the streets, gaining comfort in the sense of déjà vu. We sang *I Didn't Raise My Boy to Be a Soldier* under threat of being arrested for doing so. A year later I had to face the Women's Compulsory Service Conscription League and became embroiled in a home-front battle of our own. It was described as a 'catfight' by the press, but it was more than that for me. I was standing beside Margaret Thorp when we were set upon. At first, I was just an observer of the fury around us, the invective, remembering things I'd previously tried to forget. Then a woman came at me like a crazed bear, pulling my hair and scratching at my eyes. I found myself fighting back and punched her in the cheek with such force my knuckles split. As the police marched us away, the beaten militants, I whispered to Margaret, 'Is it violence for peace, now?' She gave me a tired smile.

'What on earth are you doing, Sister?' Matron materialised behind me in her rubber soles.

'It's just an episode of neurasthenia. He seems to have it together now.'

'That's for a *doctor* to diagnose. You know the rules. Next time, you see me and we'll give him something to settle him down. If he starts this again, we'll have to send him back to Brisbane.'

'Perhaps that's for the best.'

'Once again, that's not for you to say, Sister. You keep forgetting your place.'

I helped him back onto the bed with difficulty. He spoke some peculiar words that sounded like German. He seemed unaware of me, his teeth chattering. When I lay him down, he reached up and clutched at my throat. Matron helped me prise away the hand which had already ripped out my collar button.

'He's gone mad,' she said with a sigh and picked up her lamp. The darkness under her eyes, the thin hair of her widow's peak, were prominent under the light.

△ △ △

A few of the mobile patients went to the window to peer through mattresses and I herded them back to their spots. In the vacuum of the storm's eye, the sky directly above was suddenly clear and bright with a smattering of stars.

Outside, eerie objects lay strewn in the oppressive quiet – sheet-iron wrapped around tree trunks, mangled things with wheels, bicycles and a wheelbarrow. A couple of men were trying their luck, swinging lanterns among the debris, looking for salvageable items. I could easily run home to my daughter in this lull. My eleven-hour shift had ended hours before, and it was only a few blocks away – our flimsy shore-front home with its knocked-together wooden walls and tinplate roof.

There was a stupendous *boom* and the ground rumbled. In that moment of shock, I was back on a dark hill in Edinburgh, running down through the long grass, breathless, forcing myself forward, heart burning, ears ringing. But it was only an ancient fig tree that had fallen just short of the hospital, roots so sodden the massive thing could no longer support itself. Suddenly, the ocean edge formed into towering walls, white breaking into brown against the trees across the dirt road, bulldozing large branches before it. Surely Dorrie had had the good sense to get Evie out of our cabinet room downstairs before the ocean scrambled in. The sea-line was the same distance from the house as the hospital, but here we were saved by the security of cement and brick.

As the wave hit, another fossicker, a woman, was snatched away like an after-thought. The dot of her head appeared above the foam, sticklike arms rigid in the air. I called out, but she was whisked away and dissolved into the ocean. It could almost have been a hallucination. The longer I looked at the moonlit sea where she had been, the more I convinced myself I was just fatigued and it was only a log. But Matron had seen it too and shook her head at me in warning. Those broken by the cyclone would be tomorrow's reckoning for the staff. I felt numb with the thought of it.

The edge of the eye passed, followed by an anticlockwise frenzy. The building thumped and banged on the opposite side and the hall filled with the din of windows splintering. Before I'd left for work that morning, Evie had told me firmly that she wanted to go home to Brisbane. I'd thought about it: going back, leaving the swamps to the mosquitoes. Back to where Andy and I had lived before he marched away, convinced he'd return in a few months with a trophy enemy flag.

2

As soon as light broke and the sea receded, we took down the mattresses and returned everyone to their wards; shattered glass was swept away, and empty window-frames boarded up. My day shift was due to start in a few hours.

I made my way home, white stockings mud-coloured, scanning the sea and shore for a body or part of one. I stumbled along the flooded road, avoiding loamy pools, climbing over debris, cutting my leg.

When I arrived at the house, I saw the roof was intact. The walls of our room underneath were damp to waist height and the door was blocked by wave-washed mud and debris. It was one of three rented rooms downstairs, cheaply built and squashed together. I looked through our small window, but it was too dark to see inside. Normally it gave a view out to the foreshore where we would see trees and the ocean glittering like an animated postcard.

As Dorrie let me in upstairs there was a last bang on the roof from a falling branch. Evie was sitting on the floor in the narrow strip of a hall between the bedrooms and the dining room.

'This was the safest place,' Dorrie said. 'She won't leave it. Neither will the dogs. I settled her down with some Easton's Syrup.'

I checked Evie's eyes and breathing. The syrup contained strychnine.

'No need to worry. I was very careful with the child.' Dorrie was an incongruous guardian angel, with her gruff voice, and her hair, once ginger and now bright bottle-red, covered in a net and curling pins as if she expected new guests to arrive in the morning. Dorrie had told me in a believing way that her property and income were built on three decades of earnings as a barmaid, but later admitted there had been a generous gift from a friend, who must remain anonymous. There were also her current rental arrangements with overnight guests. Most of Dorrie's tenants were 'fly-by-nighters' – men looking for work in the mines or cane fields, women without husbands or escaping them, she told me. But when I was awake before daybreak, it was furtive couples that I saw, closing their door quietly, giving their final kiss at the gate. I was only slightly annoyed by the bumps and cries they made during spells of passionate athleticism. If I'd had no child, I'd be sharing the nurses' quarters and life would be simpler – but while I was saving as much of my wages as I could, I had no other option.

It was Dorrie who suggested she look after Evie while I was at work – provided my daughter earn her keep, which consisted of compulsory daily playtime with Dorrie's spoiled fox-terriers.

'You're not going downstairs, surely?' Dorrie said. 'I've no idea how much mud is in your room, yet.'

'I have to get our things.'

'No need, love. I took up your suitcases and Evie has her clothes and dolls. You just settle up here for a while.' She went off into her bedroom and returned with a silk scarf and a candlewick dressing-gown sprinkled with French perfume. 'Here, use the scarf for your leg.'

'Are you sure?'

'Yes, go on. I can't get into the bathroom for bandages, there's glass everywhere. Anyway,' she waved her hand theatrically, 'I've no need for silk scarves. At my age, nothing can improve me. Gotta accept I've now reached the pinnacle of my beauty.' She laughed and nodded at Evie. 'Not to worry, eh, girl? This place has seen a few cyclones – the house shakes like a clump of grass but gives with the wind like it's supposed to.'

'I'm never working on a weekend again.' It was wishful thinking.

'Cyclones don't just come on weekends, love. We'll have to start cleaning up soon, once it's properly light. I know, let's play Snap!' She went off to get a pack of cards from the dining room bureau. The house shuddered slightly, as if settling.

With our skirts hitched, Dorrie and I cleared away stray buoys, flotsam, and foamy residue from around the house. My room underneath had the woody feel of a gypsy caravan, with bright checked curtains and two cramped single beds which doubled as sofas. I swept the mud out and scrubbed the plywood walls with eucalyptus oil, smothering the fungal growth which had already mottled during the monsoon.

Upstairs, getting ready for work, I heard a male voice outside.

'And what's your name?'

The tone had a no-nonsense energy and was unmistakably American.

'Evie. But my real name is Evelyn.' She was in the cane chair cuddling her china-faced doll.

'Well, aloha, Evelyn-otherwise-known-as-Evie. My name is Leon. *My* real name is Leonid. It means *lion*.'

'You don't look like a lion.' The never-talking-back-to-strangers rule had been forgotten.

From the deck I saw a man next door on his veranda, wearing a yellow shirt and smoking a cigar. He looked vaguely threatening with an unshaven chin and powerful arms.

'Oh, I didn't see you there,' he said, when I stepped into view. 'How do you do, Mrs...?'

'Sinclair... I thought that house was vacant.'

'I arrived only a few days ago.'

'Anna, meet Leon Roberts. Just bought next door,' Dorrie said, throwing flotsam onto a pile. 'Hey, Leon, I wouldn't mind some help down here.'

'No problem, Ma'am.' He tipped an imaginary cap. 'When this critter is done with me.' He showed his burning cigar. 'Gotta clear up my own patch too.' He got to his feet and leaned on the balcony. 'That was some hurricane, wasn't it? Quite a welcome to North Queensland.' He gestured towards the sea, and the plume of cigar smoke broke into cloudy dots and dashes.

'I was scared,' Evie agreed. 'Mater, too.'

'I think you mean *Mum*, sweetheart.'

She'd picked up this irritating word from Matilda, Andy's maiden sister, just when she was learning to talk. She reserved it, as did Matilda, for company she was trying to impress. It had always been 'Mater' when my Edinburgh college friends blamed their mothers for some slight or other, and my own mother had insisted on being addressed that way – it maintained that respectable distance between parent and child natural to her class. It reminded me too much of the person I once was, of what I had done, and that version of me had to remain safely locked in the past. Besides, in this frontier outpost where life came at you in extremes, where accidents and death unravelled in unlaced country, it was even more pretentious.

Roberts stared at my white uniform, starched so stiffly that the cloth would crackle when I bent my arms. 'You obviously have important work to do?'

'It's time for me to get going,' I said, adjusting my badge.

'I hope there won't be too many injured.' He stubbed out his cigar. 'I must also go – help clear up the muck. We're lucky that's all we have to do.'

'You're not allowed to look into our backyard today,' Evie said to him. 'I can't say why.'

'Oh, I know,' Roberts said, smiling. 'The dunny with no door.'

3

'Bloody hell, Anna, what a night! A couple of hours sleep and here we are back at it.' I found Sybil hiding out in the shadow of the boiler room, smoking. Sweat had nearly swallowed up her small face.

I slumped against the wall, next to her. 'Sleep? What's that? I see you've cadged another cigarette from some poor soldier.'

She shook her head, and her veil dropped an inch which made her look like an adult gumnut baby. 'Got it off those buggers over there.' There was a group of muddy workmen across the road stripped to their singlets, rolling the contents out of a dented water tank. 'They say someone might have got swept out to sea.'

'Yes. I saw it. A woman, I think. Wandering about. Matron did too.'

'Not much we can do about it now, is there?'

'She looked so helpless, so lost. I hope someone does report her missing. Then we'll know who she was, that someone cared for her.'

'If she was homeless, she was lost anyway. How'dya know if her husband didn't send her out to scavenge stuff and didn't care?'

'Hell, Sybs, that's harsh! When did you become so cynical?'

'If you'd lived my life, you'd understand.'

Before I had the chance to ask what she meant, she elbowed me and said, 'Anyway, how's your lot at home?'

'Fine. Turns out Dorrie had it under control.'

'Really, do you think you should be doing this? I mean, I love you dearly, but face it, you can't go on nursing *and* look after your daughter, can you? How the hell you got through training for three years, I'll never know.'

'Evie will be in school next year. I've already asked for a regular shift, said I have to stop working weekends, argued I could squeeze in my forty-eight hours without doing Saturdays or Sundays. But no luck. Matron just reminded me about the big favour they did in making an exception so I could live out of grounds.'

'That'll be another cross against you in her black book of rule-breakers.'

'I have a few, don't I? I like to think of them as a line of kisses. Here – give me a puff.'

'She's not a bad old tart, really. I don't know how you always manage to get her offside.' Sybil's ability to blurt out her thoughts spontaneously was one of the best things about her. She'd largely brought herself up, and her younger siblings too, her views formed without the pressure of determinedly private and status-conscious parents.

'Maybe she's worked out that I'm after her job.'

'Steady on, girl, you're barely out of training.'

'I'm going to run my own hospital, Sybs. I've given myself a year or two to set it up.' It felt good to say it aloud, and to someone other than myself.

'You're not serious?' Now that she knew, it would be around the nurses in a matter of hours, spread like roadkill for crows.

'Face it: it's the only way to make a decent income. All this emphasis on sacrifice – no overtime for us like other public servants – we're expected to do more hours because we embody *womanly* qualities, symbolic motherhood, sacrifice and the rest of it.'

'But what's wrong with just being a nurse pure and simple? Don't you like it?'

'Look, Matron Chalmers earns barely more than the wardsmen and the porters. Wardsmen receive three times our wages simply for lifting patients and wheeling them from theatre to bed. We're far more qualified than them – even the laundrymen earn more than us.'

'Yeah, the old story: *No need for you to earn, love. Husband, father, some bloke will look after you.* Huh! Anyway, there's nothing we can do while there's a war on, is there? While so many men are out there being carved up in France, poor buggers.'

'Some women, too.'

'Yes, for sure. But it's not about us, is it? War never is. Even so, they're getting mighty cheesed off in Brisbane – the way the government treats us like a mob of bloody nuns. The nurses' union – you know I'm involved, don't you…?' She watched for my reaction.

'I didn't, Sybs.' I bowed my head in a gesture of respect. 'That takes some gumption.'

'Oh, go on!' she nudged me. 'You should join, too.'

'I can't.'

'What do you mean, you *can't?*'

I couldn't risk attracting that sort of attention anymore. Being in this faraway country had protected me so far, so long as I stayed away from politics and unions – kept my head down. I suppose I wasn't naïve in believing that protest through demonstration could bring about a better world. Throughout the country unrest grew. Strikes flared and people took to the streets – men and women, railway workers, gas workers, meat workers, coal miners, timber men. In the Great Strike it was as if the war had infected the nation with discontent, and it gripped me, making me forget for a while about the fragility of my situation. I had to stop. I left the city, its clamour and reminders, for a fresh start in the tropics.

'I'm focused on one thing, Sybs. Well, two things, really: my girl and my hospital. My own hospital.'

I'd never told her my original goal had been to qualify as a doctor – it might lead to too many questions. The more recent idea of a hospital had started as a fanciful hope while trying to live off the widow's pension – no replacement for a husband's income. As I watched other war-stricken women resign themselves to loneliness and victimhood, the idea of my own hospital became a necessary fixation. I knew that if I could create a successful business, I would finally have financial freedom. I wanted to ease life's cycle for others, to provide company and care to those on the brink of life or death. It sounds like lofty stuff, I know, but I realise now how deeply it was driven.

In the workplace, widows like me with children were considered 'still married'. It made us unemployable in some places. But the hospital board at the Brisbane General allowed me in on the basis of my apparently unblemished character, my completed second-year training as a medical surgeon in Edinburgh (my third year abruptly halted), and certified proof of excelling in Anatomy, Histology, Materia Medica and Physiology. And maybe also because of my husband, his qualification as a dead war hero. More pragmatically, there was a staff shortage caused by the rush of women who'd left for war service. There was no risk of me joining them, no stars in my eyes. I'd kept quiet about marching with the anti-conscription faction, especially now an increasing number of returned servicemen filled our hospitals.

In training, I eagerly followed every aspect of the body's complexity, like an explorer charting a map of river systems – nervous, mental and physical. Where others might see skin, hair and eyes, I began to see a series of chemical reactions, physics creating movement, flesh and bone constructed from the elementary table. As a student nurse, there was comfort in it, a reminder of what I should have been, of a childhood with my father patiently explaining the basics of medical practice.

My goal was to put a deposit on a large building that would suit the purpose. I'd often visit a run-down weatherboard two-storey near my home in Brisbane and stand on the footpath dreaming. I'd get a loan, do it up, run the wards and educate staff. The building itself would not be austere – my hospital would have a sensible but bright façade, because there'd be enough misery inside.

No one who knew my plans thought they were practical. Matilda, who at forty was childless and who'd looked after and been possessive of Evie while I studied, was furious when I took her a thousand miles north to Cairns. *How on earth are you going to cope? You're being selfish. Think of the girl.*

Sybil was equally unimpressed. 'Well, I think you're crazy. But then again, people only come to hospital to die. And death is certain. So, you'll probably make a packet. God knows, we need some sort of compensation for being up to our armpits in vomit, spit, and shit.'

'Time to head back. They're already suspicious about our "toilet" stops.' I passed the cigarette back, invigorated by the nicotine, and cleared my throat. 'Punctuality in all things, sisters!'

Sybil dropped the butt and whipped around. 'Holy Moley, that could have been Matron herself. How'd you do that?'

'Been practising. I might need that voice one day.'

'Like I said, you're crazy. You know, I used to think you had tickets on yourself, with your turned-up nose and your silly, posh accent.'

'Sybil, it was actually you I was turning my nose up at. I only pretend to be your friend because of my scientific curiosity – about what exactly it *is* that the lower orders do and think.'

She laughed with a snort.

I think she knew even then how much I valued our friendship. I could be thin-skinned at times, and was often labelled 'standoffish', what these days would be called 'introverted'. With Sybil, my clumsy self-deprecation helped her see the better part of me.

'C'mon,' I said. 'There'll be casualties for Surgical, if any can reach us.'

She kicked the butt into a bush and rolled down her sleeves. 'Yeah, we didn't even get the full brunt of it – there's a big body count in Innisfail, and Babinda has been flattened.'

4

The Victory Parade – the whole town cheering, the heat and glare, the horse and human sweat; young and old perched on ribboned wagons of red, white and blue, trumpets blasting, hats thrown in the air.

'What did we get?' a man in a linen suit bellowed repeatedly from his model T Ford.

'Peace!' roared the crowd from the dirt street, savouring the 'c' like a hiss of defiance.

Vehicles bearing dignitaries, businessmen, prominent farmers, and women dressed as Britannia, rolled over the horses' droppings. Rotund men who'd prospered by not going to war now reached out to shake hands with the crowd. Then there were the women like me, onlookers with frozen smiles.

I spotted Sybil standing beside Tom. He was tanned now, his hair barber-styled, short at the sides, sun-bleached on top. He looked taller. I'd not seen him since he was discharged months before. There were only a few veterans left at the hospital now;

some remained in the area, but many had gone back to their farms or towns to reclaim what they could of their old lives. The unfortunate sergeant had left too, shipped back in his wheelchair to dim someone else's life.

When they came to greet me, Tom walked awkwardly, not quite a limp, but leaning heavily on his left foot.

'Anna! I was hoping to see you here.' Sybil glowed with pink rouge.

'Sister Sinclair! My favourite nurse!' The lieutenant was transformed by the joy of the day.

'Oi! What about me?' Sybil nudged him with her elbow.

'Tom… Lieutenant Austen,' I said, shaking his hand.

'Not anymore. It's just plain Tom Austen now. I was discharged as unfit, of course.'

'You're not marching with the others?' I pretended to be surprised.

'My battle finished a while ago. At least some of it.' He noticed Evie who'd slipped behind me. 'And is this your daughter?'

I introduced her.

'I bet you're as clever as your mother. If I still had my hat, I'd doff it for you.'

'Would you believe he threw it up and now we can't find it?' Sybil rolled her eyes.

Tom leant down, talking with Evie.

'Sybs – you never told me!' I whispered.

'Aw, it's still new. But he's a changed guy from the one who left hospital with a walking stick a few months back. You didn't seem too interested, so I went for it. I never thought someone like him would go for me, though.'

'Anyone else thirsty?' Tom said. 'Evie and I think we should go get something to drink.'

We queued at the tin-shed cordial factory and took our sarsaparilla sodas down to the esplanade. Tom and I sat on a bench under the shade of a sea almond tree and watched Sybil and Evie poking crabholes with sticks. It was months since the cyclone, but there were still signs of destruction throughout the town. The sand was now a thin strip edging encroaching mud, but the shore was slowly mending.

'I hope you don't mind me walking out with Sybil,' he said, taking off his jacket. A starchy scent came from the dampness of his shirt.

'Why on earth should I mind?'

'She and I are just friends, you know.'

'Is that what Sybil thinks?' At the mention of her name Sybs looked over to us, but the breeze scattered my words. 'No, sorry, don't answer me – what's between you two is your own business. But I thought you'd have gone back home by now.'

He loosened his necktie. 'That's what I'd originally planned. But some jobs came up here in the cane, so I stayed. I like the work. I need it. The exercise is good for my lungs and the hard grind at the mill distracts me. Because of my foot I do mainly light work, but that doesn't stop me helping with the harvest.'

His clothes were clean and sharp, his braces new. It was hard to imagine the scarred body they covered.

'And you've thrown away your walking stick.'

'Long gone. But it still hurts after a day in boots. It's heavy work laying the mill's portable tram lines through that cane. Builds the shoulders, though.'

'And how are you sleeping now?'

He took a breath. 'Let's not go down that road.' He fixed me with the corner of his eye. 'But I'm still a *man*.'

'Of course you are.' I tried to sound casual, neutral, but was surprised by how emphatic my tone was.

When he was recovering, I'd made sure to check into his ward most days, and when he was mobile, he'd somehow manage to find me. We'd talk a little – just general polite things at first, then his fingertip touch on my sleeve, a flicker of something. I was away the day he left the hospital for good.

'Now that it's all over they'll start putting up their memorials and statues. No doubt their brave bronze soldiers will have two arms, two legs, ten fingers and ten toes.'

'You survived. What a blessing that is.'

'Perhaps. But what about those poor buggers whose last view on this earth was bloated corpses? The ones who didn't…' He rested his hand on mine. 'I'm a stupid clot.'

I slid my hand away and wiped my face with a sleeve. 'No, no. It's been a big day. I've had a terrible headache.' I'd been on the verge all that morning. And his touch, the comforting, brought it all out. Or so I reasoned. Right then, Andy, dead nearly four years, was loud inside me.

'Time is very long for those who lament,' Tom quoted, as if guessing. He had a habit of borrowing from Shakespeare when his own words failed him.

Sybil started back with Evie in tow, cradling a crab in her skirt and flipping it as it tried to climb out. Maybe Sybil was right. I was crazy working those hours and raising a child alone. *Selfish* was the word in my head. My daughter was getting some of the wild about her, Dorrie reckoned. When she wasn't playing with the chickens in the garden or the dogs on the beach, she'd disappear. I watched her once, sneaking next door to Leon Roberts'. I smacked her hard that day.

We waved goodbye to Sybil and Tom, who left to re-join the street revellers. The police had closed the pubs for the day.

'See you, Sister Sinclair,' he called, with a tone that I imagined had some regret.

Sybil linked her index finger with his, ever so lightly, as if they were a couple, neither alone nor lonely.

Dear Mater and Father...

What to say after five years of silence? A mosquito buzzed around Andy's photo on the dresser. I lit a mosquito coil and started again:

Dear Mater and Father,

I hope this letter finds you well. Please forgive me, I realise how selfish I have been in not informing you of my whereabouts. I understand how disappointed you must be.

What I could not tell them was that after I arrived in this country to remake myself, I decided never to contact them again. That was after thinking I'd found love within days of stepping off the ship.

I have made a success of my life and I want you to know I am well and happy. I received my certificate in nursing and am now working at a hospital in northern Australia. Father, you must be pleased to hear that my medical training did not go to waste.

The main reason I write is to assure you I am well, but I also need to ask you to do me a small favour, which I think you will find acceptable. You will recall the incident on the night of my leaving you. It is my intention to assist the family affected, if they can be found. I hope it is not too late. I would like to send, anonymously, a sum of money by wire to the family to compensate them in a very small way for their suffering as a result of their loss.

Dear Father, I would be grateful if you could make discreet enquiries as to their whereabouts, so that I can help them – inadequate gesture as it is. As you will understand, it is extremely difficult for me to manage this from an outpost in the tropics.

I do hope you write back – if you do, please address it to the above...

I stroked out Dorrie's address and changed it to the Cairns Post Office.

I send my love to you both, if you will accept it. Please also give my regards to Angus and to dear Malcolm. What a blessing it is that the war is over!

Signing off under my Christian name, I realised that I did not know whether my brother Angus had survived the war, or how Malcolm was – he'd have failed any army medical because of his heart condition. He was only one year older than me, my closest ally when we were growing up, the one I missed the most. He'd have understood and forgiven.

I pictured the letter arriving. It's a picture I still allow, sometimes: The envelope slides through the brass slot in the door onto the hallway carpet. My mother picks it up and recognises my handwriting. She doesn't open it. When my father comes home, she gives it to him, and they go through to the drawing room. My father sits in his brocade armchair beside the fire and puts his feet on the ottoman. My mother takes up her crochet on the other side. There's November snow in the garden and frost on the windowsill. In my favourite version of this picture, once my father has read out my letter, my mother doesn't cry – I never saw her cry – but tells him in that unchallengeable way of hers to call me home.

In the morning I dropped the letter in the post office and wondered if loneliness rather than contrition was the reason I took such a risk.

5

Evie's laughter shrilled through the trellising underneath Leon Robert's weatherboard house. I left pegging up the clothes, marched through the grass around his upturned boat, but had to stop at his trellis door while I thought of a plausible excuse to barge in.

'Where's your wife?' Evie was asking.

'Not married. Who'd have me?'

'Mater – I mean Mum – doesn't like me visiting you.'

'I don't blame her. I wouldn't like to visit me, neither.'

'You don't talk the same as us.'

'That's how we speak where I come from. Hawaii. It's a territory of the USA. It's a long ways away, a few weeks by boat. But it's as hot as here. It has palm trees, beaches, and sugar cane, too. Look it up in your atlas. My folks had a jewellery shop there. The pearls I told you about. We harvested them.'

'Are you rich?'

'You ask a lot of questions.'

'Mum needs a rich husband.'

When I stepped inside, Leon was using his teeth to hold a string taut, while he knotted another around it. Latticework squares patterned the concrete floor, lighting his bare feet, his trouser cuffs rolled above his ankles.

'Is Evie here?'

'Well, Ma'am, you should know. You've been standing there a good few minutes.'

She was sitting inside a crab pot. 'I'm helping Leon the Lion. I'm checking his nets for holes.' I lifted her out. She noticed me looking at a chamfer-board room with a slit for a window and a door fastened by a heavy chain. 'That's Leon's treasure hut. He keeps pearls and gold in there.'

'Your daughter has quite an imagination, Mrs Sinclair. My mistake for telling her about the gold mines up on the tablelands.' He reached for his cigar and took a puff.

I dragged her home. She usually took a smack without any reaction, but this time, she cried. 'My dad never belted me.'

I gathered her up and hugged her tightly. To counter classmates who had both parents living, she'd started inventing a fictional version of Andy. With no memory of him, she'd manufactured him from his photo as she stared at it, chin on hands.

'If Dad was here, you wouldn't be cranky. You'd be there with bread and jam when I come home from school.' She rubbed her nose with the back of her hand.

'I know it's hard for you, possum. But I don't want you going over to Mr Roberts' again. Do you understand? I've told you many times before and you keep disobeying me.'

'Why don't you like him? Is it because he isn't a soldier like Dad?'

'We don't know enough about him. Leave it at that.'

It was mainly a suspicion that he was not all that he made himself out to be. There were mysterious comings and goings, boat trips in the dead of night. I was intrigued, and I began to realise I was also attracted to him, and that was a complication I could do without.

'He's going to take us crabbing in his red boat when the season comes,' Evie said emphatically.

In the street, aromatic incense fraternized with spices, garlic, and overripe mangoes. Chinese vendors in conical straw hats and bright toggle jackets kept watch from storefronts garlanded with hanging duck carcasses, mounds of corn cobs, and green leafy bunches. We were shopping with Dorrie in Chinatown at the harbour end of Sachs Street. She did this every Saturday for the 'best vegies in town', rather than go to the popular local emporium.

With Evie in tow, we dodged the carts laden with thick bamboo shoots and banana-leaf parcels and headed towards a stall piled with fruit. I already felt misgivings for taking her with us.

We nurses generally avoided this part of town with its small, red-curtained shacks. Some 'soiled doves' sat by the door of one in their silk kimonos – they'd avoided the council cull after the Japanese cane workers left. Now there was an even greater variety of nations. Sex Street, as the working men called it, was where most of our gonorrhoea patients came from. The disease was prevalent enough for the hospital to have locked off its own VD ward in the Alien section, hidden by gardens at the farthest corner of the premises. The patients were mostly prostitutes. Some of them were old hands, extroverts who'd curse noisily during the Dettol douche and Mercurochrome wipe of the cervix. After a few days they'd be back in their pubs, night streets and flimsy shacks. Their shame-faced patrons were treated using a long metal catheter fed into the urethra (smothered ineffectually with Vaseline), exacting vehement promises to the world in general that they'd shun the grog and women, *so help me God.* One or two of the regulars were police who'd do raids, although as predictably as clockwork. The girls paid in opium were the most wretched and would sometimes be admitted to clinic in a muddled state. It was frustrating that all we could do was patch up the superficial injuries.

Dorrie and the vendor greeted each other like old friends. He was a small man and wore a western collared shirt and a Panama hat supported by a single long plait wound underneath. He was attended by two of his wives and four of his daughters.

'Watch me,' Dorrie said conspiratorially. She considered herself a master of the haggle and in confident command of Cantonese. She held up one, two or three fingers and spat out foreign monosyllabic words to Mr Yee who shouted back with equal gusto.

'Bad crop. Too little. Cyclone,' he snapped. The wives and daughters watched Dorrie's attempts with bored amusement, but obligingly darted around, hoisting pineapples and mangoes out of deep bamboo baskets into ours.

'No, no, those ones are bitten. I want these.' Dorrie planted her hand on an unmarked bunch of bananas. 'Those longans, too. Let me see them.'

Mr Yee cracked the yellow crust of one with his thumbnail and popped out the translucent fruit. 'Try. Dragon Eye,' he said to me. 'Better than grape.'

'They're delicious, but...' My teeth hit a large seed.

'Spit it out. Don't be shy,' Dorrie said.

'There's Leon the Lion!' Evie pointed towards Roberts who was entering a baroquely ornamental joss house beside the stall.

'Don't!' I grabbed her shoulder, but she darted off anyway, following him into the building.

'You won't find any vegies in there!' Dorrie called as I bolted after my daughter.

It took a while to adjust to the gloom inside the joss house. I started coughing – the air was filled with pungent smoke. Two men lay languidly against the wall, smoking long white pipes, too anaesthetised to care about the interruption.

Evie was already at a silk-draped altar, mesmerised by bamboo wind chimes, paper lanterns and carefully carved idols in wood and gold.

Before I reached her, Roberts appeared from somewhere beside us and hoisted her away. 'This is no place for little girls.'

'But what is it?'

'This is where you worship Chinese gods. These gods don't know you, so they'll strike you down for not showing the right respect.'

Evie reached out to a gold figurine.

'Don't touch – you'll go up in a puff of smoke.'

'Is that what the smell is?'

'Absolutely.' He carried her out to the glare and set her down.

'Did you find any god in there?' Dorrie asked, oblivious to the feelings of the family at the stall.

It was impossible to guess what sort of business Leon would have in this temple. Some Hawaiians had Chinese heritage. But he was nothing like the shopkeepers here. They lived out of town by the river, growing vegetables and other crops for their stalls. A few held illegal lottery systems. The storekeepers acted as agents, selling tickets for *fan-tan* and *pak-a-pu* in well-guarded rooms where punters staked cash in buttons, and guessed at characters on rice paper. This was where grimy canecutters went to brawl and waste their savings. I'd heard that up to forty pounds passed hands sometimes. I could easily imagine Roberts being involved where quick money was to be made.

While Dorrie finished shopping, I called him over. 'Mister Roberts.'

'*Leon*, for God's sake. No one calls me mister around here.'

'Leon, then.' His directness disarmed me, but I persisted. 'That wasn't just tobacco they were smoking in that joss house. It's opium.'

'Is it?' he said with mock surprise. Clearly framed by the sunlight were scars I'd not noticed before – a fine mounding of flesh on either side of his nose, shaped by someone's incisors. At work, we'd stitched similar bite marks after Saturday night scraps. 'I don't know what you're talking about. Besides, don't you dish out the stuff at your hospital?'

'It's regulated. It's medicine. You know that.'

'Medicine inside or outside a hospital. What's the difference?' he whispered hoarsely.

'It's not that simple, Leon.' The last thing I wanted was to deliver a self-righteous lecture on the benefits or otherwise of morphine, atropine or chloretone. 'But this place…' I pointed to the joss house, 'isn't it sacrilegious?'

'As I said, I don't know what you're talking about. But those fellows come and go here. The caretaker lets them stay sometimes. They have no jobs.'

'They need help.'

'You obviously know what's best,' he said sarcastically. 'But just consider – wouldn't the kindest thing be to leave them alone? Even if it is what you say it is, you can't stop them once they're addicted.'

'You can try.'

'I'm sure you can solve all the world's problems with a bit of a lecture and some bandages.'

He went over to pick up our bulging baskets and carried them back to his car. It was an expensive one, and still rare in the north, a beautiful dark green thing with big, polished lamps and a hood rolled down like a shawl. This was the first time in a motor car for me, even though there'd been quite a few trundling around the city when I left.

'This must cost a lot to run,' Dorrie said.

'Not considering the speed and distance you get from it. It's far better than any horse. Not as fast at the gallop but has the power of twenty nags.'

When he pressed the lever by the steering wheel we accelerated past a lazy buggy and a line of scattering cyclists, our hats flapping, the wheels stirring up the dusty road. We arrived home in a fraction of the time if we'd walked.

'Right, that's it!' Dorrie exclaimed when the vehicle was parked. 'I'm getting one!' She invited Roberts in for a cool drink from her ice chest, but he refused politely, saying he had something to do. 'You sure are busy for a man who doesn't work for a living.'

He ignored her.

There was honest work around, if you looked for it. Up at Mount Mulligan they were mining coal in great quantities, and the government had just taken over the railway to Mount Molloy and Chillagoe. All sorts of minerals were hauled on steam-trains to the port – copper, lead, tin, gold – although now that the war was over, demand was not quite so high. Jobless ex-servicemen found their way to the mines. With all the rock falls and slips, they provided regular business for the hospital. Sybil had more to do with them, as I'd taken over midwifery duties for a while. It was a happier kind of work.

There was also the sugarcane. Tom seemed taken with it,

although I couldn't understand why. He'd been a lawyer down south before the war – a barrister, Sybil told me. It was obvious she had romantic hopes for him, which, for reasons I was not prepared to admit to myself, nettled me.

With all these options of good work available, we had to assume Leon was independently wealthy, but I suspected his income was more likely connected to his hours of enigmatic sea-watching.

6

It was still light, but evening nudged in, hazy from summer fires out on the range. Leon had moved his table to the large window filled with a view of the sea. A telescope had been set up beside it. He sat opposite me, wearing a freshly laundered colourful shirt, no necktie, his olive-skinned neck and face glowing with health.

'Wine?' Leon asked.

'Thanks, but I don't usually drink it.'

'You Australians, you guys just don't know how lucky you are. You grow damn good grapes here. The temperance league over in the States has got the government to ratify a prohibition on alcohol, so the vineyards there will cop it now. As if life hasn't been made miserable enough with a war.' He took the bottle out of the cooler and poured two glasses. 'So, enjoy this.'

He had laid out silver cutlery, perfectly parallel, beside the stemmed wine glasses – two settings. There was no tablecloth, just bamboo placemats. Water had been poured from the jug in the middle of the table and drops pooled down around its base. Ants formed a regimental circle round the liquid edges. I wiped them away with my napkin. On his walls were wood-framed photographs and paintings – a steaming volcano, a blue and white lugger on the beach, and an intricate sandstone building surrounded by palm trees.

'That's the Iolani Palace in Honolulu – where our royal family lived,' he explained. 'They've all died out now.'

'That's a shame.'

'Yeah. But I'm no royalist.' His fingers tapped the edge of the table, a solid Queensland walnut, blackened in spots by cigarette burns.

On the wall at the other end of the room above his gramophone were photos of women in suggestive poses. White thighs, bare breasts and backs, Arabian silk scarves draped casually between parted legs. They could qualify as 'artistic'.

'That's actually my work,' he said, nodding at the photo of the palace.

'Almost mystical,' I said. 'And those women?'

'Yes, those too.' He wasn't embarrassed. 'I have quite a few cameras now. I nearly set up shop once.'

'What is it you do for a living?'

'I'm glad you accepted my invitation for dinner,' he said, changing the subject.

'It was the condition you insisted on when I said I wanted to talk to you, remember?'

He laughed. 'Why don't you like me, Mrs Sinclair?'

'I just want to talk about Evie.'

'Okay. After something to eat, eh?'

He went to the alcove and wrapped an ironed tea towel around his waist. He took the tray from the icebox, draining it into the sink. 'I've packed in too many things.' He took out a large, covered jar with lettuce, sliced tomatoes, cucumber, and pickled vegetables, and tumbled the contents into a bowl. 'I prepared this earlier, it's too hot to cook tonight. Otherwise, I would have made one of my famous curries.' Next came cold meats wrapped in vinegar-soaked linen – sliced ham, cold roast beef.

'This is a feast, Leon.'

'Yeah, I used to give big parties back in Oahu. Oh, if you like fish, this is my own recipe.' He indicated a frying pan on the stove. 'Barramundi in butter and mango sauce. Caught it fresh today when the tide was building.' Leon in his apron, his sleeves rolled all the way up to the biceps, was an incongruous sight.

'How early do you go out?' I'd been woken in the dead of night by the sound of his boat trundling across to the shore.

He didn't reply.

I helped him dish the food onto platters. 'Did you really prepare all this yourself?'

'What's so strange about that? Been a bachelor my whole life.'

'No lady friends?'

'Oh, plenty of them. I wouldn't want to scandalise you with the numbers, Mrs Sinclair.'

I couldn't tell if he was being serious. Even among the pots and pans he had an air of controlled threat.

'It's fine to call me Anna,' I said. 'I'm not really that stodgy.'

'Yup, about time. Your daughter has no qualms doing away with formalities.'

'Evie has no qualms at all. But she needs to get some.'

'She's a sweet tyrant. I wish I had a daughter like her.'

'Kindred spirits, maybe?'

'She does keep turning up. I don't have the heart to send her back. She's got a mind as sharp as a razor.'

'To be honest, Leon, I don't feel comfortable with her coming over here all the time.'

He slapped his hands together in the air and opened them to reveal a squashed mosquito. 'So I've heard. I better get the mosquito coil out.'

'I'm serious. Please.'

'Okay, ma'am. I'll do my best. I'll keep my doors shut when she comes round. But she knows when I'm in. I see her up on your dunny roof, looking over.' He imitated Evie craning her head, her hands poised like an inquisitive mouse, and I had to laugh.

'So why are you here? In Cairns. You're a long way from home.'

'Now I know who your daughter takes after. Both interrogators.'

'Don't worry – I ask everyone that, even myself at times.'

He whisked the tea-towel off and folded it over his arm. 'Here, can you take these in?' He placed a platter in each hand and nodded his head towards the door. His fingers brushed mine as I took them; accidental and pleasant, and our eyes met for a second.

I told him about Evie, my need to protect her. He reassured me that no harm would ever come to her if she came to his house. His voice softened with her name, but he caught himself and cleared his throat as if unused to letting his guard down. This was a side of Leon that felt good. I had no right to judge him by his mysterious activities. I'd definitely become cynical since the war. I hoped I wasn't myopic as well.

As we talked, I began to unwind, allowing a sense of release, helped by both the wine and stories we shared – the anti-bourgeoise Dada art movement, the antics of the bohemian set overseas, jazz, blues, and skirt lengths.

'The war has changed us,' I said. 'Freed us up a bit, sexually, too, because tomorrow you may be dead.'

'Maybe this country's horse-and-buggy values needed a good shake up?'

He looked steadily at me. Outside, I heard the evening breeze, heavy with salt, and the clack and pop of crabs and night creatures in the mangroves.

'My, you do have beautiful skin,' he said.

I normally would have shrugged off such a cliché, but it seemed right in the moment.

'Leon…'

'I'm sorry, Mrs Sinclair. Sometimes I can't help saying what I feel.' He stressed the word 'Mrs' as if making a point.

It wasn't just the wine that that made me reach out and touch his arm. He took my hand and kissed it. I let him kiss my lips and gave in to the moment.

I reasoned afterwards that this night was just a slightly reckless adventure that took up a fragment of time in my life and provided relief from loneliness. I convinced myself that Leon the free spirit wouldn't want more than that night, and this was a good thing because I still couldn't trust him. Maybe, for just one night, he'd restored me. But, as I was so practised at doing now, I swept my conjectures away. I avoided him for a while. I avoided all thought of lovers.

And so, I nearly dropped the eggs gathered in my apron when I turned and saw Tom in the backyard, holding a large jar of molasses.

'How long…?'

'Long enough to learn all the names of your chooks. Do they answer back?'

'How…' Up at the kitchen window, Dorrie and Evie waved at me.

'You look pale, are you all right?' he said.

'I didn't expect to see you again.'

'I'm sorry to take you by surprise like this. I was just passing and…' He held out the jar. 'This is for you.'

In the awkward silence he finally said, 'Look, can we go across to the beach, just you and me?'

It's the openness of the foreshore which affects you, I think. You feel free when your words are blown out to the horizon with no coming back, no judgement.

In mid-sentence talking about the cane, he suddenly stopped and said, 'Anna, Anna, Anna.'

'Has it been so long you have to practice my name?'

He laughed. 'You've no idea how good this feels to me, looking at you.'

'Really? But where is Sybil?'

'Sybil? I haven't seen her for a little while. We're just friends. She's great fun.'

'Does she know this? She talks about you all the time.'

He threw a shell into the water. 'I'm here because of you, not Sybil.'

'Why?'

'Maybe because you are also my friend. Except you understand me. She doesn't, couldn't.' His body beside me felt close, solid. 'I'm sorry you got caught up in my mess at the hospital. I kept away because the more I started feeling for you, the more I wanted to protect you.'

'I don't need protecting, Tom.'

'Sometimes it's the ones closest to you that hurt you the most.'

I waited for him to explain this cryptic comment.

'There are things… there are times when I am not who I want to be.'

'I think that's true of everyone.'

'What you saw when I was in hospital, that was only part of it. There are other things… sometimes I find them hard to control.' And so, he told me about his debilitating anger and frustration, triggered by the slightest thing, how those feelings refused to disappear.

'But have you ever actually hurt anyone?'

'Outside the war, no. But sometimes it's there, the feeling that people better keep their table and chairs pinned down when I come into the room!'

'I think the most important thing is that you're aware of it. This other man the war created, he's not really you, is he?'

'Only you would see that. Sybil would never get it.' He turned his eyes towards me, and I looked away, afraid mine might give me away.

'Oh, look,' I said. The waning tide had exposed a small army of pipi shells that had attracted a flock of seagulls.

It happened gently. He'd drop in now and then, talking but not talking, while my natural desire to be held by him grew. It felt peculiar, as if I'd put my clothes on inside out. He trusted me with his vulnerability, and I was desperate to expose mine, to tell him everything about my past. He'd understand fear and loneliness. But I realised the enormity of the confession would ruin the equilibrium of our friendship. Only now do I realise how badly I wanted to love and be loved. To depend on that love.

7

Sybil tried to talk me into a full bob. We were moving forward now, and 'your bank manager must not see you looking so dowdy, like an old widow, a relic of war.' Everyone adored her new style, she told me, her turquoise eyes bright.

She snipped away, humming a victory tune. 'Strawberry blonde and not even out of a bottle, you lucky thing. But what are these? They look like scars?' She had made a part, exposing a white, hairless, jagged line.

'Oh, nothing. I was born like that,' I lied.

'Hmm,' she sniffed. 'Poor you. Perhaps Madame would like me to do the back now?' She had cut the hair slightly longer on one side, not quite matching the indolent model in the Home Fashions magazine.

'No, stop. I'll wear the back in a barrette. Just neaten up the sides.'

As I twisted to check my profile, my heel caught something under her bed. It was a book.

'I see you're doing your bit to become a modern woman,' I said, lifting out a copy of *Married Love* by Marie Stopes.

'We girls have all read it. Smuggled it in, hot off the press. But I think to be really modern it should be called *Unmarried Love*. It's full of advice about birth control.'

'That sounds more modern than modern. I'm not sure the curmudgeons we work for could handle that.'

'Love doesn't have to be married to be blissful,' she said. 'In fact, the book goes on about how married couples become bored with each other. We girls have to keep our mystery. When Tom pops the question, we'll have separate bedrooms and I'll swan into his room in a silk negligee whenever *I* feel like it.'

'Oh. I didn't realise you were so close.' This was not the right time to tell Sybs about Tom, and I didn't want her to read more into it than there probably was.

Tom and I would spend the time laughing. I'd never thought it would be so easy to be just friends with a man. I liked the way we could stand eye to eye, no contradictory strategies of charm and denial. He was my new pal, my chum. The gentlemanly acts and kind words I'd receive from society men had often come with an undercurrent of sexual expectation. But Tom was different. And anyway, I felt safe from involvement because of Andy's tangible presence in the wedding ring I still wore. After all, I had managed to put Leon back in that same compartment – a friend, of sorts. But I should have realised I was fooling myself with Tom. The dazzle of this new man reached further than friendship. His ready smile, his tightly woven musculature that was so like Andy's.

'He always seems to be busy lately.' Sybil sniffed. 'But, here, borrow it.'

'Thanks, though it's a bit late for me.'

I could see her point. I was swept away when I first met Andy and it became something else pretty soon afterwards. 'It needn't be boredom, Sybs. It can be deep friendship. The nitty gritty of marriage comes when you get to know and accept each other's faults. Andy had a few, but I didn't find out until after he died.'

'Tell me?'

'Nothing really interesting.' Keeping it in its box had worked for me, so far.

'The important bit is that Stopes says we should compound our alchemy… ooh I like that… *compound our alchemy*… at least three or four days a week, or even more often if you're in the mood. Easier if you're married, I guess. You must miss all that.'

'It sounds very regulated. It doesn't always work that way.'

'Ooh, do tell me.'

'Well, let's just say Andy and I had a healthy alchemy.'

'Thought so. Thought there was a good-time-girl under that stuffed shirt.'

Sybil knew nothing of my night with Leon. Or my life in Edinburgh – didn't question why I never mentioned my family. Maybe because she barely mentioned hers.

When we met, we were training as first year staff nurses in Brisbane – 'green around the gills' in our striped green uniforms, according to the registered nurses. We didn't become close then – I was in mourning and dull company and the baby gave me no time to socialise with the others. Sybil was a North Queenslander from 'out in the sticks' as she described it, west of Townsville, but unlike me she'd not been posted to Cairns by preference. She was so intent on escaping the bush that even the sleepy Brisbane sprawl appeared to be an exciting metropolis. She considered our common posting in the north as a sign that we should be best friends.

In looks, we were opposites. I wondered if that was the reason Tom did not pursue me as a lover. Maybe I was not his type. Sybil was short, and in uniform, her chest was pressed flat by the stiff apron. Because she was dainty, her actions appeared as quick as a honeyeater. Even her speech was clipped, not the usual rural drawl.

She straightened my shoulders with both hands and assessed her handiwork. 'Perfect. Now, you are completely remade!'

'I wish it were that easy.'

In the reception area, a bank clerk shuffled papers and stamped cheques behind his caged counter. I had plenty of time to admire his diligence, because my appointment with the manager was now thirty minutes overdue and no one had come to explain or apologise.

There was a framed painting opposite, a landscape, stereotypically British, with heavy oaks and decorative figures in eighteenth-century clothes. I could see my head reflected in its glass, disembodied. I kept tucking my hair behind my ears, but it soon fell loose. After forty minutes watching bank customers come and go, I rose to leave. Maybe this was all too premature anyway. I was almost at the door when the secretary appeared.

The manager's face was pockmarked with childhood scars and he wore a white linen suit and a tight necktie, just like any banker in a southern city, although the temperature gauge on his wall showed it was ninety degrees. He offered a slim hand and a seat opposite his desk. Beside a pith helmet hanging on the wall was a photograph of him in military uniform, the pips of an officer on his shoulder. On the desk his wedding photo was prominent.

'A nurse? Did you serve? Admirable lot, those sisters.' He wiped moisture away from his moustache with a hanky.

'No. I couldn't – I have a child…' *Idiot.* 'But my husband served.'

'It would have been better if he'd come, Mrs Sinclair, it's very unusual for the wife to come in alone, or at all.'

'I don't really understand why. Married women can now deal with property in their own right, Mr…' In my irritation I'd forgotten his name. I glanced at the engraved wooden block in front of me: *Mr Ernest Hall, Bank Manager.* My mother's favourite saying came to me: *You catch more flies with honey than vinegar.* 'Mr Hall, what I meant to say was that I'm a widow.'

'Oh, that is very sad to hear.' His hard eyes blinked. 'The Front?'

'Gallipoli.' The name was getting easier, its impact further away. 'Ninth Battalion, Third Brigade.'

'Oh, yes. We lost a hell of a lot of officers at the Dardanelles. Heavy gunfire from the Ottomans. Deadly operation.'

'My husband wasn't an officer.'

'Oh?' He took up a pen and his notebook and placed them on his blotter. 'Now, Mrs Sinclair, I understand you are here about a loan?'

I took a breath. 'Yes. I'm intending to establish a hospital. Here, in Cairns.'

'Really? Is there not a fine hospital here already?'

'There's a need for certain patient cohorts to have longer-term care. Lying-in arrangements for pregnancies, returned servicemen, the less serious cases which take places away from equally deserving patients at the District Hospital.'

'I see. Your qualifications?'

'I'm a registered nurse – with the Nurses Registration Board.'

'That's a fairly new course, isn't it? You'd need a properly qualified medical practitioner for the running of such an establishment.'

'I'll have the support of medical staff from the District Hospital for appropriate cases.' This was an untested truth, a necessary invention, because there was no one yet I'd approached or who I had strong reason to think would support me. 'And medical qualifications are not always required to establish a hospital.

The children's hospital in Brisbane was founded by a grazier's wife, a grandmother. But it took her years of fundraising, and quite frankly, I don't think Cairns can wait that long for decent medical support.' *Quite frankly?* I was turning into my mother.

He bombarded me with a series of blunt questions about my training and personal background, forcing me to be selective about what I disclosed.

'Mrs Sinclair,' he said eventually, 'before I can begin to consider your loan request from a financial perspective, and I must say it is an unusual case, I would need statutory declarations from at least two medical practitioners verifying their support. And I would need to make sure you have complied with all legal requirements for the running of such an establishment.'

'Yes. As a registered nurse I'm entitled to apply for registration of my hospital with the local authority. And of course, I intend to form a medical board.'

'Allied to the District Hospital board?'

'No, fortunately – and unfortunately. I do intend to invite District members to my board, but neither they nor my hospital will receive government funding.'

'In that case we have to review your financial situation closely. Is there no father or brother who can attest for you?

'My brothers and father live in Great Britain.'

'I must say, this is quite a venture you propose to undertake by yourself, without backing and medical qualifications. Have you really thought this through?'

'As I said, I do have appropriate nursing qualifications. And I don't think it would be so different from the lying-in hospitals elsewhere in this state. I intend to start a maternity hospital but then apply for a broader licence as a general private hospital – to admit men maimed from the war, non-infectious diseases and the like.'

'Pregnant women and soldiers are an odd mix, are they not?'

How to explain to him that this was not merely a business venture. What interested me medically now that the war was over were the things I didn't understand; how the mind affected the body, and vice-versa; how tough men were now filling the mental wards. 'Mr Hall, I'm sure you'd agree that life in both its beginning and end has an urgent fascination. And as I mentioned, I wouldn't limit my patient categories – I'll also cater for bush folk.'

'Ah. A veritable Florence Nightingale.' A crooked smile. 'But she had the backing of a wealthy family.'

'We certainly practice under her principles, Mr Hall. But I have no illusions about myself.' I scraped my chair noisily to rise. 'I'll have the medical references to you when available.'

'I haven't finished, Mrs Sinclair. There is the matter of your current financial arrangements. Income? Assets?'

'I've been penny-pinching and saving for a while now… since starting my position in the town.' One decent dress, one unscuffed pair of shoes, one plain lipstick.

'Yes…?'

I shifted on the edge of the seat. 'My wages are a hundred and three pounds. Per annum.'

He scrawled down the figure in a notebook and looked at me. 'You mentioned children?'

'One.'

'Hmm. Boy?'

'Girl.'

'How nice. Now, Mrs Sinclair, under normal circumstances the weekly cost of living would be about two pounds eight per week for you and your daughter – that's approximately one hundred and twenty-four pounds per annum – and your current wage does not even meet that.'

I shook my eccentric, half-bobbed head. 'It won't be long before I qualify as a senior sister and my income will increase to that figure.'

'Is that it? What about a bequest from your husband?'

Andy's share of the family business had gone to Matilda. This had always been the arrangement. When Andy was preparing to leave for the Gallipoli Campaign, I'd been too distracted by him, by the dull pain in my core, to worry about wills or consequences. Someone told me afterwards I could make a legal claim, but I had no money of my own to make one. Besides, Matilda was the trustee of a small endowment for Evie on which she sat like a bush turkey at her mound. I was thankful for that.

'There's my widow's pension. That's seventy-eight pounds per annum.'

'While you remain unmarried, of course. Assets?'

'No house, yet. I'm saving for the hospital, in which we'll live. I have a little savings.'

At this, his expression strained. He recapped his pen and laid it on the table.

'I can do this, Mr Hall. A private hospital can earn a decent income. There's a need for more up here. I'd have the patients. Don't you provide mortgages as a routine arrangement?'

'You are aware, of course, that this town is being crippled by the seamen's strike? It's been going, what, two months now, and businesses are closing. Timber mills have stopped, logs backing up the inlet. There are no steamers, there's no flour to feed us. These are not good times and you have been the only person to approach me about a new business venture for quite a while now.'

'There's some flour, Mr Hall. We're grinding it locally. And the strike will resolve.'

'Anyway Mrs Sinclair, to state the obvious, and I'm surprised this hasn't crossed your mind, even if you had the collateral, even if times were not so stressed financially, how could you possibly look after your child?' It was an accusation. His signet ring flashed in the light as he tugged the collar of his shirt, laundered and ironed by a regulation wife.

'I really don't think that's any of your business…' He'd hit a nerve. 'I've thought this through, many times. I'm no fool. It will start as a simple affair with low outlays. I will build it up from there…'

'Mrs Sinclair. This is really a waste of time. For us both. Come back in better times, when you have some collateral and decent references, and then perhaps I'll reconsider.'

Doctor Jamieson examined the shivering girl on the outpatients' stretcher – he was one of two surgeons at the hospital, the other being the outgoing Medical Superintendent, soon to be replaced by one from the south. He ran his stethoscope down the girl's chest, palpitated her back and pulled down the lower lids of her jaundiced eyes. He wrote on his pad and handed me the prescription. 'We'll be running out of quinine at this rate,' he said under his breath.

'My daughter…?' the girl's mother asked.

'Yes, malaria. She'll have to be quarantined with the other cases.'

'Leave her here with us and we will do the best we can,' I said. 'Check all your mosquito nets. Make sure they are always tucked under – darn any holes. And empty out all unnecessary water vessels in your garden.'

'Good advice, Sister Sinclair, but you really must leave that to the medical staff.'

'Of course, doctor. But this is just domestic common sense.'

I followed as Jamieson walked ahead, his legs slightly bowed as if under pressure of his tall frame. He shook his head when we came to the children's ward – every bed was occupied, with two extra set up in the aisle. 'Ah, the joys of working at the ends of the earth. We need more wards here. This hospital is understaffed and undersupplied.'

'I agree. And we need a laboratory. We'd be able to test diabetics here rather than plying them with Oxo and sending them south to the city. Overseas researchers are making big discoveries there. Or we could even conduct the Wassermann test for syphil—' I realised I was within the hearing of a boy whose bed was cordoned off from the rest. He was about thirteen and was wheezing. I lowered my voice to a whisper, '… for spirochaetes. We also need some sort of pressure ventilators for the poliomyelitis cases. Machines are being developed overseas using motor bellows, I understand. But I doubt this hospital would get any new type of machine. I'm sure young Bill here'—I motioned discreetly to the boy—'would find that more helpful than a daily massage on his paralysed leg with olive oil. And…' I stopped when I noticed Jamieson was staring down at me through his spectacles.

'Nurse, are you quite done?' The light caught his ears from behind, giving them the appearance of pink wings.

'Sorry, doctor, I was rambling.' I'd broken my own rule, revealed my depth of medical knowledge, and irritated Jamieson. But at least I had his attention. 'I think we agree a new hospital is needed in Cairns. Look, I was wondering if I may speak with you afterwards?'

'What's this about?'

'It's a private matter.'

I hated asking favours. As a new widow I'd had to. It wasn't that people did not mean well back in Brisbane with their small gestures – calling on my sister-in-law, bringing home-made jams and cakes and news of their own little worlds, telling me everything would get better. There was nothing they could do about that aching emptiness inside. They would say how well I was taking it, how admirable I was, as they sat on Matilda's floral sofa to knit bed socks and sleeping helmets for the soldiers. I had no niceties to give back – my smiles were not felt, there was nothing to rattle out of myself. It was as if someone had come to me with a large spoon and scooped away the marrow.

'How do you find practising in tropical medicine, Sister Sinclair? I take it from your accent you weren't born here.' Jamieson smiled at me in a way usually reserved for Matron and more senior staff. He was a very private man himself and like the other doctors, tended to limit his conversations with nurses to basic orders.

'It's an area I would like to explore, and that's one of the reasons I'd like to talk to you.'

'Yes, later, obviously.' He walked on to the next ward.

Following behind him, I had a click of memory – times as a child with my father visiting patients on his house calls, helping fetch and carry, going to Georgian homes or street tenements where there was no distinction made in appreciating the desperation of his patients. I'd listen intently to his diagnoses, always asking for explanations afterwards. I hovered beside him at his microscope, then on his lap viewing thinly sliced skin tissue, saliva or blood samples, the balls, rods and spirals of bacteria wandering, assembling, attacking white blood cells. 'This is how you find the source of the complaint,' he'd say. 'But you have to be patient. Sometimes you have to experiment.' My father was progressive in not advising me against studying medicine. I'd planted the idea in his head long before, so that when my oldest brother, Angus, chose to follow Father's calling, I slipped quietly into his wake. Or maybe I was another of my father's experiments.

Here with Jamieson, there was something familiar in his unobtrusive proficiency. 'I understand your keenness,' he said. 'But when I see so many of these malarial cases I often wonder if this environment really suits white colonisation. And it's not just the pathological risks – the diseases, the ulcers – it's the tropical neurasthenia brought on by the monsoon in summer. I'm seeing too much dissipation, alcoholism, and anxiety.'

'We've just come out of a war, Doctor Jamieson. I don't think that has helped.'

Sybil's theory about Roy Jamieson was that he was 'deliciously criminal', in that he had romantic relations with men, 'for sure'. Unlike the other hospital doctors, he was not married and had no apparent love interest. This alone constituted proof of her theory, confirmed by the fact she'd used all her flirting techniques on the good doctor and none had worked.

I took a deep breath. 'Actually, I'll stop babbling now and get to the point.'

'Quickly then, Sister.'

'What I really want to see you about is my hospital… a private hospital.' My attempt at casualness came across as too flippant.

'You mean, you're going to take up a position in a private hospital?'

'No. I intend to establish one.'

Jamieson stared at me, lost for words.

8

My father's name was stamped squarely above the adhesive seal. *Dr Gordon Huntly, MB, ChB, FRCSE.*

I thought I'd be prepared, but I spent the day as if I'd been punched in the stomach. I dispensed medication and helped with rounds – the unopened letter stuffed into my pocket.

I made sure Evie was asleep before I dared read it. It was brief and to the point:

> *Your mother and I are glad to hear you are well. You will be pleased to know that Angus has come back from the war unscathed and has returned to practice with me. Malcolm, on the other hand, is frail. He contracted pneumonia and now has chronic ulcerative endocarditis. He had to relinquish his administrative position at the University. He's still here at home, where we can care for him.*
>
> *We were worried for a very long time and hoped to find a trace of you. I will not, of course, advise the police of your whereabouts, even though I believe*

they are still searching. What you did is something we do not speak of here and it pains me to say that you must get on with your life in Australia and do not communicate with us further. If you do, Mater says to tell you, any letters from you will be burned. It is too upsetting for her. As for me, I had hoped you would make us as proud as Angus has. You had the ability and opportunity.

I will do what you have requested and report to you if I am successful.

I think I had always expected this – the surgical separation. Malcolm's prognosis was terrible. I wanted to write to him, but no use. Too late for letters. Too late to tell my parents they had a granddaughter.

Next door, Harry Lauder sang jauntily from Leon's shellac disc.

'Seventy-eight revolutions to the minute,' my father said, smiling, when he played a similar record on our new gramophone. He'd danced me round the room, my feet on his.

9

'We're not together anymore.' Sybil stubbed out her second cigarette in the sand.

'Why not?'

'He told me he had feelings for someone else.'

'Who is she?'

'Don't know. I mean, who the hell would Tom meet in a cane paddock?'

'What did he say about her?'

'Only that she was the most *incredible* person he'd ever met. Incredible! Gives me the shits. I mean, does she walk on bloody water? Does she have snakes for hair?' She drew up her own hair, combing her fingers through it, letting it fall back into a frizz.

'Perhaps it's for the best,' I said, knowing how feeble this sounded. 'Perhaps it wasn't meant to be.'

'P'rhaps schnapps – what rubbish, Anna. The bitch. The friggin', stinkin' bitch.'

I waited for her to calm down, to stop digging small sand pits so I could tell her about Tom. 'You're angry now, but it'll pass.'

'You don't know me. I'm good at bearing grudges. Anyway, it's time to get out and about again. Mustn't deny the men of this town my *incredible* beauty.'

I'll have to wait a while, I thought. 'That's a good idea,' I said.

'There's a dance on at the Strand Hotel tomorrow night – want to come? There's a band up from Brisbane.'

'I don't like dancing.' Without Andy I hadn't seen the point for years.

'What use are you as a friend, then?'

I looked away towards the mangroves; in my ears the sound of small mud creatures as they moved about.

I poured more water and watched the moisture run down the carafe next to Sybil's empty glass. She'd smuggled gin in her handbag to take care of 'the temperance league's six o'clock drought'. Somewhere in the cigarette smoke a saxophone was being tortured while I watched the dancers from the table, as desolate as the diesel generator outside, an awkward introvert among these high-spirited people. I'd refused two offers to dance, explaining I had sore feet, which was true after a day on the wards. I was only there to guard Sybil who was now out on the floor, skirt kicking up past her knees, pretending not to care.

Earlier, when she was sober, I'd finally told her about Tom. She'd responded at first in stiff silence, then downed a straight gin and by the fourth could hardly pronounce his name. I tried to explain that I'd done nothing wrong. Tom had visited us only as a friend, and we'd received him as a friend. I'd said this with my face burning, because it wasn't entirely true on my part, and Sybil was my closest friend. I tried to explain that Tom was a hope, a desire. And who knew if I'd ever see him again, especially if he'd met someone else. I'd be stupid to think it was me he meant, and I honestly believed that. But she still accused me of being 'the most *monstrous* bloody man-stealer under the sun'. I swallowed a large mouthful of gin and was ready to tell her more, but she was dancing again. I wasn't used to spirits – having been brought up by strait-laced teetotallers – and felt the sway and nudge of the room.

When the band stopped at interval Sybil shouted at them to start again, while her partner, a young man who looked barely eighteen, guided her back to the table.

'Time for us to go, Sybs. You've had enough analgesic.' I picked up her purse.

'No.' She snatched her purse back. 'Don't be an old cumbudgeon.'

'Curmudgeon.'

She leapt onto a chair, extended her arms towards the ceiling, and turned in a slow pirouette. 'I'm on top of the world! Come all you fellas, catch me, if you can.' I reached over to steady her, but she toppled to the floor. Blood from a broken glass smeared one leg.

'Time for you *ladies* to leave.' It was the hotel manager, righting the chair and indicating the door.

Outside, I propped her up under a gas light and wiped her leg with a hanky. 'I shouldn't have let you drink so much. You behaved like a right old good-time Charlie, Sybs. It's not you at all, and you don't deserve to get a reputation.'

'Reputation? That's a bit rich coming from the man-thieving tart of tin pot town.'

The esplanade was beginning to fill with men returning from waterfront pubs where the six o'clock curfew was easily ignored. Judging by the yells and scuffles coming from the 'Barbary Coast' end of the street, a fight was brewing between sailors and wharfies.

As we weaved our way beyond the lights towards the hospital, the sky blackened with a new moon rising. We picked our way along the kerb, bumping past carts and bins. I took off my shoes, damp from dew. The grass felt pleasantly spongy until I stood on something cold and reptilian. I jumped back in fright.

Sybil chortled. 'You scared of frogs now?'

As we got farther from the hotel, it became quieter. No one was out except us. Slits of lamplight fell through the curtains of houses, giving us some direction. I had the sense of being watched. In the last few years I'd sometimes verged on paranoia about being observed or followed. And here it was again.

'We're not alone,' I said.

I smelled the beer before I saw them. Two men, the vague shape of them, following us. They came closer and the bigger one started a low song – about a farmer's daughter and shaking sheaves – and eyed Sybil. His partner lit up a cigarette and waved it at me like a dart. 'Hey, where's your nun's outfit?'

It was then I recognised him. 'You mean *uniform*, Mr Tate.'

His mate ended his song in a low wolf whistle.

A railwayman, Tate had been a patient admitted a couple of months before for severe gastroenteritis and early onset cirrhosis of the liver. One of many drunks who'd come in after a few days' bender. He'd shuffled in, dry-retching and grey, hanging onto the shoulder of an Aboriginal girl wearing a mission's calico dress. She looked no older than sixteen. I asked her where she belonged, but the girl didn't want to linger in another white man's trap and slipped away without answering.

'Hey, where's me black velvet goin'?' Tate had roared 'Gwan! Run back to the bush like a kangaroo, ya slut!'

Now he came towards us, bellicose, his friend leering vacuously behind him.

My hand shot up as if I were a guard at a checkpoint. 'Stop right there Mr Tate!' Emboldened by gin perhaps, I assessed his height, bulk, and pointlessly remembered Angus's boxing lessons. *Keep your left up to block, punch with your right, and put your shoulder into it.* No use in a street fight.

'Whasa matter? Don't you girls wanna party a little?' He stood closer, his back rigid.

'It's time you went home to your wife and kids.' I stared into his gravy eyes, feeling my complete lack of authority outside of the hospital.

'Huh. That lazy bag-a-bones!' A spray of spittle reached my face.

'You ought to be ashamed. You take beds away from good people, drinking yourself into an early grave.'

He faltered. How different he was from his sober self, which, after a week's delirium tremens was almost unrecognisable in its politeness and circumspection.

Sybil stepped forward as if she was ready to tackle the man.

'C'mon, Sybs.' I took her arm and pulled her away. 'We've got to get home.' I gave the railwayman a look of disgust as he and his friend stared after us, muttering 'sluts'.

We'd gone another block when a car pulled up and Leon hopped out, insects dancing around him in the headlights.

'Mrs Sinclair? Is that you?' He had taken to calling me by my married name since that night.

'Hello gorgeous,' Sybil said. 'Who're you?'

'Sybil, meet Leon Roberts, my next-door neighbour. Leon, this is Sybil Drake. I'm afraid she's had a few too many.'

Leon laughed. 'I'll say. What's that perfume – eau-de-gin? I'd never have taken *you* for a night-bird, Mrs Sinclair. How come you two young ladies are out without an escort?'

'I'm not so young. And the night doesn't scare me.' This was true these days. 'I'm Sybil's escort. I'm consoling her.'

She murmured, 'Hmm,' sardonically.

'Her heart is broken,' I added for no reason at all.

'Oh, that explains it then,' he said, butting his hand, open-palmed, against his forehead. 'Is there anywhere I can take you two damsels?'

'You can take me anywhere, Sir Roberts,' Sybil cooed.

'C'mon, Sybil, it's already past curfew. If Matron hears of this, it'll be the end of us.'

Leon pushed aside the boxes crowding the back and helped me get Sybil into the car.

She sank into the leather seat and gazed at the canvas roof. 'What model is this?'

'General Motors Holden. American Chevrolet chassis. Australian built. You guys – your authorities – won't import a fully manufactured car.'

'It's no secret that we need manufacturing work for our boys home from the war,' I said.

'Gorgeous, ain't she?' Leon rested his hand on the smooth green door.

'She?' Sybil asked.

'Look at her lines. Says it all.'

Sybil popped her head up. 'This must've set you back at bit?'

'About five hundred pounds Australian,' Leon said matter-of-factly.

She whistled in admiration. 'American chassis, eh? I bet.'

I tapped on the window of the nurses' quarters to get someone to open up. Sybil's room, one in a double row of five, was a cement-floored cubicle with a bland cotton curtain at the door and was within hearing distance of Matron Chalmer's private room. Sybil's laundry-pressed uniform hung on a coat hanger from a shelf beside the 'wardrobe', a thick cretonne fabric slung over the same shelf. Another nurse and I worked quietly to haul her into bed. When it came to sneaking in or out at night there was a code of silence among the young nurses. Sybil's legs were free of the bloodstained stockings she'd unrolled and hurled out of Leon's car. She'd regret this in the morning; not just the hangover, but stockings were always saved up for and mended into extinction.

Leon parked the car on his kerb.

'I'm sorry about my friend,' I said.

'No need. She's very entertaining – not all stuck-up.' He turned in his seat, arm on wheel, eyes willing me to a challenge. 'Just the way I like 'em.'

'It's all right, Leon. No need to worry about *me* knocking on your door with a broken heart.'

He blinked. 'What makes you so sure that's what I'm thinking?'

'I hope moving those boxes didn't damage your leather seats.'

He didn't reply.

△ △ △

Eclampsia is a dreadful way to die – in convulsions, and doubly tragic if you aren't quick enough to deliver the child or complete a caesarean section. But at times it felt like we were fighting the devil when a woman wrenched herself out of bed with phenomenal strength; it required two nurses to hold her down and prevent injury or a premature birth.

Daisy Russell was brought in preterm, nauseous, high blood pressure, giddiness, and oedema of the eyelids and ankles.

Doctor Daniel Fuller, a junior doctor one year out from his medical degree, told her that it was just dropsy, that all she needed was a bit of rest, to put her feet up, and that women obsessed too much about their housework. As she worsened, I could tell it was more than exhaustion. I didn't wait for doctor's next round and a further dubious prognosis. In the washout room, I took a spoon of thick urine from her bedpan, lit a candle and did the test I wasn't authorised to do. High albumen level, bloody casts.

By the time I got back to the ward, her fever was high, her pulse rapid, and Deputy Matron Timms had appeared with Fuller.

'It's more than dropsy. I'm pretty sure her kidneys are compromised,' I said.

Timms, who was slightly built, straightened. 'Don't you recognise the symptoms of pre-eclampsia, Sister? The kidney issue will go away once baby is delivered, provided it doesn't worsen of course. Doctor knows best.' There was no sign of the woman terrorised by a cyclone. Timms had served at the Front, her colours already faded and silvered by it, and with only a few more years' clinical experience than me, she had been promoted quickly. She deserved her Military Medal, but the real survivors, the homecoming nurses I admired most, were those who hadn't allowed their compassion to be rubbed away. That's what I thought about her at the time, but in retrospect, I realise I had confused the effort of bravura with detachment.

'I tested her, the sample's downstairs. You know how easily pregnancy can mask Bright's disease. She needs diuretics now, the right diet...'

'You checked her albumen, you say?' Fuller said, as if he had just swatted a mosquito.

Timms stumbled when he brushed her aside to charge downstairs. I caught her before she fell, and to my surprise, she shot me a look of thanks.

Down in the washout room, Fuller swirled the specimen jar. 'What have you done, you idiot?! This is probably contaminated.'

In my haste I'd poured the sample into a clear jar not usually used for testing and hadn't checked if it was from the sterilisation cabinet. 'We can take a sterile sample when she's settled. But we have to stop assuming these episodes are just pre-eclampsia. Patients can die…'

Fuller cut me off. 'No need for melodrama, Sister Sinclair, pre-eclampsia also produces high protein levels. We're always on the watch with the kidneys. I expected you to know this.'

At university, I'd studied with people like Daniel Fuller, elite boys who obviously thought women's brains weren't competent to handle the complexities of a medical degree. Some lecturers appeared to agree. In those green days, I assumed a strategy of alliance. My brief friendship with our tormentors ended when they realised they'd get no further than an intelligent conversation. I was accused of being a flirt and this took me by surprise because flirting was an artform practised by interesting and worldly people – not tall, gangly girls who made peace offerings of tea and sandwiches at the refectory. Women who persevered with their medical training earned a mindset of steel. I reminded myself of this as heat now crawled like insects under my veil.

After Mrs Russell was reinspected and my diagnosis confirmed, I received a reprimand from Matron in the presence of a select guillotine committee – Fuller and Timms. Fuller gave a speech about uppity nurses trying to be doctors; how my interference was nothing short of inept, not to mention, dangerous; that it was sheer luck that my guesswork had been right in this instance. Timms remained silent, neither defending nor damning me, but her eyebrow slowly raised in disapproval as Fuller continued his attack.

Rules, protocol, were never to be breached, Matron told us. Sloppy hygiene not to be tolerated. I agreed with her on the last point but was cut short with: 'If you step out of bounds again, you *will* be suspended.' Court-martialled for bruising a doctor's ego.

I'd never been able to insinuate myself into the closed guild of live-in nurses. And it was no use trying to get Sybil to commiserate – her cold shoulder because I had 'stolen' Tom was permafrost now. Even though I hadn't heard from him in weeks, and I insisted this person he adored couldn't possibly be me, she didn't believe it, or didn't want to. My treachery had been to accept him into my home.

I was disappointed he hadn't contacted me but I didn't want to appear desperate by sending him a note, to step out from behind my screen.

◠◠◠

Two silverfish fled from the photo album when I took it out of my suitcase. I'd grabbed a family portrait from my chest of drawers along with some clothes before I closed the door on my father. I don't know why I took it. It was never meant to be the last time.

The photos were chronologically arranged in the pages. The one of my family, one of Andy in uniform (another on our dresser), and a few of our wedding day, a baby photo of Evie, then me and a group of nurses in uniform just after receiving registration.

Evie used to ask who the people were in the photo of my family. I told her they lived far away, too far for visits. It was taken just after Angus enrolled in medicine. My mother stares severely from her chair, while Malcolm and I sit on the floor. Malcolm looks down, his face almost obliterated. My father has kind eyes. I'd sometimes catch him proudly watching me as I studied at the kitchen table, or daydreamed on the front steps, near where squirrels hid in the oak tree by the garden wall.

I suspect that my mother was envious of him, the obvious enjoyment he got from his profession. She was different from the other doctors' wives she invited round for crust-free sandwiches and Madeira cake. To them she was just another dutiful wife. But when the suffrage movement gained force in Edinburgh, she didn't join in her circle's tut-tutting. They thought these raging harridans were unwomanly, that no man could possibly find them attractive. I heard her respond how interesting it would be if all women had the vote, had a free choice of vocation, and how women in Britain, Europe and America had only managed to get medical training against much abuse and despite rules being changed to exclude them. Just look at Elizabeth Garrett Anderson, a suffragist, she said, or Doctor Sophia Jex-Blake, Scotland's first registered doctor who had to come up here to Edinburgh University thirty years ago, the only place in Britain to admit a woman.

Her friends looked puzzled. *Wasn't she a lover of women?* one whispered.

My mother's influence on my father was gradually persuasive. I'm sure she encouraged him to tolerate my unladylike interest in medicine, and even influenced some of his recommendations at university council meetings. One day there'd be my hospital. And one day, ran my narrative, they'd forgive me.

Andy looked cocky in his slouch hat, as if he'd finally joined the ranks of the accepted ones. The glory only lasted a while for the survivors until they were accused of bringing typhoid back from the war. In reality, it came from badly drained towns where flies deposited faecal matter on people's noses and lips, and cooks who seldom soaped and washed their hands after a visit to the toilet. It was sometimes difficult to diagnose, with similar symptoms to malaria and tuberculosis. On confirmation of a rose-spotted torso, the patient was wheeled into an airy ward and confined strictly to bed. Typhoid patients were given soft hair mattresses with extra blankets under rubber sheets, and plied with water, barley water and lemonade. Everything they touched was boiled – sheets, gowns, plates and utensils.

It was convenient in our insular country with its short-term memory to blame the ex-servicemen. Some of their injuries were self-inflicted – a cut to the jugular or ulnar artery. There was something less measured, less visceral in a bullet. But we could only fix the damage, if we were lucky, not its cause – that would be admitting that our war was wrong. They'd be brought in by stretcher or in the arms of a kind and bloodied passer-by. We saved one and lost a few.

I'll always remember the one we saved up here, in the District. His face had been split open by shrapnel, quilting his right cheek into misshapen pillows of flesh when the stitches healed. His lips were grotesquely twisted, and his eviscerated eye covered with unconvincing prosthetic spectacles. I was the first on duty to attend to him, when he was only a few pumps of the heart away from death. When I checked, I saw he'd managed to slice his trachea. While we waited for a doctor, we lay him down with his head and shoulders raised. I pressed his head forward onto his chest to stem the blood flow. I compressed the bleeding points and used a dilator to keep the windpipe open, to relieve the dyspnoea and discourage the clots that were quickly starting to form. This wasn't so hard while he was passed out in shock, but when he roused with an intake of air, it took two orderlies to hold him down. It was the quick skill of the Medical Superintendent, Doctor Albert Clarke, that saved him. He ligatured the bleeding vessels with silk thread, sutured the cut, then fed a laryngectomy tube down the man's throat through a separate, fine incision.

'Why did you bother? I already died at the Somme,' the man said, when he eventually could speak.

As he was recovering, he talked in a slur about his new reflection in the faces of terrified children. Doctor Jamieson would sit with him and listen intently, murmuring questions. I wished I could hear. Jamieson once told us it was the stigma after the event that was often the worst for the patient. 'It's not just Christian attitudes. Blame Aristotle,' he said. 'He thought the act of suicide was deplorable, that it angered the gods, and even worse in his eyes, it weakened the economy.'

Even the man had to laugh.

I tucked the album into the suitcase and slid it back under the bed.

I made the mistake of thinking that after so many years I was safe. Then the first letter, one of three, arrived. The envelope, bent and smudged, was postmarked 'Edinburgh'. There was no return address, and the handwriting wasn't my father's. There was no official police seal, but my heart was beating so quickly I had to sit down. The marks on the envelope looked deliberate, an inky fingerprint mark by the stamp, my name spelt out in uneven bold capitals. They'd used my maiden name, Huntly, which was not surprising, considering I hadn't yet told anyone at home about my marriage.

> *You murdering COWARD. You thought you were so clever. You thought you'd escaped. But I know where you are hiding. Through me, the Lord will PUNISH you, just as I have often prayed for his judgement to be visited upon you. You think crossing great oceans can save you? His EYES ARE NEVER CLOSED. Reflect now upon HIS WORD:*

The Lord is slow to anger, and great in power, and will not acquit the wicked: the LORD hath his way in the whirlwind and in the storm, and the clouds are the dust of his feet.

—NAHUM 1:3.

The paper shook as I turned it over to the signature page. *You know who I am, and if you don't, you should.* It was impossible to tell whether a man or a woman had written it. Obviously, it wasn't anyone from my family, but it couldn't be a coincidence that it had arrived a few months after my note to my parents.

The accusations were not all madness.

10

The train almost stalled in the steep section of the range, belching coal dust on the passengers. We rested at Stoney Creek and brushed ourselves down. A waterfall thundered from the sheer mountainside, fed by recent heavy rains.

'They're not here, but we'll definitely see them at the top of the mountain.' Tom held Evie away from the flimsy railing.

'I think I saw one there.' She pointed to the wide leaves of a stinging plant clumped to the cliff-face. 'It'd be good to hide in there. No one would ever want to chase you.'

'Aha! Since you understand fairies, Evie, you must know where they all lurk,' Tom said. 'But to see the ones we're looking for, we need to hike a bit after the train, then cross a river. You just wait.'

I closed my eyes and breathed in the crisp air rising from the gorge, clearing my mind of that awful letter. The trip was Tom's suggestion. He told me he'd been away and had just returned from a trip to his parents'. He insisted on paying. I was so thrilled, I'd mentioned it to Sybil, not expecting her to still claim ownership so many months after their break-up. But she turned away, rigid with indignation.

We arrived at Kuranda station for sandwiches in a weatherboard hotel. An intense little man showed us a pinned butterfly collection. He tilted the cases of aqua, pale blue and yellow wings, all sorts of colours, to catch the sunlight.

We crossed the Barron River in a whooshing riverboat, and Evie pointed to diaphanous wings above the water, a fluorescent red blur.

'Not yet. That's a dragonfly,' Tom said.

The humidity closed in over the water. He put his hand on mine and I didn't move it away, feeling our perspiration mingle. He said he missed me. I didn't mention Sybil. Evie looked coolly at us. I imagined Andy beside her, sturdy arms crossed.

The riverboat thudded into the embankment and Tom hoisted her up onto his shoulders. We climbed steep wooden steps to a path shaded by huge tree ferns as old as the Earth, still competing for the canopy. There was something sweet in the air, like a million petals. Orchids crowded on bark, drooping low enough for us to see their pinks and purples. Nature's rules were more complex in the rainforest, its birdsong clearer. We stopped close by a tree, its trunk smothered in honeyed white blossoms reaching to the apex and out onto its branches. A breeze let in chinks of sun, which released a syrupy smell and gave glimpses of red forest plums growing between the blossoms. And then, glinting in the light, far up in the leaves, hundreds of tinsel wings.

'They're here!' Evie danced with joy, pointing at the butterflies.

A short walk ahead there was a carved sign: *Fairyland Tea Gardens*. It was a glade filled with chairs carved out of sections of tree trunks. The tables were laid with white tablecloths and crystal vases, eccentric in this natural setting. When scones, cream and jam arrived, Tom reached for the teapot.

'Aha,' I said and turned it three times one way then three the other. 'It tastes better if you do this. I've always had a thing about threes, a sort of superstition I suppose.'

He poured the tea from the china pot with large, awkward fingers.

'My teacher says I hold my pencil like a bunch of bananas,' Evie said, assessing his grip on the teapot. She studied us as she ate, looking from Tom to me and back again.

'Go and play,' I said.

Tom leant down to her. 'I'm sure there are other fairies to be found around here. They're often where you'll least expect them. They might even be sitting at your table. But you have to be looking for good things to recognise them.' As he watched her skip away, he frowned.

'What is it?'

'She reminds me of someone.'

'Who?'

'Anna.' He paused as if looking for words. 'I've known you for a little while now. We never mention it these days, but you know my...' He paused again.

'Your...?'

'NYDN. Not Yet Diagnosed Nerves. That's what they call it in the army now, apparently.'

'It's been given a few names – we're not allowed to call it shell shock anymore. Too much of a stigma.'

'That'd be right. Another stigma.'

'Another? What do you mean?'

'I'm a walking stigma, according to some. Mostly because of where I come from.'

'But you were born here in Queensland.'

'Yes. But my parents are from outside Vienna – anglicized our surname when they became naturalised British subjects – Augstein to Austen. My parents were clever enough to change our surname before nineteen-fourteen, while it was legal. They emigrated here before I was born – my mother, a farmer's daughter, and father, an accountant with dreams of a dairy farm. They struggled a bit at first – my father couldn't get a decent job. They started a small farm and eventually moved out to Jardine when the German settlers arrived; they were mainly tradespeople and dirt-poor. It was a pretty awful place to begin with. They all copped it because of their accents. When the war started my parents had to leave the scrub farm once a week, losing a day's work, to report to the nearest police station. I'd been sitting my bar exams when Britain declared war on Germany. I tried to get the Barrister's Board to grant a concession so I could complete sooner, but they refused. And here I was, Tomas Augstein, stuck in the city while all my mates were enlisting.'

'Tomas?'

He was a bit embarrassed, but I loved his other name. It was the way he pronounced it, lyrical, fluid, as if it belonged in a romantic alpine meadow. It also made me realise how much we had in common, but I chose not to say it.

'To be honest, Tom, I don't really believe in any war. Defend your principles, yes, but to waste people's lives for them…' I stopped, realising my hypocrisy.

'If I'm to be totally honest, neither do I – as unfashionable as that is to say. But we won. At least I wasn't maimed for nothing. I actually tried to enlist at the start – I would have left my training at the bar – but they found all sorts of excuses not to accept me. Even though I was born and bred here. It wasn't until so many of our men didn't return home that they resorted to aliens like me.'

'But why even enlist if you don't believe in it?'

'It wasn't what you think. I did it mainly to save my family. To stop them being imprisoned in an internment camp. I was at risk, too.'

'Did it work?'

'Not really, Uncle Max was sent to Sydney and interned in the camp near there. It might have been better for him if he'd become naturalised and changed his name like we did. He was a proud Empire man, too sentimentally attached – I'm not talking about the British Empire here – and this had been perfectly acceptable before the war. His whole bearing smelt of it. They were going to "repatriate" him back to Austria with all the others.'

'And did they?' I was still processing him, trying to rebuild a picture of the real Tom.

'Luckily he had contacts and was owed favours. His appeal against deportation succeeded. He became naturalised and set up his practice again. If he's bitter, you wouldn't know. He's grateful he got to stay. Who'd want to live in Europe right now with it falling apart, the food shortages? I'm convinced my parents only escaped deportation because they were so far away in the bush no one saw them as a threat. But my father has a different theory. He says it's because of my mother. She's a fearsome woman, you know, not to be crossed.' A slight smile. 'One hand on her and she'll take you down with a swipe of her streusel pan.'

I laughed, a loud belly laugh. He joined in until the diners around us turned their heads.

'Sorry, sorry,' he said to them, waving his hand in apology.

'So, do you mind if I ask who Evie reminds you of? That girl in the drawing – the one you had in hospital. Is that her?'

He looked at a point beyond my shoulder. I'd never noticed before how pale his eyes were. 'She was my younger sister. She drew it, her first self-portrait.'

'Was?'

'She died when she was twelve. Used to go around the farm barefoot, just like that.' He motioned his head towards Evie, who'd already removed her shoes. 'Ran over a shovel full-pelt and her foot got infected. Imagine that. A bloody shovel. The fever took her. Real tomboy, she was. But gentle, too. A better person than me.'

'Oh, I'm so sorry.'

'That's why the pressure has always been on me. I've had to make up for two.' The scar on Tom's neck reddened as he wiped his face with a hand.

'Does that still hurt?' I pointed to the mark. 'Bayonet? Bullet?'

'Er... that's enough of my bull. Why ruin such a glorious day.'

I picked a slender leaf off the table and put it in his saucer.

He leaned closer to say something when I felt a sharp nip on my foot. I kicked off my shoe and pressed my other foot against my ankle. A green ant had stung me, despite the sweaty stocking. I swore and hoped the intimacy of Tom confiding in me hadn't been ruined. I apologised, but he just smiled.

'What I can tell you is that the realisation that I was no warrior happened gradually. I can pinpoint the day that I think it started. My company had left the trenches, half-full of the dead, and we'd headed towards no-man's land. It was foggy but we were still visible in the forest because the leaves and branches had been blasted away. My mates were falling around me. I took cover behind a mound of earth, out of sight from the others. The crossfire was getting closer, ricocheting off the ground – it was frost-hard. Then all the firing stopped, and I slid out for a better view. I had my rifle but took my pistol out of its holster, cocked it and tucked it into the back of my belt. It was difficult to see with all the grey trunks. One of them turned into two, a German soldier. He was standing on a mound with a rifle. Smooth-faced, not even twenty, covered in dirt.' Tom's voice was breaking.

'Hey,' I gripped his hand, 'you're doing fine.' In the clear green of the rainforest, his face was vivid. Across the table I felt almost too close to him.

'It's… not easy. And I don't want to burden you.'

'I'm a nurse, Tom. I've seen pretty much everything.'

'You've seen *me*. You've seen a real coward, Anna.'

'No, never. Look, let's leave it be – I won't interrogate.'

In the murmur and clink of diners, his fingers unclenched, his shoulders relaxed. 'I'll tell you this, this one *small* thing.' It was as if he were convincing himself. 'That German kid, he hesitated like it was his first time at close range. But when I got to my feet, he stepped down and pointed the gun at my head. I dropped my rifle and put my hands in the air, slowly, slowly. He was short, almost swamped by his feldgrau jacket, if it was even his. He yelled something at me, something incomprehensible, and I do understand the language. I stood firm, not moving and he kept yelling. I could feel my pistol hard against my back, and I waited for a chance to reach behind. Then I responded in German, something like: "Don't make me kill you." He might have recognised the Viennese in my accent. He let out an odd sound, like a laugh, but there was no humour to it, and all I could recognise in myself was a scared schoolboy playing "do or dare" in the playground. I dropped my arms, waiting for the shot. He quietened, recognising the game. He lowered the rifle to my heart. I was ready, ready for my chest wall to smash open. But then he turned and sauntered away, almost arrogant. I tried to hate him. I took out my pistol, took aim at him, but couldn't do it. As it turned out, there was no need – someone from my company shot him in the back before he got very far. He collapsed, then the stillness. There was a photo of his mother tucked into his pocket – she could have been mine. Perhaps it should have been.'

'It wasn't your fault; it never could be.' I wanted to reach over and hold him.

'After that, I couldn't do it anymore. I just stopped. Then I got shot.'

'Your scar.'

'Which one?' He looked away. 'When I tally the people I've killed, some *literally* by my own hands, as melodramatic as it sounds, I enter my own circle of hell. And there's no one else there but me.'

I lay on my back on a mountainside staring up at a clear sky. Ice water began to seep through my dress. I got up, my hands and feet, numb. All around were uprooted trees. No birds called. A man with no face appeared in the silence, his arms severed at the elbow. 'How can I do my job?' he asked me. 'I have to bring water from the well – how can I now? You did this, you did this.'

I woke up in the night, head throbbing, nightie soaked in sweat, the heat stifling. My faceless man had come to me before, with a similar message. This time he was on another hill, the one where Andy died, breathing in dirt, bleeding into it. Would it be better to have a hero's quick death than to live like Tom, still trapped in the forest? I got out of bed, lit the lantern and dimmed it. The clock said half past two.

I poured a glass of water from the pitcher and took two aspirin. A glow came through the thin curtain, then a flashing. I pushed the curtain aside. The sea was invisible in the blackness but the tide was high. I could hear splashes at the water's edge. The light source was distant. It wasn't a regular on-off pulse, as there would be from a beacon, but systematic long and short flashes, stopping and starting as if in short sentences. Then it stopped. I wondered if someone was out there on a boat, in serious trouble. I heard movement at Leon's place, the unlocking of the gate under his house, then the sound of something heavy rolling over the footpath onto the road. I made out the shape of his boat on a trolley – he was pulling it over the sand. The dim beam of his torch found a curlew standing sentinel-still as he passed by it. He slipped into the quiet sea and started rowing.

I dreamily realised it was too early for fishing and tried to get back to sleep, watching the slow line of light breaking over the horizon. I must have been awake for an hour or two.

I heard Leon return before the clanking of the night cart drew near. It made its way up the street, stopping and starting with clacking hooves. The cart always appeared before the flies were awake. It pulled up outside and a man with a lantern jumped out with an empty pail and disappeared down the back of the house. He quickly returned with our stinking contribution, which he hastily slammed into the covered section at the back of the cart, then bolted the door with a clang.

I shut the window and rolled onto my side, willing sleep to come. I thought about Andy.

And now there was Tom. When I wasn't working, he would take me out to the pictures or for a walk. As I got to know him better, I saw more clearly how he hid his vulnerability from others. He brought out something in Dorrie, who'd never had a family of her own. She'd got into the habit of baking biscuits on the weekend just in case he'd drop by. He was working at a cane mill in Hambledon, a few miles from Cairns. The work had been a release, he said – igniting the mature plants with a torch, flames high above him, the black smoke filling the air like all the dirtiness of the world disappearing, then hacking the stalks low down until he was exhausted beyond pain. But his bad foot became infected with tropical sores, and he had to give it away. He had a full-time job in the office now. Working indoors suited him better. When I'd asked him why he didn't go back to his profession, he simply said he wasn't ready.

He reassured me, told me I was doing the right thing, living with the living, and Andy's voice began to fade. I might be falling in love with this broken man, at least love was what it felt like. It had been so long I couldn't be sure. But sometimes it felt like betrayal.

11

I'd spent the day under the house washing our laundry. For the average housewife, Mondays were wash days, but for me it was whenever I had the chance. I'd crammed so many sheets and towels into the boiler that it overflowed into the back yard, sending the chickens scrambling back to their run. I had to start again. Just before dusk I dragged the sheets off the line before the black mess of fruit bats glided in from across the bay with their treacle droppings. Tired and grumpy, I ironed the damp laundry until it stopped steaming.

In Matron's office, with seven hours still to go of my night shift, I already found it hard to stay awake. I rubbed my eyes, hoping the burning sensation wasn't the onset of influenza. Four nursing staff had just been diagnosed with Spanish Flu. There was no proof where it actually began, but with this enemy, our smug post-war scruples wouldn't allow for self-blame. The virus hitched a ride around the globe, launching wraithlike into the atmosphere, feasting on lungs and lives. It exploited even our remote patch, where children wore home-made masks to school, by necessity breathing their own exhalations rather than the charged air of a rainforest town.

Our isolation hut couldn't contain the beds starting to block the aisle, so two temporary influenza hospitals were opened. One was allotted for whites, the other for non-whites, as if separate specialities were required to cater for the same bodies, the same suffering.

As I took over the duties of reallocated staff, my shifts at the District drew longer. I helped train Red Cross volunteers, explained the precautions, distributed surgical masks for their ward rounds. Many patients recovered, but we lost a few, their depleted bodies purple, chests streaked with bloody sputum coughed from disintegrating lungs. It could have been worse, as it was in the south, but Queensland's bubonic plague ten years before was still fresh in its collective memory, and the authorities quarantined our borders. A little too late, but it helped slow the spread. The greatly anticipated inoculation program seemed to have helped very little.

When public meetings were allowed again, there were some curious measures. The picture theatre removed its roof (to release circulating infections), so screenings were in the open air. Dramatic scenes where the victim hid from a killer while holding their breath, were punctuated by casual slaps at mosquitoes, and intense love scenes were blurred by the censorship of flapping moths.

Even the stalwart Timms had been laid low, but she'd avoided influenza. She was diagnosed with 'exhaustion', and I helped nurse her at the District. Her reaction to the cyclone that night, her nightmares, her odd shivering, indicated it was more than weariness. One day when she was brighter, sitting up in her bed telling me it was time for her 'to get on with the job', I mentioned neurasthenia and that it did not discriminate between the soldiers or nurses who had served in the war. Later, I quietly arranged for Jamieson to 'stop for a chat' with her on his rounds, and this became a regular event.

'I want to say thanks,' she said, one day. 'You and Doctor Jamieson are the only ones in this hospital who seem to understand what I went through. You were kind to me in the storm and I never thanked you.'

'We both have our storms to deal with,' I replied, and she smiled.

The eerie hush in the ward near Matron's office was disturbed only by the occasional snore or fart of sleeping men in the ward nearby, the air already stale because the fans had been switched off hours before. These men were crippled from years of trauma to their backs, knees and hips while working in the cane, mines or workshops. The women, too, bore twisted fingers and arthritic knuckles, swollen from a lifetime of labouring. I had little appreciation back then of how gradually your body turns on you, without you noticing.

Clouds floated past the moon, Matron's windows like cataract eyes. Her paperwork was waiting. I was about to start when a deathly scream sounded beside the open casement, like a girl in pain. I rose instinctively. Then a movement at the office entrance. I grabbed my weapon, the hospital's bulky *Manual of Medical Procedures*, and the scream faded. At the same time as I realised it was just a curlew's call, the intruder bustled in. A familiar shape, short and slim with frizzy hair.

'You on night duty, too?' she said. It was not really a question.

'Sybs! Are you looking for Matron Chalmers? She's on duty at the new isolation hospital.'

'Yeah, I know that,' she said flatly.

'I'm filling in for her.' I put the manual back on Matron's desk. 'This'd be no defence against *you*.' I gave her my warmest smile. For a month or so I'd been trying to catch her for a chat, like the old days.

'Did she ask you specifically?'

'Yes. It surprised me too. It was Timms who recommended it.'

She nodded at the ward and said flatly, 'Easy work for you. I've got the children and babies.'

'Of course,' I whispered, although I didn't really agree. 'Shouldn't you be back keeping an eye on them? The little ones sometimes sneak out of bed.' I regretted this as soon as I said it. 'Sorry, I didn't mean to be patronising. I think the spirit of Matron has inhabited me!'

'Yeh, well you are a bloody Madam.' Her irritation was palpable. 'If you think Matron's giving you favours, you're up yourself.'

'Sybs, please. This is silly.'

She shook her head in disgust and headed for the door.

'Bloody Hell, Sybil!'

She stopped, her back to me.

'Talk to me for goodness' sake.'

She turned, her face ruddy now.

I wanted to tell her I missed her. Instead, I blurted out stupidly, 'I know you're stirring up trouble.'

'*What* did you say?'

'It's all about Tom, isn't it? You've been on a whispering campaign against me. You and the staff nurses. You know I'm trying my best, but you're deliberately trying to stuff things up!'

'You need your head read.'

'You need yours read and then explained to you in big print.'

'You think you're so smart, don't you? Hanging around here all night with your lantern, playing Miss Nightingale.'

A man groaned in the ward. 'Can't you girls take your catfight somewhere else?'

'Shush,' I called. 'Go back to sleep, now.'

'Anyway, Matron has noticed how slack you are.' She swept out of the office.

There really had been criticism from Matron Chalmers that had worried me. Matron had made me close the door when she called me in, which always meant bad news. *Yet another complaint, Sister Sinclair. You're far too familiar with the doctors. You are forgetting your place. Or do you think you are too good for us, hmmm?* Maybe I'd been too bold in approaching Jamieson. In this place where I was becoming the proverbial misfit, I'd thought he was the one person who'd understand. She wouldn't tell me who'd made the complaint but said the only reason she hadn't pursued it formally was because there were *precious few sisters to do the job.* Then, shifting a bundle of papers to the side, she'd said, *Now, don't you get any notions about what I have to say next because Deputy Matron Timms has impeccable judgement and for some reason has strongly recommended you replace me in my absence. She is too ill for the job, as you know doubt know.* Either Matron also saw potential in me, and this was a test, or, more likely, she hoped I'd do enough damage in one week to allow her to get rid of me.

I knew that Nora Owens, a charge nurse and one of Sybil's roommates, had complained and I thought I knew why. I'd discovered Nora's carelessness – forgotten patient requests, wrong allocations to wards. I took it up with her directly, thinking it was fairer than reporting it to Timms or Matron. None of us had it easy during those times, all facing the same enemy – sheer weariness – and now we were turning on each other. I hoped that in my own hospital things would be different; the hierarchy fluid, everyone responsible for their own duties. Discipline, but not just for its own sake.

I watched a night beetle whirring in a crooked circle around the desk lamp until it slammed into the bulb and fell. I picked it off my desk and put it in the basket.

As soon as I saw Doctor Jamieson leave the operating theatre, I threw off my apron and trailed him across the grass towards the facilities block. He was followed by Timms and two nurses. An orderly emerged behind them, pushing a stretcher with a sheet-covered body towards the makeshift mortuary.

Jamieson turned when I called him, his white gown spotted with blood spray, his spectacles smeared.

'May I take your gown to the laundry?'

'No, it's all right for the moment.' He went inside the kitchen and poured himself a large tumbler of water, glugging it down.

A fly had followed him in and buzzed at the mesh door. I waited while he shooed it out and opened the zinc-lined ice chest, where there were surplus hospital meals. He took out a few folded newspapers from the corner shelf and slapped them on the table beside his plate.

'How can I help you, Sister?'

'Sorry to interrupt.'

'Please excuse me. I'm starving. Just come off an all-nighter – four emergencies, all from the same brawl. Not enough staff to help – everyone's at the isolation hospital.'

He was already forking down last night's mince, despite having spent long hours cutting, boring, cauterising and sewing up human meat. He'd been on call when the patient now under the sheet was brought in. We all knew that surgical duty was not Jamieson's favourite.

Without looking up he said, 'Help yourself to a plate, Sister.' This had to be London manners – no other doctor would bother to offer.

'No, thank you.' My stomach was rumbling, but I wouldn't eat for the rest of the morning – not after bedpan duty. 'Do you mind if I get straight to the point?'

'Please.'

I took a breath. 'Remember when I mentioned my hospital plans to you?'

He looked blankly for a moment. 'Oh, yes. How're they going?'

'I hope I wasn't overstepping the mark in telling you about them?'

'Hmm. I have to admit, I thought this was only a pipe dream of yours.'

'I didn't quite get the chance to explain everything to you before and I was hoping… well, *now* would be the perfect time for you to provide me with some sort of reference.'

He stopped, mid-bite, and looked at me. 'You leaving already?'

'Not quite yet, if I can help it. But I'll be starting arrangements for my hospital soon and I need to secure support now.' I said this quickly, getting it out.

He pushed his spectacles onto his forehead and rubbed his eyes. 'Already?' he said again. 'Are you serious? I'm sorry. I'm so tired I'm not sure whether or not I'm dreaming.'

'Absolutely. I've spoken to the bank.' It was not his business to know, at least just yet, that it hadn't gone well.

'I see.' He chuckled. 'How audacious! But I do wonder, why ask *me?*'

'Having worked with you now for a couple of years I respect your practice. And opinion.'

'Ah, flattery will get you everywhere!'

'No, I mean it.'

'Since we are speaking directly – do you consider yourself qualified enough?'

I was prepared. 'As it turns out, that question relates to the second part of my request, but I'll come to that. It'll be a lying-in hospital, at first. I'm one of the most experienced midwives in our area now. I'll also take other, less urgent cases – manage the overflow of the District Hospital.'

'Well, we certainly need one. I've been trying to talk the board into doing something similar for years. But have you really thought this through?'

I checked my watch. My second shift was about to start. 'You've seen how I work, Doctor Jamieson. I think you are able to provide comment. If you will?'

'Can't say I've ever had to haul you up over anything technical. I can certainly say something positive about your nursing practice to whomever, Sister.'

'That would be wonderful! Thank you a million times!'

'And the second part?'

'Oh, yes. When the hospital is established, it'll need consulting medical staff. I was hoping you'd be able to assist me there. It would be paid pro rata.'

'You mean, you want me to be your employee?'

'No, no, not at all. That would be ridiculous. A hospital board would have to be established, and hopefully you would be interested in becoming a member?'

'Part of me thinks you're quite mad!'

'It's been done elsewhere in rural areas – lying-in hospitals are becoming quite common. And it's also common for regional doctors to assist.'

He flicked his fork over a few times as if thinking. 'Perhaps you should come to me once you've developed your plan properly.'

'Please take your time to think about my request. I agree there's quite a bit of planning to do. But this is our chance to improve medical services in the north. The hospital here can't always cope – especially with the malaria epidemics and mining accidents – and we are in the midst of a pandemic.'

'Yes, yes, I'm aware of that. All of it.'

'Once it's established, I intend to expand the hospital to other patient categories. It would help build a solid platform for informal medical progress, encouraging new techniques. Treating neurasthenia, for example. Since the war I've gained a particular interest in it and my hospital could provide support for any medical practitioner should he wish to develop that area.'

I saw this spark his attention. He'd trained in England, and had once told me about experiments with returned soldiers there, advances in their treatment.

'Don't trip over your ambitions, Sister.' But now he was smiling.

'I'm no starry-eyed idealist, Doctor Jamieson. The stars faded away a long time ago. Besides, I'm a superb hurdler.'

There was delight in his laugh, a kind of ripple.

'I'm just giving you something to mull over. I can provide all the required facts and figures, if or when you want them.'

'Fine. And I'll get back to you in due course. But this is a huge undertaking you have in mind.' He untied his gown. 'Don't get your hopes up.'

'And don't give up on yours, Doctor Jamieson.' I was growing bolder.

'Oh, by the way. I think you might appreciate this. Keep you in touch.' He indicated his broadsheets, *The Times* and *The Scotsman*. 'I get them every couple of weeks from overseas. I've usually read the ones here, so please, help yourself whenever you're feeling a bit homesick.'

12

Miss Marchant's timber shack school was very different from the one I'd attended, but the way she appraised me as I entered her office was vividly familiar.

At George Watson's Ladies' College, a large sandstone house in an Edinburgh town square, girls like me had big plans, way beyond revenge pranks on boys from the Royal High School on Calton Hill. That school was eight hundred years old when my brothers enrolled there. They'd enter classrooms guarded by colossal Doric columns and statues of steely heroism on horseback. It was Angus who shone there. Malcolm, who was slight for his age, was bullied.

The note signed by Marchant simply stated: *I wish you to attend at my office in the children's lunchbreak this coming Friday sixteenth to discuss the serious conduct of your daughter, Evelyn Sinclair.*

As Miss Marchant rifled through papers on her desk, I heard a jumble of playground shrieks, thudding of balls, and the snort of horses from a nearby agistment. Evie was standing outside the door, waiting for judgement to be handed down.

The headmistress's voice was like ironbark. 'This,' she said, brandishing some sort of charge sheet, 'is Evelyn's last chance.'

Another last chance.

The talcum-powder and lead-pencil air was suffocating, the coloured ABCs and 1, 2, 3s on the wall militant in their certainty. My headache worsened.

'Just last month she had to be disciplined. I don't like to use "Fred", but...' Her eyes flickered to where the school cane hung like a warning on wall-hooks.

'For laughing, as I understand it.'

'For laughing at another's misfortune. Mr Lewis's to be accurate. Slipping down the steps.'

'Yes. That was not kind. But – and I do not say this as an excuse – I understand quite a number of children were also laughing at Mr Lewis, and Evie was the only one who owned up to it. She came home with some misguided wisdom from the other children to the effect that it was silly to tell the truth.'

Miss Marchant referred to her sheet. 'Perhaps you've forgotten the slingshot incident?' Evie had stolen a catapult and shot its owner in the buttocks with dried peas. There were mysteriously no witnesses to the preceding bullying, but a few who'd secretly congratulated Evie on her righteous aim. 'And here we are again, Mrs Sinclair, discussing your daughter's conduct. At six years of age, she should know better.'

'I made sure she was punished.'

'That might not be enough. It hasn't been so far, has it? And to return to today's task – are you aware she has been completing other children's homework, and not very well either, charging a fee for it? This is simply *dishonest* behaviour.'

'I wasn't aware. But surely, it's the other children you should be punishing. They are the ones passing her work off as their own.

'If you... if *that* is her moral compass, then I can see why she is losing her way. You must acknowledge there has been a series of delinquencies. We've spoken about her rebellious attitude before.'

Blood rushed from my head, and I felt faint. 'Evie has been through hard times, Miss Marchant. She lost her father a few years ago. And with our move up north, she has had to deal with great changes.'

'Evelyn is not the only fatherless child at this school, Mrs Sinclair. We have just been through a war. The advantage the other children might have, if you can call it that, is that their mothers look after them properly. I understand you are working?'

And there it was again. The dizziness grew and I couldn't breathe. As I swayed, clutching the seat with both hands to support myself, Miss Marchant's face became a blur.

'Is there something wrong with your head, Mum?' Evie was on our steps beside me with her jam sandwich, her book, *Wild Birds of Town and Country*, open on her lap.

'I just had a little episode, that's all.' Panic attacks had started with that letter from Edinburgh.

'The janitor had to tidy up Miss Marchant's broken flower vase when you fell.'

'Not our finest hour, was it?'

'I had to give the money back.' She rested her head on my arm. 'But it was for us, you know – for you, Mum, so you didn't have to work.'

I kissed her salty hairline. 'Evie, I don't think motives, no matter how good, matter to your school.'

'Mr Lewis, he was tottering all over the place like Charlie Chaplin, holding onto his books. And I only hit Enid with her slingshot 'cause she did it to me first.'

'Poor Enid. That was really stupid. There's no need for you to take matters into your own hands, Evie. It never works – I know this from my own experience.'

'How? Did you hit bullies too?'

'Never you mind. But did you know Enid has been admitted to hospital with trachoma? She's had punishment enough. Not that you can go around telling anyone I told you. That's between you and me, you hear?'

'What's trachoma?'

'It's an infection in the eye. She's nearly blind in that eye now. The doctors operated on her, but it didn't help. You're lucky you didn't catch it. Some of your school did. How you all managed to avoid the flu, I'll never know. But that's why I make you wash your hands all the time.'

'Was it because I hit her with a pea?'

'No. Not unless she has eyes in her bum.'

She giggled.

'But, young lady, don't you ever have me dragged in there again – you'll be the death of me.'

'Dead like Dad?'

'I only mean that you'd better behave, or they'll throw you out. That was a warning. There are no other schools up here, so what will we do then?'

'Your fainting didn't do any good. Miss Marchant caned me anyway.' She lifted up her checked skirt, exposing two red welts on her thigh. 'See.'

'Oh, Lord! We'll put some salve on that.'

'My teacher cuffs me all the time.'

'Maybe because you're usually planning mischief?'

'She picks on me.'

'Then I think you should make yourself less visible, Evie. Being naughty will draw attention, as sure as fire. Just go to school, sit quietly, speak only when you're spoken too and do your homework. No playground warfare. This is the first rule of survival. If you do that, then Miss Marchant will have nothing to complain about.'

But then, who was I to lecture. I sometimes caught myself repeating my mother's stock phrases and worse, remembering her remoteness. All I knew about my own child was that I loved her beyond anything else, and that I would not become like my own mother.

'She doesn't like me. Neither does Miss Marchant. Teacher told me my plaits were scruffy and I looked ugly.'

'What nonsense! You look just like your father, and he was the most handsome man I've ever known. Don't you believe a word of it.'

'Mum?' She sat up as if about to make a pronouncement. 'If you won't marry Leon, I think you should marry Tom.'

Mentioning Leon in that way, she caught me off guard. 'Possum, this might come as a surprise to you, but marriage isn't always the answer to a girl's problems.'

'Why do we have to be so different?'

'From what?'

She shrugged and turned the page.

There was a familiar magpie, white on black, brilliant against the grass, hopping towards the steps.

'Why is its shadow so dark?' Evie said, looking at the bird.

'The brighter the sun, the darker the shadow. Though some people have shadows you can't see.'

I threw a crust down for the bird, but Evie immediately objected: 'You're only teaching it to be a beggar.' She showed me the page in her bird book.

'Sometimes I make mistakes, Evie.'

'Then why can't I?'

'We just have to be strong and keep our heads down.'

'Ouch, don't hug me so tight.'

Doctor Albert Clarke was surrounded by a perfumed band of paste-beaded nurses. Like magazine-cover girls, their calves were emphasized by fashionable just-below-the knee dresses, and even Matron Chalmers was glowing, trussed in mustard taffeta and sipping gin and tonic by the drinks table.

Clarke had made a point of summoning all the nurses to his retirement party in the ladies' lounge at the Pacific Hotel because, in his words, 'the ban on fraternisation is generally not conducive to the esprit de corps required of a well-run hospital'. I liked his modern take. Up until the war they'd rope off formal functions into two sections, so that 'trade' and other 'riff-raff' were quarantined from the professional and merchant class.

The craze for jazz had reached the far north, but the local band hurried the notes along like ragtime. I would normally have settled for signing the card of well-wishes and an early escape, but I was here on a mission. My 'uniform' was a navy linen dress – long-waisted with black trim, elbow-length sleeves, the hemline cut just above the ankle – more utility pole than beacon. I would have to make my move quickly, before word spread to the doctor about my latest dressing-down. I'd been called to Matron's office that morning as she was looking for extra volunteers for the night's shift. She obviously thought I'd accept but, in return, I politely requested a wage increase for all the extra duties I'd been covering. Two nurses had married, and although temporarily taking on their roles was good experience – assisting at operations and covering more wards – I was only being paid for my current role in pre-natal and midwifery. And with babies not caring about night or day shifts, I now had to pay Dorrie handsomely to help with Evie.

If you choose this work, Sister, you choose its hours. For Matron it was another chance to hammer home my indiscretions: *When I hear that one of my nurses is too opinionated or talks too much on the job, you can be sure this nurse is a danger. She doesn't know the difference between herself and the doctor.* Etcetera. There was no use complaining. And no matter how amiable and courteous I tried to be, it didn't work.

I stood by the door, as far as possible from the stifling crush of people, and took out my sandalwood fan. Over in the corner, Clarke looked younger than his fifty-odd years. He was a handsome man, known for his way with women, his attentive focus which made you feel you were the only person in the world. This had probably helped in recently securing a much younger wife. He cycled to work every morning in a peaked cap and with bicycle clips on his ankles, an athletic testament to healthy living.

Sybil wasn't among the coterie around him, instead standing near the band with her rosy Queen of Hearts cheeks, talking to Roy Jamieson, while the weedy accounts clerk looked on in awe of her. She drew occasionally on a jade cigarette holder sourced from Chinatown, blowing the smoke in a long thin stream, narrowly avoiding the clerk's face.

A group of young doctors stood to the side with Fuller, as if they hadn't heard that the days of segregation were over. I nodded to them, then made for my first target.

'Doctor Jamieson, can I talk to you please?'

I shoehorned in next to Sybil who turned her back, suddenly deep in conversation with the clerk.

'Ah, Sister Sinclair! I thought for sure you'd be on duty tonight. Would you like a gin and tonic, or perhaps a shandy? Be quick, drinks close at six.' He raised his voice over the music.

'No thank you. I need to keep a clear head.'

He followed me to the door, away from the jazz.

'I was hoping to have your answer soon.' I'd already given him a rough plan of financial estimates, infrastructure requirements and patient load a few weeks before and had heard nothing back.

'Oh, that.' He made a gesture of acknowledgement. 'My response is quite simple, Sister Sinclair…'

'You may call me Anna, if you wish.'

'I'm hoping to get to my point.'

'Sorry.'

'Subject to your funding, to government approval of your venture and to our hospital's sanction of my outside hours, I'm happy to provide medical services at a second hospital. It would have to be on a strict roll basis, of course.'

I stepped back to restrain myself from hugging him. 'Oh, thank you so very much.'

'But you must know that I'm agreeing to this for selfish reasons only. It will be an extra outlet for my own practice, as you have already shrewdly suggested.'

I wasn't completely convinced. Even with the details of his face blurred by gas lighting, his kindness was clear. At that moment I was in love with all crooked-toothed doctors wearing tortoiseshell rimmed spectacles.

'This is wonderful. You see, I'm in a chicken and egg situation. I need the commitment from trained doctors for the hospital loan and the loan to secure the trained doctors.'

'How many practitioners do you need?'

'Just one other. Like you, with good general and surgical skills.' I was already filled with the niggling prospect of failure, of funding being refused, of embarrassment among the medical community. 'I was hoping you might be able to put in a kind word for me with Doctor Clarke. I haven't been able to get hold of him.'

Truthfully, I hadn't tried too hard to capture Clarke's attention. I'd see him in the hospital, but a senior sister always seemed to be glued to him, or he'd be rushing off to some appointment or another. The more I wanted to talk to him the harder it was for me to summon the courage. His progressive ideas about the nursing profession set him apart – there was no one else so senior who was like that, and consequently a lot rode on gaining his support. He energetically encouraged continuing education for all staff. Matron Chalmer's formal training sessions were often sidelined by emergencies or other commitments and so, seeing the new staff left to their own resources, he'd take every opportunity to tutor them on the job. To Matron's annoyance, he allowed nurses to ask their questions directly, rather than take the proper course via her. *I'm prescribing this medicine, nurse, because… The reason I'm using the clamp on this particular vein is because…*

'Yes, he might be interested,' Jamieson said. 'He's only retiring because his new wife is always pressuring him to take her away on exotic holidays.'

'Isn't she here this afternoon?'

'Home with their baby. It's her first. She was a war widow before she met Albert. Just like you.'

'A baby? I didn't know – no one told me. And he's retiring from the profession, not just the hospital?'

'I believe her ex-husband left her an impressive inheritance. By the way, where's your little one this evening?'

'Being looked after.'

'If you want to talk to him, you'll have to make it quick before he downs another beer.'

I ordered a large shandy from the waiter and found Clarke, still with a circle of women gathered around him, a fence-line of giggles. Matron stood resolutely at his side, all restraint and decorum but with a genial gin flush. I now regretted not bringing Tom with me for moral support, even at the risk of aggravating Sybil.

'You look lovely tonight, Matron,' I said, launching into business venture flattery.

'Well, I certainly hope I don't look *too* festive. We may have endured a pandemic and have much cause for celebration, but this is a rather sad occasion, losing Doctor Clarke.' The last three words elegiacally broke the silence as the band finished a number. Clarke turned to us.

I waited for him to speak but he took a swig of beer. I held out my hand and he shifted the glass to shake mine with a cold, moist palm. 'Sister Sinclair, are you enjoying the evening?' His hair had started to flop out of its Brilliantine slickness.

'Oh, yes.' I knew this was my best chance, but Matron was still within earshot. 'I believe Doctor Jamieson is asking for you. Shall I take you over to him?' Sweat rolled into my collar, brought on by subterfuge rather than heat.

'The fellow can come here and speak to me if he wants. Now tell me, how are you enjoying life in the tropics? You're looking a tad hot, there.'

'Yes, I have a fan,' I said stupidly, under his intense gaze.

Someone came from behind me in a rush and bumped their shoulder into mine, making my drink tumble down my dress. It was Sybil. She strode on without apology.

'Oops!' Clarke said, looking at the wet patch on my bosom. 'You better fix that up, Sister.'

I found a napkin and dried what I could, but the moment was gone and so was the doctor.

When I found Roy Jamieson, he was taking out a small notebook from his pocket. 'I'm giving the speech,' he said. 'Any luck?'

'No. Not yet. I'll need your help.'

'You'll have to make it quick. He's nearly three sheets to the wind.'

'I should have spoken to him much sooner. Can you spare me one of your scraps of paper?'

He tore off a page and gave me his pen.

'Thank you, you are sweet.'

'Sweet? That's not usually the adjective people apply to me.'

'Well, I think so.'

'Then you definitely don't know me, Sister Sinclair.'

'Again, please call me Anna. After all, we are to be business partners.' I scribbled my note and gave him back his pen with a smile.

I waited for Clarke to move to the bar, where women, even matrons, were not allowed. When he collected his last drink and returned to the reception area, I blocked his path.

'Doctor Clarke.'

'Sister Sinclair. Have you been taking a bath?' He'd forgotten my spillage just minutes before.

'Doctor Clarke, I have an important matter to discuss with you. I think it's a proposition you will be very interested in. At least Doctor Jamieson thinks you might.'

'*That* old Bertie?'

'Excuse me?'

'Oh – just joking, nurse, just joking. Now, a proposition from you would be of more interest to me.' His voice was muffled by the cigarette dangling from his mouth.

I realised I'd missed my chance.

'Please, I'm quite serious. I'd like to meet with you at a more convenient time to discuss something – in the next few days if you're free. I could meet you at the hospital or, if you like, at the esplanade café on Saturday.' I put the paper in his top pocket, 'I'll be there at this time. This is important to me. I hope you'll be so kind.'

He pressed it to his chest with his free hand and headed off with a tilt towards the dais where Jamieson was about to give his speech.

13

'I'm settled here now.' Tom hoisted a leg onto the broad arm of the canvas squatter's chair, as if to emphasise how comfortably settled he was.

Beyond the sagging porch of the worker's hut, sugar cane fields, green and regular as a giant's lawn, met the rainforest where a creek trickled through the morning air. Clay-stained shirts hung from nails, drying above a hooked cane knife. The other two men, temporary workers, had already left for the paddocks, leaving Tom and me to enjoy the solitude.

'But your family must miss you.'

'Yes, they might. But they remind me of everything I don't want to be reminded of.'

'Don't you miss the law?'

'Sometimes. But thinking of it also reminds me I'm my family's creation. At least I was.' He exhaled as if in relief. 'It's more peaceful here.'

'The scenery around here makes elsewhere redundant, doesn't it?'

He reached over and squeezed my hand. 'Mutter sends letters. She's threatened to come up here for a visit, bringing her parcels of Gugelhupf cake. I've managed to fob her off.'

Down in the scrubby yard, Evie was playing by an oleander bush, poking a row of yellow flowers into her hair.

'Take them out, they're poisonous,' I yelled.

'One should always obey one's mother,' Tom shouted helpfully.

'Yes, Tom. So why don't you let yours come visit? I'll help you eat the goo…'

'Gugelhupf – her rosewater marble cake. But, no thanks. She'd kick me back to Brisbane and drop me, or what's left of me, into my uncle's firm. When I last went down the pressure was bad enough. They disapprove of me wasting my time up here, as they see it. If I'm not going to do law then I should be on the farm, helping out. You remember my father was an accountant, couldn't get much employment in this country, but he's happier with his animals and crops and has done pretty well. Down to his hard work and nous, really. I was hardly there – they boarded me at a private boys' school in Brisbane. They did all that for me. Now I'm giving them trouble again.'

'I doubt that.'

'I've been nothing but trouble for them… Lieselotte… my only sister. Liese, for short.' His face was hidden by his fist as he leant on it, but I thought I saw a shadow in his expression.

'Tell me about her.'

He turned quickly towards a whipbird's echo. 'Look, enough of me. What about you? I still don't know much about your background. Just that you came here from Scotland for some mysterious reason, lived in Brisbane, got married, and he died in the war. I've heard more about him than anyone else in your family.'

'I came to Queensland for my health. I met Andy a week or two after I arrived, so I stayed.'

'Your health?'

'Yes. I wanted to get away from all that damp sooty air in Edinburgh.' I glanced at him to see whether he believed this lie.

Knowing that the best lies contain some truth, I added, 'My family has a history of heart disease.'

'Are you well?'

'Oh, yes. It's much better in this warm climate.' The panic attacks were coming sporadically now. I figured they were similar to symptoms found in wartime soldiers, the 'Disordered Action of the Heart' caused by stress. Drugs were available, extracted from foxglove, but they weren't needed for episodic tachycardia such as mine.

'Glad to hear it. I can see why you moved to Brisbane. You never know, a few years ago we could have passed each other in the street down there.'

'I doubt you'd have noticed a married woman with a pram.'

'I definitely would have noticed *you*. Did you come out with your parents?'

'No.'

'So, they're still back there?'

'Yes, they and my two brothers, Angus and Malcolm.'

'What does your father do?'

'He's a doctor.'

'You never mentioned that before.'

'You didn't ask.'

'Usually that's something daughters have no hesitation in declaring – the ones I've met, anyway. But it explains a few things.'

'You mean about my nursing.'

'That… and more. You know, some women are becoming physicians now?'

It took me a few moments to gather my thoughts. 'They are few and far between,' I said flatly. 'Medicine is an expensive course – and impossible with a child.' I couldn't trust that what I wanted to tell him should ever be told.

'So, what do your family think of you being all the way out here?'

'Probably the same as yours do about you being all the way up here.'

'So, we're refugees together!' He looked at me as if expecting me to continue. 'I won't press,' he said after a while. 'But you'll have to tell me all about your family one day.'

'One day.' I relaxed again.

'You know what I like about this place?'

It was a rhetorical question, but I shook my head anyway, glad for the change of subject.

'That.' He pointed to the triangular-shaped mountain, rising abruptly above the cane.

'The Pyramid?'

'My aim is to climb it if my foot ever regains its full strength. It's not a mountain with a fancy name, but a pyramid, pure and simple. The settlers call it as it should be; there's no pretence. We're all in it together. Living off the land. Surviving. There are other veterans like me in the mill, an ex-dentist, tradesmen, shop assistants. The Australia we imagined from the trenches was not the country we came home to. On the ship back we were told it was a Land Fit for Heroes. Arrived to find that our soldiers were heroes only for the day's march; that the ones who stayed had pinched our girls and taken our jobs, thank you very much. We were on the scrap heap, scrounging for jobs, some with not enough limbs to be employable anyway.'

'But surely you could've taken your old job back?'

'Hardly. People say to me "pull yourself together" as if it's that easy. Sometimes I think the ones killed had it the easiest…'

I made a gesture of annoyance.

'Sorry,' he said, 'that's self-pitying nonsense.'

I pointed to The Pyramid. 'One day you'll reach that summit, you'll master all of its tranquillity.' I was thinking also of myself.

At that moment a locomotive hauling crammed cages of cane shunted down a distant tram track, hissing loudly as its small engine headed towards the mill.

Tom and I looked at each other and laughed.

The afternoon breeze brought a sweet scent like molasses.

'What's that smell?' Evie yelled from below.

'They're burning sugar cane for the mill,' Tom said. 'They do it when it's ripe. Gets rid of vermin – rats and snakes. Makes it easier to cut down.'

Orange tipped flames gradually filled the skyline, then sparked and spat out black smoke. While Evie stared at it, mesmerised, Tom leaned over and kissed my lips softly, quickly.

'Sorry.' He smiled, his face still close. 'I'm such an opportunist – had to steal it from you because you're very slow in the offering.' Then, ignoring my obvious surprise, and loudly enough for Evie to hear, he said: 'It feels good to be taking your day off when the others are still hard at it.'

After a pause, I said, 'Speaking of work, Sybil hasn't talked to me since you and I started walking out.'

'Ah, Sybil. Wonderful girl.'

'She's my closest friend. At least, she was.'

'I never made her any promises. She's far too much woman for me, tiny as she is. She'll come around – just give it time.'

'I doubt that. She's on a mission to punish me.'

'Sybil,' he said lightly, 'is someone who needs purpose and zest.'

We watched Evie spinning with her arms out, like a whirling seed. In the relative silence, and with me now thinking about that molasses kiss, I asked, 'What are you really escaping from, Tom?'

'You say that like someone who might understand.'

'How are your nights?'

'Lonely.'

'No, I mean…'

'I know what you mean.'

'I've been reading about medical trials with returned soldiers in Great Britain. Some say it helps to talk it through. Relive it and keep reliving it until you talk it into exhaustion.'

'Sounds like an idea hatched by someone who's never been at the Front. Medicine men in white coats theorising behind safe walls.'

'I know it sounds too easy, but it looks like there's been some genuine success. When I open my hospital, I'm going to take in out-of-work veterans. Give them a place to recover before they go back into society.'

'Oh, so I'm an experiment, then?' He chuckled unconvincingly.

'Seriously, I wish you'd talk to me about it. It might help.'

He reddened. 'What? Let you into my cowardly little world? Lay out my despicable weakness for you to scrutinize?'

'I'm on your side, Tom.'

'You know how to ruin a moment, my Anna. May I call you that?'

'Of course.'

'There's a reason why I chose to remain in the north. Apart from your lovely face.'

'Oh, yes?'

'My friend, Jim Miller.'

'Does he live here?'

'His bones were blasted all over a field in France. But he came from here. I've got a tin cup with his name scratched into it. That's all that's left of him.' Tom let out a long deep breath. 'He let himself get blown to bits. Sometimes I think that was the final straw. We'd had a rough morning and bodies of our men were littered outside the trench. He climbed over the parapet – he was trying to drag his dead mate back inside. We shouted at him to forget it, but he was too high on adrenaline. He was one of the Cane Beetles, they called them. Farmhands who dropped their cane knives and took a five-day march to the port at Cairns, singing songs about the King and his Empire, collecting more glory-seeking suckers on the way. He was a simple man, called a spade a spade, didn't have two bob to rub together, but he had guts. I see him here, around the fallen banana plants and squashed mangoes.'

I sat on the arm of Tom's chair and massaged his shoulder.

'Oh, that feels good,' he said, bending his neck. 'I'm not a whole man, Anna. And I'm not just talking about my half-foot and gassed-up lungs. You can see that, can't you?'

'Nonsense. You're a great man. Terrible kisser, though.'

He grabbed my hand and rubbed his chin stubble against it. 'Changing the subject, I've got something for your little whirlybird down there.'

He got up and headed inside the hut. I noticed his slight off-kilter gait was accentuated after he'd been sitting for a while. He came back with a wind-up tin dog.

'Here, Evie, a present for you.'

She bounded up the steps, took the toy, then gave him a long hug. I wanted this picture, of my girl and the man I was trying not to fall for, to remain just so.

With a shriek, Evie sprang away from Tom, pointing. I saw it a moment after she did. Absurdly, I registered a garden hose uncoiling itself from behind a tub on the porch. A snake the colour of dead leaves was skimming towards my chair.

'Don't move, anyone!' Tom yelled.

I watched the creature come alongside me. Impulsively I lifted one of my feet in defence, to which it responded with an uplift of its head.

'Evie, you must stay still,' I said.

She stood screaming.

I heard the crack first. The cane knife had come down on the boards, slicing the reptile's head from its body.

'Taipan,' Tom said. 'Venomous as hell. It must have been chased out by the burning. They come to the cane for the rats.'

He picked up the remnants with a shovel and flung them into a dirt hole.

'Thank you, Tom. I owe you.'

'No – we look after each other.'

Our relationship was nascent and unbroken then, and the flow of it, his kiss, was nudging away the memory of Andy and all my shadows. But I still wondered if I'd enough to offer, because with Tom it would never be straightforward. We might always come to each other like this: me with my child and my ghosts, he with his battalion of demons.

The woman sat with one hand rocking a pram covered in muslin. She appeared to be about my age. Two strands of pearls rested perfectly upon her pink silk blouse and her crimped hair was clasped in a thick bun. She crowned this gentility with an aerophane-edged flop hat.

'Mrs Clarke? Clarissa Clarke?' I asked.

In the distance behind her, a group of indigenous children played tag near the ramp for the ferry, wet shirts stuck to their skinny chests, legs slick with mud. They revelled in their day release from the mission.

'How do you do. I received your note. I'm Anna Sinclair.' Up close, her lightly powdered skin showed no sign of freckle or tan, no hint that she had even a passing relationship with the punishing outdoors.

I held out my hand, but the woman kept both of hers on the pram handle. The child was swathed in white and whimpering.

'I thought the note was from your husband, Albert, at first.' I immediately regretted my over-familiar reference to him.

Mrs Clarke motioned to a wooden café chair, saying, 'Please sit down,' like a hostess inviting in her guest.

'I only have thirty minutes – it's my lunch break.' I took a seat, smoothing my skirt under me to avoid the tell-tale crease. Uniforms were not allowed out of hospital during breaks without permission. 'Please forgive me, but I have no idea why you wanted to meet.'

She produced a note from her bag and held it disdainfully between her index and middle finger. 'It's about this.'

I looked at the hovering paper and waited for an explanation. But she merely scrutinised me, in the way a grand lady might regard a scullery maid who'd failed in some duty and was now expected to burst into tears. I'd seen my mother with the same expression.

'May I see it?'

The note was crumpled and stained. I unfolded it and laughed with embarrassment.

Her cupid mouth tightened.

'I'm afraid that your husband was a bit under the weather when I gave this to him,' I said.

No words, just a look that said she would slap me if she could.

I realised my gaffe. 'I'm sorry, I think you've got the wrong end of the stick. May I buy you a lemon squash?'

She waved my offer away.

'This is not what you think, Mrs Clarke.'

'Then I think you owe me an explanation, wouldn't you say?'

'It's really quite simple. I'm not sure what you're thinking, but I can assure you it was benign.' *Benign?* 'Look, I wanted to meet with your husband to discuss a business proposal. But he didn't turn up.'

An eyebrow raised. 'You? Business?'

'I was told it would interest him. I think it could be a great asset to this community.'

The baby quietened and I stopped, afraid to rouse it.

'Go on.'

'I'm a war widow, like you,' I said. I couldn't tell if this attempt at common ground eased the situation, so I hurried on, explaining my plans for the hospital, my need for her husband's help.

Her expression was watchful.

'I should have chosen a more suitable time to discuss my plans with your husband. But I'm new at this, you see.'

The breeze died and the air fell on us like a clammy net, a reminder of the oncoming monsoon season. 'Another hospital? The current one is quite adequate, I would say.'

'It is, indeed. But as we've just seen with the recent influenza outbreak, hospitals become overcrowded and toxic very quickly in an epidemic. And the last cyclone brought its own diseases – mosquitos breeding in backyard bins, the badly-drained mudflats around us brought…'

'How bizarre.' She sniffed. 'You want to put a *private* hospital here, in these mangrove flats.'

'Yes, indeed,' I said. 'It's good enough for the District Hospital.'

She pushed the pram outwards as if widening the distance between the baby and me. 'How on earth does someone like you afford to have their own hospital?'

Now she had me.

'I think I should save you the embarrassment, Mrs Sinclair, by telling you that my husband will absolutely not be interested in your proposal. He is done with medicine. We are travelling.'

I slid the note back across the table. 'I understand what you are saying. I would not expect him to be attending my hospital full-time. I just thought he might like to keep his hand in. He wouldn't be the only medical officer on call.'

'On call? My husband will not be *on call*.'

'I don't want to interfere with your family life…'

'What makes you think you have the ability to do so?'

'… but I would really like to discuss the proposition with him first. There are others who believe Doctor Clarke will find it of great interest.'

'You are not getting my message, Mrs Sinclair.' She clipped her bag shut and rose.

'My project is a serious endeavour. This settlement is in need of so many more health facilities. We serve a very large district, including the tablelands, and we don't have enough medical services to cope. You were here during the last cyclone? The hospital was packed. We had to put critical patients in the hallways. I saw your husband at work during that time. He's so committed and such an excellent physician.'

'It's hardly your place to comment upon my husband's work ethic. And hospital facilities are our government's concern, not yours.'

'There are many lying-in hospitals being established in the country regions for exactly this reason. And someone has to run them.'

'As I said, not our concern. Goodbye.'

As she walked off towards her home somewhere at the 'better end' of the esplanade, the baby woke and started to cry. It took me back to midwifery classes during the war, where we practised on a linen torso stuffed with horsehair, a white linen 'baby' curled in the pink satin uterus, ready to be drawn out through a pudendum quilted in labia lines. Trainees from conservative homes, protected from the horror of bodily functions, were appalled at the absurdity of it all, this linen and satin outrage. They began to realise there was no room for airs and graces when a woman was birthing like a cow.

14

A half-asleep mare and a scraggy carthorse were hitched up to Leon's fence, snorting and flicking tethers as they nuzzled towards his new hibiscus bushes, imported from Hawaii. Cheap cigarette smoke and Tchaikovsky's symphony competed with husky voices, drifting down to our yard. I coughed and a window closed with a click of the catch.

Leon was generally a quiet neighbour – I'd gauge his daily coming and going by the cranking of his car engine, usually two or three turns, then the rumble of his return and brisk scraping of horse droppings from its wheels. At that time there were only a handful of other cars in Cairns, mostly General Motors Holdens and model Ts owned by the mayor, a few shop owners, some farmers and doctors, as well as the new hospital ambulance. Pictures of the vehicles with well-dressed drivers and admiring passengers tantalised in the weekend newspapers. But the numbers here were nothing like the southern cities where dirt roads were sealed with tarmac, making the drive as smooth as air.

'He's having one of his boys' parties again,' Dorrie said, startling me at the fence. 'I wish he wasn't so damned noisy; he'll wake up the dogs and then they'll be hell to pay getting them to quiet down. But I need a break, anyway. Want a cuppa?'

'Thank you. Good timing – I was coming up for one.'

She cleared her account books and silk fan from the kitchen table. 'At least you miss his racket when you're on night duty. Happens now every second Saturday.'

'What's he up to? Do you have any idea what he does for a living?'

'He's still vague about that, love. Seems he comes from money.'

She laid out two china cups and saucers, the overdecorated sort that a fiancée would bring with her trousseau. As she put the teapot down, white roots parted her hennaed hair. She might have been an attractive bride, but I didn't ask if she'd married, afraid it might open a wound. She didn't talk of a husband and there was no sign of family of any kind, giving the impression that she'd always been mistress of her own life. She wasn't involved in women's organisations, never went to church, and seemed to enjoy socialising on the fringe of society at the mosquito-infested shanty town by Alligator Creek. From her visits there she'd bring home a basket of strange dried objects – twisted leaves and desiccated animal parts – for whatever ailment afflicted her at the time.

'So, how's this hospital of yours going?' She took out a jug from the ice chest, milk curdles floating, the iceman not due till Monday.

'It's stalled. I thought I'd enough backers, but apparently not.'

'Backers? Financiers you mean?'

'No, well, yes. But firstly, I need qualified medical practitioners to give me references and support – it's the bank's requirements.'

'Who did you have in mind, then?'

'I work with them – at least with one – the other has just retired.'

'Who's that?'

'No one you'd know, I don't think. Doctor Clarke?'

'Albert Clarke?'

'You know him?'

She poured her tea into a deep saucer and took a sip. 'He was a familiar. Long time ago. Between wives.'

'I met his wife a few days ago. She seems… constrained.'

'Let's hope he can keep this one.'

'You seem to know a bit about him?'

'More than I want to.'

'Now I'm intrigued.'

'Ah, that'd be telling.'

'Surely you didn't have a thing with him?'

'Good Lord, no!'

Leon's windows were open again, judging by the increase in volume, and we sat listening. Another Russian concerto.

'They're on to their Cigares de Joy again. Didn't think so many of them were asthmatics,' Dorrie said wryly.

'Yes, they're hallucinogenic – but stramonium is supposed to give some relief. I doubt that smoke for inflamed lungs is really the answer, though.'

'They must be having a riot – with all their imaginary friends.'

'How d'you know about those cigarettes? They're not common over here.'

'You'd be surprised what I know, love. I'm no spring chicken.'

'It's times like this I realise how little I know about you, Dorrie. You're kind, perhaps too kind, but that's really all I know.'

'Perhaps it's best that way.'

'The rooms you hire out, next to ours. They're usually never occupied by anyone longer than a night. Why is that?'

'Itinerant workers. I told you. They don't disturb you, do they? In all your time here, you've never complained. I have the cheapest clean lodgings in town and the condition is that they keep quiet.'

'But they usually arrive at night and are gone before light.' This was a statement of fact rather than a question – a question I'd always carefully avoided.

'That's the other condition – better for you and Evie, don't you think?'

I looked at her steadily.

She raised her hands in the air in a gesture of defeat. 'You're a smart girl. I'm sure you've worked it out. If you don't like it, you're always free to leave.'

'Is that how you know Doctor Clarke?'

'As I said,' she tapped the side of her nose, '*that* would be telling.'

I wondered what the town knew, what the conservative sorts deduced about me and Evie living here; wondered if that's what lay behind the starchy disapproval from school principals and matrons.

Dorrie brushed away a moth. 'Tom, he's a good 'un. What's holding you back?'

'It's complicated…'

She broke in. 'The heart always knows what it needs.'

'A whole heart might. Mine's in bits. So's his.'

'All the better reason to join them.'

We clinked teacups, sealing a kind of pact.

The music stopped and men thumped down Leon's stairs to their horses. I counted five – it was hard to make them out in the dark.

Maybe it was time to make a go of it with Tom. Live somewhere else, away from the goings-on at the mangrove end of the esplanade. Away from Hawaiian shirts.

'I'll lose my job. And my widow's pension too.'

'The pension? What, a pound a week?!'

'And my job. I'm up for a senior sister position soon, if Matron Chalmers doesn't give it the kibosh.'

'How much extra will that really give you? If your hospital plan goes ahead, you'll be your own boss. And no one will lord it over you.'

'*If.* Everything hangs on *if.*' My skin prickled under the woolknit bathing suit and my legs, basted in coconut oil, started to tingle – they felt as overheated as our argument.

'That's nothing more than semantics, Anna. I just offered you my soul and you quibble about grammar.'

'You didn't offer me anything, Tom. You only suggested it. *What if we got engaged, what if we got married?*'

'I'll get up on my knees and do it properly then.'

'No!'

'You're the best thing that's ever happened to me. I love you. And I think, although you haven't admitted it yet, you love me.'

'Once, I would have thought that that was enough. But what about the rest? Are trips to the pictures and excursions like today a basis for marriage? Besides, when we've been alone, we've not really… you know. We've kissed but…' It came out too clinically. And it was only an excuse.

He looked away to my daughter splashing in the sandy shallows of the island, but I saw the sting of my words in the set of his mouth. Andy would have hated it – knowing another man had stepped in, was helping me erase him. I even wondered if I'd encouraged Tom simply because he reminded me of my husband, dead now five years; and that subconsciously I felt that healing this soldier would bring back the other.

'Is it because of your husband? The reason I've had to wait so long. Or is it because I'm a cripple?'

Tom's perceptiveness and intellect were largely what drew me to him. But physically, too; his tensile body as he leant back on his elbows, his honey-brown legs on the bamboo mat, even his feet – his foot and a half, currently covered in bucket-shaped sandcastles – I found everything about him attractive. He was a different man to the one I'd nursed in hospital. At the moving pictures, watching the double viewing of *The Fourteenth Man* and *The ABC of Love*, black and white mistiness through the cigarette smoke, the piano's final chords, Tom reached his hand across the canvas deckchair. I'd held it to my cheek, our shy distance broken. His lips were on mine, our first real kiss and my head was spinning like an ingénue's. Later, with his hand on my breast, my hand on his thigh, I realised how deeply I felt. And I felt it almost every time I saw him now.

'Feet are over-rated,' I replied. 'You're just the way I like it.'

'What do you mean?'

'Easy to catch.'

'You…!'

I got up and ran into the sea, sinking up to my ankles in soft wet sand and slowing, so that he was able to catch me and pull me down with him. Briefly, as we kissed, he pressed his body into mine under the ocean, as if we were naked. I released myself and swam away in a four-stroke crawl, he following, over to the coloured coral forest under the jetty, chasing the shoals of tiny blue, yellow and orange fish, keeping an eye on a lethargic sand shark. There was transient distraction in this alien world.

It was as if the cay had been formed for a perfect afternoon walk. Where there wasn't beach to cross, there were narrow sandy paths winding through the scrubby trees and rainforest, beaten down by the feet of visitors and increasingly now, scientists hunting for clues and specimens. The three of us circumnavigated it at a pace Tom found comfortable, my daughter on his shoulders.

Wrapped in towels, we held hands, passing only one or two others. We fantasized about what it would be like to stay here, living off fish, birds, and molluscs, sleeping in gunyahs, and even planned a strategy to miss the launch back to Cairns.

'There's a legend that guarding spirits live here,' Tom said with a smile. 'They say that's why it's unpopulated.'

Under that goblin sky I devised my words. But it wasn't until we were in the boat watching the island become smaller, gusts of sea-spray stinging me into action, that I found the courage.

'I think it's time we got to know each other… properly, intimately.' I said this in a rush, and it didn't come out the way I intended. Too formal, out of context.

Tom shook his head, startled. 'What?'

'I mean it. The way you make me feel makes me want you more each day.' *And this way, you might help me let go of the past.*

'Want? But I thought…'

'Want. All of it.'

'That's… very *progressive* of you, Anna.'

I felt myself blush. 'I think you should accept my offer before I change my mind.'

He smiled.

'Good. Next weekend, Evie's staying with a friend. How about I come over to your place?'

'I'll pick you up Saturday night after work.'

It was too easy, like buying a favour, and I regretted it almost as soon as it was agreed. This was not how I imagined it would go, me half-begging for sex – that's what it must have looked like to Tom. But then, nothing had gone the way it was meant to. I barely had a shilling to spare for Evie's shoes which she seemed to grow out of too quickly, and in our hot little room under Dorrie's house we ate sandwiches for dinner more often than meat.

If I'd been more vigilant that night in Edinburgh, if I'd not ploughed on with blind self-righteousness, I'd never have had to leave the place. My medical degree would be finished, and I'd be truly free. I'd probably also be a surgeon's wife, but more importantly, with an enlightened husband, a practising doctor myself. No doubt we'd have a large house with at least one servant, and he'd vote for the Tories, though we wouldn't debate that. My husband, the archetypical do-gooder and Mason like my father, would be highly regarded and our children would attend the 'right' schools. The boys would go to his old school, the girls to mine. We'd all drive to St Giles' Cathedral on Sunday for Morning Service to take Communion. Sex would not have to be proposed.

It would have been some kind of happiness – the sensible kind.

15

HUNTLY. – At Morningside, Edinburgh on 24ᵗʰ inst, MALCOLM JAMES HUNTLY, aged 29, second son of Dr Gordon Huntly, MB, ChB, FRCSE. A valiant heart to the end. Funeral private. (No Flowers)

It was in Jamieson's Edinburgh newspaper. Malcolm, the brother who taught me chess and draughts in front of the fire, who used to slide me along the ice outside our house on a board, who backed me up in arguments with Angus. He hated flowers, they made him sneeze and set his heart racing.

I was late now. I raced upstairs to the ward holding the Mount Mulligan survivors. A whole contingent of miners had been killed, a double tragedy, since some were men previously nursed at the hospital and sent off, only to end up back in that choking labyrinth. Only a few, those near the entrance when the coal mine exploded, were not entombed. The handful of blast survivors in our ward had been brought down from the tablelands, red-raw, skinless under the black coal dust, and blind. These hard men with their solid sinewy muscles rejected all sympathy.

My own skin was still tender with trivial sunburn as I tried to reassure a barely conscious man that he would soon be whole again; but I recognised the fading jugular pulse. He was in the bed occupied by Tate the alcoholic just the night before. Tate had lost his job at the railway and then his wife threw away all the grog. A few days without it and he had to be admitted with delirium tremens – yelling, shaking, feverish, and with his pulse racing. He was too advanced to save. He had an infarction and died in this bed of widows.

I was jolted by a trolley butting me. It was Sybil, going too fast again.

'Now you've done it,' she said loudly, as zinc oxide plasters, swabs, blue bottles, green bottles, tincture of iodine and Listerine toppled and fell onto the floor. '*I've* finished the beds and dressings for you,' she continued with emphasis.

My thoughts scrambling: *My brother is dead, and all this is so petty.*

'If anything's broken, Sister Sinclair, you'll pay for it.' Matron was at my ear. She'd arrived on the scene with the new Medical Superintendent's grand round of the wards.

Behind her, in military ranking, stood Nora Owens, now promoted to sister and the new Deputy Matron. (Verity Timms, encouraged by Jamieson, had returned to her rural hometown shortly after the influenza epidemic. She'd given up nursing to pursue her dream of running a milliner's shop). Matron shook her head as the superintendent, taking up the rear, watched with dispassionate boredom while I retrieved the bottles from the floor.

'Where have you been?' Chalmers asked.

'Sorry, I was on duty in hospital services.' *My brother is dead.*

'I hope I don't have to remind you of your schedule again. Perhaps if you weren't in such a rush, you wouldn't be destroying hospital property.'

As they turned to go, Nora shot Sybil a conspiratorial smile.

I caught Sybil's arm but she snatched it away. 'For goodness' sake, we used to be friends.'

Her eyes narrowed. 'A friend is not someone who breaks your trust. Who carries on with your boyfriend behind your back, all the while pretending to sympathise with you because he's left you for her.'

'You're right. I could have been a better friend. Please, let's not waste what we had. Life's too short.' I don't know what she made of my tears.

She took off across the hall.

'Slow down. You're missing Women's Medical.' I caught the trolley and stopped it abruptly outside the ward.

'If you're upset, it's all your own doing,' she barked.

'I'll explain later, if you'll let me.'

'Maybe.'

'Look, I know this is no excuse, but it just happened with Tom.'

'For Crikey's sake, be bloody honest for once. Nothing *just happens.*' She shook her head.

'No, wait. Please. I'm sorry. This is crazy. Come for dinner tomorrow, won't you? I've got a cut of roast and I'll cook up some vegetables.'

I waited for the rebuff.

'Do you have sherry?'

'I'll get some. And there's cream. I'll make a treacle sponge.'

'Hmm, all right. But don't expect things to be all pally again.'

A fly, trapped in the syrup-and-resin-soaked paper hanging by the kitchen window buzzed intermittently. It was a close night, and I'd politely declined Dorrie's invitation to use the dining room, allotted for her 'official' guests, though I'd never observed any. It was a stuffy shrine to the turn of the century; a mirror framed in chipped gilt reflected the occasional glitter of the Welsbach lights; small framed prints hung almost floor to ceiling; and polished side-boards were smothered in fringed damask. Dorrie's two dogs would sleep under the relative cool of the dining-table most of the day. Her only concession to modernity was a set of crystal glasses with a matching soda syphon criss-crossed in silver. No one could blame her – Dorrie's best years had been lived when Victoria was queen.

'I think you better put that thing out of its misery,' Sybil said, pointing her spoonful of cream in the direction of the stuck fly.

I screwed up the flypaper and put it in the bin. 'No, don't get up,' I said as she went to scrape the dishes.

She lit a cigarette, inhaled deeply, contorted her mouth, and blew out the smoke. 'I'm really sorry about your brother,' she said.

'Thanks. It was expected, but that doesn't make it any better. I'm sorry too, Sybs. About… you know.'

'Tom was the best I ever had. Hard to forgive that.'

'I should've been more honest with you. I wasn't really sure about him at the start, but I guess deep down I knew he'd ditched you for me.'

'That's the biggest cut, me pouring my heart out to you and you pretending you were so innocent. I was probably more upset about you than Tom. After all, I only knew him a flea's lifespan. Mind you…' she fixed on me until I stopped rinsing, 'we did… you know…'

'You did?'

'Yes. How does that make you feel, huh? Not too good, I see. You've gone a bit green around the gills.'

'It doesn't matter. I deserve it, I guess.' But I felt it in my gut, a twisting jealousy.

'So… you *haven't*, have you?'

'No…'

'Well, I won't tell you how it went for me, then.'

'I'd rather you didn't mention it again.'

'I suppose you want me to say sorry, too? For being such a bitch. I was getting bored with it all, anyway.'

'No need, Sybs. But you know how to hold a proper grudge – I can hardly believe it's been nearly a year. I've missed you. Your bump and run offensive made you hard to catch.'

She laughed. 'If you're going to do something, then you should do it well. That's *your* saying.'

Leon's gramophone started up and the sound of male voices came from his windows.

'What's that noise?' she said.

'It's next door having one of his card games – at least, I think that's what they are. You remember him? You met him – but you were drunk as billy-o after the Strand Hotel that night.'

'Oh yes. Vaguely. He's a looker, right? I remember a Rudolph Valentino type driving a fast car. Or maybe that was my gin-eyes.' Sybil stretched her neck out the window, scanning Leon's back yard. 'Can't see anything.'

'I think he likes it that way. More sherry?'

'No need to ask.'

Dorrie came in from the sitting-room to fill her glass with water and take some cake. 'The smell of this pudding has been driving me wild.'

'So, how's your lying-in hospital idea going?' Sybil asked.

'Work in progress. Still saving. It's hard but I'm getting there. I'm planning for more than just maternity. There are so many tropical ailments here. And as you know, many people up here tend to shy away from hospitals – can't afford them – so there's small chance to improve treatments.'

'Isn't there a tropical diseases centre in Townsville?'

'I'm not so interested in the research as the care, for all types of cases, if that makes sense. The haphazard stuff I see going on at the District sometimes…'

'Oh, yes. I'm with you there.'

'But I've criteria to meet to get the bank loan and I'm having trouble getting interested practitioners. Jamieson is keen. I nearly had Clarke, but that fell through – his wife was a wet blanket.'

The din from Leon's house grew louder – orchestra at full volume. Dorrie shut the windows.

'Lousy taste in music,' Sybil said. 'Are you giving up on your hospital, then?'

'Absolutely not. Even if it kills me.'

'You'll get there, love.' Dorrie finished her drink with a noisy gulp. 'I know what it's like to be on your own and struggling. It's hard to see it now, but you'll get there.'

'It's stuffy in here, now,' Sybil said. 'Let's go out on the veranda.'

'It'll be even noisier there.'

'Blow it! I'll fix him.' Sybil was out the front door and charging down the steps before I could stop her.

I followed, calling for her to come back, but then she was at Leon's, pounding on his door.

The gramophone stopped, the voices quietened, and Leon opened the door with a furious expression, bringing with him the smell of beer and cigars. A group of men were at the end of the room around a table which was covered in bottles. Their hands were empty – no decks of cards, just a typewriter, pamphlets and an open exercise book by Leon's vacated chair.

A single wolf whistle came from the group.

Sybil appeared lost for words, so I spoke. 'Sorry to disturb you Leon, but could you please keep the music down a bit, my daughter is trying to sleep.'

'She never complains about it.' He was looking at me coldly.

'How would you know?' Then I realised. 'We've talked about this, Leon. You *are* aware she's not allowed to come over here.'

'I'm no monster, Ma'am.'

'Do you mind!' Sybil had planted her feet firmly on the threshold and Leon was taking her by the shoulders to turn her away.

'Hold on, I know you,' he said, his voice rising. 'You're the gal with the broken heart.'

'Not anymore.'

'And an admirer of a well built chassis.'

'Would you mind removing your hands,' Sybil said.

'Obligingly.'

'C'mon, Sybs. Time to go.' Sybil was released, but neither she nor Leon moved.

'Hey, Leon!' someone called. 'Are we not pretty enough for you.' A deep guffaw.

He regarded Sybil in a way that made me feel like I was trespassing.

'C'mon, Sybs, let's get going.'

'Hang on a moment, ladies.' His expression turned to amusement. 'You know where I live now, Sybil, isn't it? Feel free to pop over anytime. With Mrs Sinclair if you like.'

'Watch out for him, girlie,' a man said. 'Take me instead.'

Downstairs, Sybil said with a sigh, 'He could have asked me to the flicks, at least.'

16

He wasn't there, just the impression of his head on the pillow. There was the hollow tick of the alarm clock, set for five, and the call of foraging doves outside the open window. The sickly smell of rotting mangoes brought me fully awake.

'Tom?' Through the mosquito netting I saw no sign of him in the barracks' room, just the shaving-mirror and coffee pot glinting in the lazy light.

In the chirrup of the evening before, twilight darkening, he'd laid his head on an upstretched arm. I traced my finger round his nipple and up to the scar on his neck.

'Why won't you tell me?'

He put his finger on my lips then followed them with a kiss. He caressed me slowly until a long time later my body arched in pleasure, our mouths parting, our tongues touching in eager exploration, the narrow bed our only world. When I reached the point where my body wanted all of him, he pulled away from me.

'Sorry,' he said.

'Am I too forward?'

'That's not it. Believe me.'

Each time that night, it was the same. I found myself craving nights in another place, the memory of vigour and Andy, feeling the dark pressure of loss.

We lay together, now feeling awkward.

I said, 'Is it me?'

'No, never.' He rolled away from me, his shoulders rigid. I curled into the musculature of his back and hugged him.

Hours later, when I was pretending to sleep, pretending I was content, aware of the moonlight on my face, I heard him whisper, 'You're beautiful.'

His demons arrived in a dream. He flailed and fought and called, barely coherent. I hushed him and he woke, and I held him close until he drifted off again. Anna the healer. Anna in charge.

In the dawn, shapes, thoughts, came fuzzily – memories of little things I'd tucked away since the day the pink telegram came from the colonel. When the newness of our relationship was spent, when we no longer needed to impress, Andy had the habit of talking over me, telling me what to think, selecting which clothes I should wear out. He hated my friends, what few I had. I'd sit on the deck with the baby tucked in for the night, possums skittering down branches onto the roof, right on cue with sundown, his beer ready for him, waiting well past dinnertime. It took me a while to learn how to negotiate the imperfections of marriage, to learn its perplexing language, how to lose myself in it.

The colonel's official notice was enclosed in the parcel of Andy's belongings. Folded inside the band of my husband's cap was his cryptic unfinished page to 'Georgia', the words, *secret*, and *reunited*, glaring from it. I was too grief-stricken for their meaning to register straight away. Even after I threw it away, that letter haunted me. In time, that discovery helped galvanise me. I suspected I'd been grieving for something I only thought I had. Death sanitised life, mourning acted as a shield for the dead.

There was scratching on the floorboards and a small bush rat disappeared through the hut door which had been left ajar. I got out of bed, naked. On the chest a bowl of water was filled with frangipani petals, there since the night before and now half-submerged, a bar of soap on the towel next to it. I went to my overnight bag and took out a dressing gown.

Between unwashed dishes from our lover's dinner there was a note and a button. I recognised the button from my starched work collar. Tom had kept it since the cyclone. With a sense of foreboding, I opened the note. *I cannot*, it simply said. A tug in my belly, every part frozen.

His clothes were still draped over the chair, his shoes under it.

Outside, I picked my way, barefoot, walking and hopping through the damp stubby grass, the early sun edging solitaire palm fronds in light, distant white cockatoos squawking away from the mountains. The chimney from Hambledon Mill was quiet, smokeless. Tom's buggy was abandoned beside the hut, and the horse, left unhobbled in our hurry to get inside the night before, had broken its tether and left a trail mark through the grass to the creek. I followed it as branches scraped my legs, bindi-eyes stabbed my soles, and sticks moved when I stepped on them, coiling and uncoiling in my imagination.

I saw a man through the jungle growth, or had an image rather than seeing him, a grey man in baggy undies, hanging from a noose made of vine.

'Tom! Tom!' My voice echoed down the gully.

I eventually found him, sitting on the forest floor, naked, head bowed, his skin supernaturally pale against the dark green backdrop, the tattoo of a coquette winking at me from his arm.

His left hand held something heavy, half-hidden by his leg. His mouth drooped and his face had the expression I recognised from elderly patients in the rag doll minutes before their end.

'Let it go, Tom. Let it go. Here.' I reached down to take the revolver.

He looked blankly at me.

'Let it go!'

He gave a start. Rallying, he said, 'It's for wild boar, they charge at you out here.' He made no attempt to make it sound convincing.

'Please.' I reached out my hand.

Slowly, I prized the gun away from his fist and put it out of his reach.

'I don't even have the guts anymore.' His voice croaked.

I checked to see if he was wounded. 'It's fine, Tom, please. You'll be fine. You will be. I hope this isn't anything to do with last night. Last night was just the beginning. There will be more, many more wonderful times.'

'I'm a wreck. Can't keep a woman happy. Surely you can see this? I fudge my way through life. Put on a show. I can't pretend anymore.' His chest rose as he sucked in a deep breath then exhaled gently. 'It's the images. They never leave, even when I'm with you. The stench. Cadavers, decomposing limbs, holes for eyes. It's stuck in me.'

'It's only been a couple of years, Tom. It'll take time.'

'Some of us couldn't wait to get to the Front. Eighteen-year-olds, some seventeen, champing at the bit to show everyone they were men. This was a chance to prove what we were made of. Brave warriors, all of us. Bloody idiots. Some are born to it, I think. But we were all full of it, the politicians egging us on, telling us it was for glory.'

As his breathing settled, so did mine.

'Didn't think it at the time, but we were just pawns sent out to save politicians' blunders.' He shook his head. 'My unit was assigned as trench raiders for a while… you can't ever understand… in the quiet of night, plunging your knife into a man's guts, hearing his realisation, his pain, him writhing, you twisting it again and again to make him stop, the smell of blood everywhere, flesh coming out on the blade, mince-meat.' He paused and gave a long sigh. 'Stop the agony, that's what you're thinking. It's him or you.'

'Oh, Tom,' I whispered. How could I tell him that I knew what it was like to take a life? An unsanctioned killing, if there's such a thing. No glory attached.

'Afterwards, some of us sporting their helmets like barbaric death trophies.'

I put my arm round him and pressed my forehead to his.

'It's useless. I'm useless. I've nothing to offer you, Anna. I'll always be dodging that next shell. See that tree there? It could come from behind, right now. And that,' he indicated the Webley revolver, 'I'm so low, I souvenired it from a dead machine-gunner in my own battalion.'

He'd invited me in, revealed his core, its devastated, emasculated state. We held each other, surrounded by the rattle of frogs and early cicadas. He heaved in great gulps of air and gave a cry of unselfconscious anguish. It reached into the corners of the rainforest but silenced nothing.

PART TWO

1921–1922

17

The isolation hut was crammed with children, faces livid with fever and unable to stop scratching their abdomens. Doctor Jamieson, gloved and masked, checked temperatures, arterial pressure points, throats, and white tongues while I noted the charts.

'The parents are saying it was a bad batch of milk,' I said.

'Unlikely. Measles is airborne. That's why I insist on masks. We're lucky there have been no deaths, so far. We can't stop the spread, but we do need to find a way to strike it within the body itself.' He patted a boy on his shoulder and moved on to the next patient, a girl no older than three, draped limply in a cot and sweating profusely.

'No one seems interested in this little one,' I whispered. 'Her father committed suicide recently and the mother has been spirited away by relatives.'

'He was in the army, no doubt.' He gave a nod of recognition to no one in particular.

'I don't know – but he was out of work.' I placed a damp cloth on the girl's forehead and propped her up to take a drink of water. The girl moved her head away from a shaft of sunlight, moaning. 'Come on, Maude, sweetheart, just a little sip. I'll lower the blinds for you.'

'I used to treat attempted suicides in a military hospital in Devon,' Jamieson explained. 'Some patients had a few goes before being incarcerated there. At first the favoured treatment was electric shock therapy – "faradisation" – sometimes administered by a sister, like yourself.'

'There's a view, doctor, not one that I agree with, that these men are already predisposed to weakness.' I'd read everything I could find about neurasthenia, for Tom, for both of us.

'That's a common theory even among specialists. There's not much sympathy for these soldiers at all, partly because there have been so many suicides, and foolish people think that's a sign of weakness. It doesn't help that tens of thousands came back with gonorrhoea or syphilis. After the Front, the prostitutes of France must have seemed like goddesses to those men…' He turned away. 'Let's take our conversation away from Maude's hearing.'

Jamieson put the chart back beside the cot. 'Get the children's nurse back from her break when we're done. This one needs a close watch.' We left the whimpering girl and walked to the main building, throwing our gowns, masks, and gloves into a linen bin which I tied securely for the orderlies. 'Personally, I think this attitude towards veterans is ignorant codswallop. I can't imagine how any man, weak or not, could cope with the daily bombardment of trench warfare.'

I was encouraged by his willingness to confide. 'Can I ask how the electric treatment works?' During Medicine, I'd studied experiments on frogs' hearts with a string galvanometer, the ectopic rhythms shocked into regularity. But heart muscle was a simpler biology. With the brain so complex, the attempt at beneficial rearrangement by faradisation seemed as implausible as Frankenstein's experiments on his tragic monster.

'I'm not a big fan, although it's been mooted for the hospitals down south. I don't think we still fully grasp how it works. The idea is to shock the affliction out of the patient. He lies on a reclining chair or bed with conductor pads resting on the head, or the thighs, depending on the particular ailment. There's a sliding scale attached to an electric board with a generator and the sister, or whoever, applies the level of electricity according to the dial at the bottom. It's done gradually, over a period of minutes.'

'Could we do that here?'

'All we'd need would be some decent generators. I've heard a local power station may be on the cards.'

'But do they work – these shocks?'

'In a few cases that I've heard of. It's not a pleasant experience. The men I saw were kept in solitary confinement in a bare room, mainly because they were prone to fitting. I'd rather adopt the new method: hypnosis, persuasion, and massage – that combination has had reasonable success. Soldiers who could barely walk without falling to the floor in a terrified paroxysm, men with rotating Von Graefe's eyes from war-induced hyperthyroidism and hyperadrenalism, they've walked out of hospital, apparently cured. For a while anyway.'

'I've read that they think the disease can be divided into two groups.'

'They classify it as neurasthenic or hysterical. They say the second kind affects privates more than officers. I think that's too simplified a view, influenced by attitudes about class, although logically it's the sappers at the front who bear the brunt, and they do far outnumber officers. I find it tends to be the younger ones, often the daredevils.'

'But rationally, wouldn't kindness and acceptance be important in tackling such an illness? Wouldn't electrotherapy and isolation traumatise the patient more? Of course, I'm no expert.' At some cost I'd sent away for Freud's *Introduction to Psychoanalysis* and had heard of Jung now tackling the cryptic life of the mind, its neurosis and psychosis.

'I tend to agree. I suspect that the few supposedly cured patients probably frighten themselves into recovery. The trouble is that so few people actually recognise it as an illness.'

'We're a strange species, aren't we? What we don't understand we either vilify or lionise.'

'You know, Sister, I think we could work together extremely well.'

'That would be wonderful! But may I ask why you came out here to Australia, especially given your interest in psychotherapy?'

He stepped back a little, as if instinctively. 'That's a reasonable question, I suppose. I just needed a change.'

A bandy-legged doctor from foggy London seeking the sun. I imagined him as a child with rickets. But clearly there was more to his story. 'Well, North Queensland is as far away as you'll get from anywhere.'

'That's the whole idea, Sister.'

'This town seems to be a hiding place. Once you get here you don't want to leave. There's something about it that's both exquisite and cruel.'

Cairns was a promising centre of middle class comfort for some, but it also attracted outcasts who became stuck here, as if stuck in the mud. A bit like myself. Its shanty town was still filled with families descended from the cane labourers of the last century – Japanese, Chinese, Pacific Islanders.

He looked at me with a curious expression and I blushed. 'Sorry, I wasn't meaning you.'

'You're quite perceptive.'

'But why come to a small regional hospital, where you have to be a medical jack-of-all-trades?'

'Good question. Surgery is not my first choice. But Albert Clarke. Now there's an excellent surgeon. Seems to relish the slicing of flesh and sawing of bone.'

'I met his wife.'

'Ah.'

'It's a long story. She put the kibosh on his involvement in my hospital plans.'

'He's now just back from their first trip. Europe. You should try again. He's not the type to rest on his laurels. You might save him from his wife's intentions.' He looked like he was about to say more but stopped.

'She made it abundantly clear to me that she did not want her husband involved.'

'You could widen your net, but then again, he's the most likely to want to assist you. And he is the best medical professional up here.'

'I've tried other staff, but I got the cold shoulder. If I can be frank, my being a woman does not inspire confidence in the fraternity.'

'I'm sure Clarissa Clarke has become totally fed up with her husband rattling around the house by now. And your venture can open up all sorts of possibilities for a doctor wanting a second base, you know, to develop a specialisation… tell you what… I'll talk to him.'

'Thank you,' I said, surprised by his generosity. Emboldened, I asked, 'Doctor Jamieson, given your interest in the field, would you consider seeing someone I know, just for a chat? To see if you think there's anything that can be done for him? He was an officer in the war. I think he's been affected.' *Affected: touched by, moved by.* The truth was that the war had wormed deep into him. But in those days, you'd say nothing to jeopardise a brave soldier's dignity.

'It would be my pleasure,' he said without hesitation. 'Give him my details and he can contact me whenever it suits.'

He turned to walk away then stopped. 'Oh, by the way, congratulations on your promotion to senior sister. It's well deserved.'

'I didn't know! I wondered why I was given the seniors' rounds today. I thought...'

'I asked for you, actually. Matron Chalmers obviously hasn't passed on the news yet. We confirmed it at the board meeting last night. And...' he reached into his shirt pocket and took out an envelope. 'This is for you. Read it later.'

I opened it as soon as he was out of sight.

This is to certify that Mrs Anna Sinclair has been known to me for the past three years. I have formed the opinion that she is a person extremely proficient and painstaking in her profession and is capable of efficiently holding the position as matron of a private hospital.

I would be happy to assist her in this endeavour as and when she requires.

⌒⌒⌒

For the first few days after my promotion, I felt two feet taller. I'd almost check the ground to make sure I was still attached. I think my voice gained a new certainty, but I was careful not to look smug, especially around Daniel Fuller and the other juniors, whose low opinion of me hadn't changed. Fuller would lope over to Jamieson or Clarke whenever they came near, opening an obsequious conversation. He was already known for blaming nurses when things didn't go smoothly with his patients, and he got away with it. As the treating doctor in maternity while I was stationed there, I couldn't avoid him.

'Rose' was brought in with a stubborn breach birth and extreme pain. Normally, prostitutes about to give birth were too poor to pay hospital fees – their clientele tended to dwindle during pregnancy. This was her first child. She fought and screamed while we tried to settle her. Fuller proscribed a further dose of tincture of opium.

'Isn't that a dangerous amount?' I asked quietly.

'She's an addict. Her resistance is up. Can't you see that, Sister Sinclair?'

'We don't know that. And she's no heavyweight.'

'She's been in the clinic before.'

'I really think we should wait.'

'Do as I say! The woman's squealing her head off and needs to be calmed!'

I couldn't risk suspension and he seemed so sure that she could take another dose. I administered it and watched.

She started struggling for breath and Fuller disappeared to get a surgeon. Even before the baby was delivered, she'd sunk into a coma. She was stitched up and the child given to a wet nurse. A prostitute friend came unsuccessfully to claim the baby girl, whose future now lay in an orphanage.

It was when Rose was transferred to Townsville Hospital, her face as ethereal as a mannikin's, that I was placed under formal investigation by the board.

18

Tom and I had reached the outskirts of Babinda and were travelling in his box buggy up the clay track to a small farmhouse at the end of the road.

'Jim didn't like me much at first. He found out my real surname. Overheard me talking to another officer. I'd let it slip somehow. He believed all the propaganda – how German soldiers cut off the hands of little girls pleading for their mothers' honour. How they gouged out the eyes of an old Belgian man who said he would not betray his country. Anyone who was a "Hun" was a monster.'

'Propaganda's the fuel of war,' I said.

This trip was important to Tom. He said it had been Jamieson's idea. Since my intervention he'd seen the doctor regularly and they had formed a bond. It was one-on-one time, Tom said. Most of it not for my ears, but Jamieson told him how to take deep breaths when something or someone began to irritate him. How to let everything go, by talking it through with him – a kind of controlled catharsis. And also, a script for night sedatives.

'We must be nearly there.'

'Hopefully it's at the end of this track. To be honest, I'm only guessing from what Jim told me about the westerly position of Bellenden Ker and the mango tree at the turn-off.'

The horse whickered and started tossing its head as if trying to rid itself of the reins.

'Easy boy,' Tom said, but the horse continued to whip its neck.

He stopped the buggy and got out. 'He's smelling the grass here. It's as sweet as can be. May as well have a rest, anyway.'

'Are you sure? It looks like it might rain.' Clouds were forming, dulling the bright day, a dank sweetness breezing in.

'The wet's coming, I guess. But we've got a canopy. And it doesn't hurt to have a breather; we don't know how far we're going.'

'You're too soft with that animal.'

'Funny you should say that. That's exactly what my father used to tell me. Sent me off to Uncle Max in the city instead of mucking out, or maybe mucking things up, at home.'

We found a rock under a tree and slumped against it, watching the horse eat its way around the tether, buggy still attached.

'This is not just about that guy,' he said, nodding towards the animal. 'You know how much I care for you?'

'Yes…?'

'Anna. My wonderful Anna, the best Anna in the world…'

'Okay – enough buttering up – get to the point.'

'Roy Jamieson tells me I shouldn't give up on us.'

'He's a wise man.'

'But…' He looked at me gingerly from the corner of his eye. I noticed the swollen veins in his temple.

'But?'

'About what happened a few weeks back.'

'It's fine, Tom.'

'No, but…' he faced me now. 'You see, I *am* a wreck. You know I am. From talking this through with the doc it's become obvious that any woman would be wasting her time with me…' He leant down to pick up a small stone, feeling it as if trying for words. 'I have to set you free.'

'You're ending this?'

'I've been dragging you into my misery. I'm holding you back. And seeing you with your plans, how excited you were when you made it to senior sister, when you knew you had support for your hospital… you don't need me… I've *nothing* to offer. I will always fail you. You can see that, can't you?' He seemed strangely energised.

I laughed. It was not what I meant to do.

'What?' he said.

'I thought you were going to suggest I marry you, again.'

'I'm sorry.'

'No. I understand.' I was lying.

'That's not the response I was hoping for.'

'No?'

'A few tears would have been nice.'

'But I'd like…'

'What?'

'… to always see you.' I just wanted the last few minutes dusted off and replayed.

'Darling Anna, you will. You are my very best friend, and more. There will be no other very best friend for me.'

While I was trying to absorb his message, a rumble sounded above us. Lightning buzzed in a copse nearby, charging the air with acrid burning, followed by a ground-shaking clap of thunder. The horse tossed and screeched, and Tom whistled it to settle. We ran through heavy rain and climbed into the buggy, pulled up the canopy and watched as the road around us turned to rushing red mud.

I huddled into the seat, my wet blouse pressing heavily against my chest, anger beginning to stir. 'Why now? Why this on top of everything else? In this wretched storm!'

'I didn't…'

'This is crazy.' Realising how Tom might interpret that, I said, 'We were about to do something very important today.'

'I didn't intend this when we started out this morning. But I've been thinking about it for a while… suddenly it just made sense. I'm sorry, Anna.'

Shivering in my blouse, I felt his arm wrap around me.

'No, don't,' I said, and shrugged him off, pretending I was wiping rain from my eyes. 'Tom, we were working towards something. Don't give up.'

'I'm not giving up. And that is the very reason…'

'Yes, you are!'

'I thought you'd see the sense of it. All I've been hearing from you is: *What's the point? I'll lose my job.* It's as if that's the only thing important to you. It's as if the only reason you're staying with me is because you're sorry for me.'

'That's not true!' But I knew there must be some truth in what he said. I had, after all, been making him wait. I'd rationalised that there was little prospect of me being free to marry until… I didn't know when. 'You *really* don't know me, Tom.'

'If I don't, it's not my fault.'

I couldn't argue with that. I'd played the healer, getting close to him that way, not allowing him to get close to me.

'You don't find me attractive anymore.'

He was silent. 'You're beautiful,' he said, eventually.

'I'm too tall, aren't I?'

'Every inch of you is beautiful.'

'Obviously not.'

He was stunned by my bluntness. Then, almost pleading he said, 'I *am* working towards something, Anna. When the time's right, I intend to go back to the law. Who knows what that may open up.'

A raindrop rolled down to his eyelash. Once, I might have kissed it away.

'I think you should also buy a car,' I said.

△ △ △

After an hour, the storm subsided and the lightning stopped. We urged on the bedraggled horse and ploughed over the muddy track in drilling rain.

We arrived at a low wooden house and knocked on the latticed veranda door. There was a rattling sound from inside. We knocked again and a dog started growling behind the inner door. It opened ajar and the muzzle of a gun showed through the gap.

'Who are you?'

'Hello,' Tom said in his best private schoolboy voice. 'Are you Jim's mother, Mrs Miller?'

Clearly unimpressed, she asked again, 'Who *are* you?

'My name is Tom Austen. I served with Jim.'

'I don't know any Tom Austen.'

'I was Lieutenant Austen then. Jim served with me in the battalion. He talked about you a lot. Told me all about this place. The dam over there where he used to fish… your dog… Buster, isn't it?'

'Buster?' she said.

The dog stopped barking.

'Please, we are very wet. Got caught in the rain.'

The door opened and the woman stood behind the lattice with her rifle in one hand, grasping the dog's collar with the other. She stared at us for a while then told the dog to sit.

Leaning the rifle against the wall, she said, 'Yes. I'm Jim's mother. I don't welcome everyone like this. It's just that I'm on my own at the moment, the husband's out helping neighbours, and we're always getting ne'er-do-wells trying to scrounge something out of us. If I had my way, I'd line 'em up against a brick wall and shoot 'em.'

She let us in to the veranda. Close up, with her cracked and sun-speckled arms, she looked too old to be Jim's mother, but she can't have been more than fifty. 'Oh, do come in,' she said, as we stood dripping onto the floorboards. She ushered us inside the house while eyeing Tom, his uneven gait. 'So, *Lieutenant* Austen. And this is… Mrs Austen?'

'No,' I said, trying a smile. 'I'm Mr Austen's very best friend, Anna Sinclair. How do you do.' I held out my hand to shake hers. His very best friend. Just like that.

'So, what are you two doing in the back of beyond in a storm?'

'Hoping to find you,' Tom said.

She drew up two wooden chairs and handed us towels while she sat on her sofa, Buster at her feet, grey nuzzle on paws, looking at us with suspicion.

'You knew Jim?'

'I did indeed. He's the reason I'm here today.'

'He was our only son, our only child,' she said, looking at his photograph on the sideboard.

'I was with him when he died,' Tom said plainly.

'Oh.' She gave a guttural sound as if words caught in her throat. 'How…? Was he brave?'

'He was a very brave soldier.' Tom didn't mention how Jim had gone over the top against orders. On the day he died, Miller had been happily firing potshots at the enemy with a, 'Look, Lieutenant, I got his helmet – yeh, where's yer manners, take yer hat off to me, ya gutless Jerry,' or, 'Ha, I made him dance.' Only an hour later he was crouched, head in arms, at the bottom of the trench wall.

'My brave boy. He saved us, our Jim. Saved our country. On his march to Cairns with the Cane Beetles, they cheered them the whole way. He was a hero even before he left – children lining the towns waving Union Jacks, brass bands, speeches, cigarettes, tobacco, the whole thing. He had a fitting farewell. Not like those cowardly curs who wouldn't sign up.' She looked into her lap and shook her head. 'But you survived, Lieutenant.' It was more like an accusation than a statement.

Tom took out Jim's battered tin cup from the knapsack. 'Here, I kept this for you.'

She turned it over, gazing at the initials scratched into it and pressed it to her cheek. 'I was hoping he wouldn't pass the medical. Some didn't.'

'Can I make you some tea?' I asked.

'I'll do it. I've got some beef sandwiches, too, if you can stomach 'em. My husband says they'd stop a bullet.'

There was an awkward silence. Mrs Miller crossed the room and placed the cup beside the photo of her son.

19

Weeks of monsoon rain trapped us in. It tumbled remorselessly from the blanket of low cloud, threatening to dissolve the town with warm leaden drops, pooling under doors, morphing roads into muddy rivulets, and causing sodden-rooted trees to lean precariously. People ducked in and out of houses with an umbrella or a hastily snatched piece of cardboard to take out tins of rubbish, or to check the hoods on their cars and sulkies. The hospital lawn, mowed only a week before, was already drooping seeded heads. The rain broke momentarily, and doves, currawongs and parrots exulted before another onslaught began.

I hadn't seen Tom for weeks. Every time I thought about him, about that day at the Millers', I felt a weight forming deep in my belly. Humiliation, but much more, a profound longing. It had been a curt dismissal, but maybe he was right – there was no room for us yet, that union of the wounded. I didn't deserve him, or any other.

The deluge finally stopped. Evie's voice in my head: *When rain dies, trees cry.* Evie was the queen of half-wisdoms.

Unlike Andy, Tom hadn't wanted me as a possession, as a thing to control, and despite the challenges, there had been freedom with him. I'd married Andy in haste. I was a runaway, arriving in the country with one bag stuffed with clothes, all double-lined, woollen, unsuitable for this climate. But Australia was a progressive country, or so I thought at the time, where the battle for suffrage had already been won. That's what attracted me to it. Hell, I would take every one of my twenty-one years and vote as soon as it was time. I did too. I voted for Billy Hughes, warmonger, much to my later regret.

I'm not sure at what point I became altered. Perhaps it started when I met Andy the day after I stepped off the boat in Brisbane – the end of the line. I'd avoided Melbourne and Sydney, more reminiscent of my own genteel city, and headed straight for Queensland, where I could reinvent myself. That was a deliberate, purposeful change. But something else happened along the way. I think this must be common for those who disappear and lose connection with the past.

I wandered the wide streets created by a penal colony, where workmen wore singlets rather than jackets, where voices were sharp at the edges like crows, the pace of the city set by a river so languid that even steamers seemed to float without purpose. I was wearing my mother's small earrings, the silver ones I wore that last night. I remember pressing them as if to feel her reassurance. I thought I had proved my point, that I could survive without her, my family, without overseers. As I stared up at the mill tower where convicts had been hanged, I was aware of the irony in my own banishment.

That cold Edinburgh night, my ears were ringing as I ran breathlessly, my bag blown from my grasp by the force of the explosion. The police found it later and were intrigued by its contents. Currant biscuits (for my long vigil) and the utopian flyer I'd picked up at the meeting: *How beggarly appears argument before defiant deed. Votes for women.* I'd abandoned any last thought of returning home to throw myself on the mercy of the court. That would be a life sentence.

I entered Andy's shop – a decorator's business – to ask for directions. We talked, and later had tea. With his attractive honesty, he told me he was smitten at first sight. I let him fall in love and I thought I loved him too, but now I see it was the exoticism of him that caught me for a time, the easy manner. He said my accent reminded him of his mother, who'd died a year before, and asked me to repeat some of her favourite sayings. Within a matter of weeks, we were married in an impressive building with a sandstone façade. So much for being self-sufficient. I allowed myself to be dissolved, like one of his paint colours, into the marriage mix. No longer the absconding delinquent. Andrew Sinclair, painter and tradesman, gave me a new name and respectable identity. My parents would have thought him totally unsuitable.

I became pregnant with Evie on what must have been our wedding night, too soon to know the real man I had married. Now here I was, years after his death, stuck in my life, moving neither forward nor backward. Here in this fluid green town, I missed the solidity of stone – cobblestones, stone houses, stone walls, sentinels to guard the greyness. I missed living in a house where generations of hands had worn the banister smooth, where coal fires were set in the parlour before daybreak. I even missed those frosty mornings when the cart delivered our milk, the cream frozen hard.

I blamed myself for many things, for leaving, for not leaving, for letting Andy go to war, for never stopping to properly grieve. The guilt of my past was too easily transmuted into remorse about my husband, who died thinking he was completely loved.

'Sister, why aren't you in the ward?'

I jumped involuntarily, not at the question but the cold-blooded way it was spoken. It was Daniel Fuller with his imperious glare.

He still hadn't forgiven me for convincing the board that I'd acted involuntarily under his instructions. He'd noted his prescription on Rose's chart, thank goodness. In those weeks while the investigation took its slow course, I felt the eyes on me. In the end, they found I was not responsible and Fuller only received a warning. That didn't stop me remembering Rose's inert body, her dilated pupils. As far as I knew she was still in a vegetative state in Townsville and bound for an invalid home.

'Sorry, Doctor Fuller, I left to get an Aspirin for my headache. It was quite severe.' My head was fine, but I'd felt the familiar commotion in my chest, the buzzing in my ears, and found a place to sit down. It had become worse during the investigation. I hoped Freud was right – symptoms like this were often psychosomatic, and I wouldn't deteriorate like my brother.

'Well, you're not the patient today, Sister Sinclair. Get on with it.'

I went back to the ward and found distraction in the precise administration of laudanum, belladonna, and arnica.

Before that awful night, there'd been official visits to my family's house in Morningside – helmeted constables on the doorstep. My alleged smashing of windows, setting fires, acid poured into letterboxes – my father's 'quiet word' with the bobbies in the drawing room. I didn't admit any of my involvement which, at first, was far less dramatic. I assisted the steadfast doctor, Jane Landy (whom I would never betray) at her home, as she tended to injuries acquired by our militant sisters in the Women's Social and Political Union. I confidently sang *La Marseillaise* at rallies.

I remember clearly the day I decided to join the WSPU. At university I'd heard about Aletta Jacobs, a suffragist who'd pursued a medical career long before me, in the Netherlands. I was in the library reading a translation of Jacobs' dissertation and as a male student went past, he bent down and whispered: 'You're not fooling anyone by pretending you understand that.'

I was full of the cause, and a fall had to come. If I'd waited for the police to return after that black night, I'd soon have been imprisoned. Since then, my colleagues, Ethel Moorhead and Maude Edwards (the slicer of King George's portrait), had been held in Calton Gaol, force-fed with rubber tubes rammed down their throats, made to swallow their own shattered teeth with the milk.

When I arrived home with the taste of blood in my mouth, my face and blouse covered with it, my father, the introspective man of calibrated demeanour, realised what I'd done. Past the limit of his tolerance, he thundered the responsibilities of the Hippocratic Oath, and pointed to the door: *Get out of this house, and don't come back!*

Somehow, and not through him, I'm sure, the university suspected I'd been involved. I'd wondered about Malcolm who worked as a clerk in the administration section, but quickly dismissed that idea. It was much more likely when they discovered potassium nitrate and sulphur had been stolen from the chemistry laboratory right before my disappearance. I was expelled in absentia even before I set foot on deck for Australia. But both the university and my father, who had a position on the university council, kept this quiet. They must have done, because the police offered a reward for evidence leading to the identity of the perpetrator. In one mad night, my passion for the cause had destroyed my career, and brought shame to my family.

When the newspapers reported the tragedy, my colleague Jane helped me get away. I ran from all reminders of a man pierced to death by the shattered windows of the Edinburgh Royal Observatory.

⌢ ⌢ ⌢

I don't know what made me follow Roy Jamieson home. He must have thought I was a bit unhinged. I rationalised that it was Tom's mysterious scar, not my frazzled heart, which led me to knock at Jamieson's door when everyone else had the good sense to be at home preparing their dinners.

Roy didn't seem surprised when he found me standing at his threshold. 'Anna,' he said, not 'Sister Sinclair.' From this familiarity which he'd previously avoided, I guessed he knew more about me than I realised. It must have come from Tom.

He took me into his house where metal gleamed, wood shone, the ceilings were high, the rooms airy. In a central room which was dim, relying only on a window to the veranda for some light, there was a couch, a comfortable chair and various medical texts. He led me past this room into a sitting area where a vase with black geometric patterns sat alone on a circular table.

'Gin and tonic?'

'Thank you,' I said out of politeness.

When he went off to get it, clattering and banging ice chests and glasses, I slipped into the inner room. It was set up like a consultation surgery. Jamieson obviously provided therapy treatment in his house, in breach of his contract with the hospital and possibly without a specific licence to do so. This had to be where Tom was meeting him.

There was a filing cabinet in the corner, locked when I tried it. There was a key poking out of his pencil holder.

'Large or small?' he called from the kitchen.

'Small, please.'

The heavy cabinet made a grinding sound as I opened the drawer too quickly. There, Tom's life was bundled up in a loose-leafed dossier. I heard the soda syphon and flicked quickly through the folder. There was one page which caught my interest: Tom saying I was enigmatic. He'd never probe, didn't have the right to. I scanned the rest quickly. Most of it was indecipherable doctor's scrawl, but I saw something about cowards and snipers. I couldn't imagine Tom being a coward, but before I could really make sense of it, Jamieson's footsteps drew near, and I closed the drawer.

When he arrived with two glasses, I was hovering at his bookcase, not being quick enough to have made it back to my seat and too late realising I'd left the cabinet unlocked.

'Great collection,' I said, lamely.

'You look flushed,' he said, guiding me into the sitting area. 'Here, this will cool you down.' The glass clinked with ice.

I felt a mixture of foolishness at what I'd done, and curiosity over what I had seen in the folder.

'So, Anna,' he said, 'what brings you here?'

I took a gulp of gin. I'd start on a high note. 'We're so fortunate to have someone with your medical experience here in the north, with your London training. Out here, we're a far cry from civilisation,' I said.

He avoided my subtle probing and said, 'I think studying the mind, particularly its reaction to trauma, is the only hope we have for our soldiers.'

'You didn't feel the need to serve?'

'Not after my friend in London was killed…'

'In the war?'

'No. He was back on leave. His mother thought sending him away to the front would toughen him up. As if he could be changed. It took me a while to realise he was suffering neurasthenia. The war did that, but it didn't kill him. He was murdered by a street gang. I was with him…'

'Was he a close friend?'

He paused, waiting for me to stop tidying loose hair behind my ears and when he had my attention, said, 'The closest I'll ever have.'

I coloured as I realised his meaning. 'Oh, I understand. I understand everything now.'

He coloured too, then took a sip of gin.

The sun was setting and cast a glow over the room. The warmth surrounded us, connecting me to him. He and I were both fugitives from the law in our own ways. Nothing more had to be said. I would never betray this aspect of him to anyone else, and I think he sensed that. Making light of it, I said, 'I see now why you're interested in this area. Did you know a centre for psychoanalysis has been established in Tavistock Square? Sounds very progressive.'

'Yes, the centre was created a year or two ago. But is this really what you've come to discuss, Anna?' The expression in his voice made it obvious that Jamieson the professional, was back.

'Well, no, to be honest. Although I can see how this development might inspire someone to set up a practice here.' I glanced meaningfully towards the consultation room.

He sat back, cleared his throat, and crossed his arms. I realised then I'd make no ground in asking him to divulge any of Tom's private records, with or without my feeble threat of professional exposure. Jamieson was in every respect a decent man and I'd already made enough of a fool of myself.

So, I pretended it was about my hospital. 'Wouldn't it be marvellous if my hospital were to have such a clinic?' I prattled on about it, all the while picking at an undone thread at my skirt seam, Tom catching in my words. I was sure that the good doctor could see right through me.

I knew from the wild uneven printing, my name pressed deep into the envelope, who this second letter was from, so I didn't open it straight away. The script began with another quote from the Old Testament, then:

> *I went to GAOL for you, while every night you slept in a COMFORTABLE bed with soft sheets. But God saw my goodness and I know in my heart HE has told them everything. The POLICE are coming for you. I tell you this so you may REPENT.*

An elaborate 'V.S' was scrawled at the bottom of the page. I knew no men by that name. There was my old friend, Victoria Duncan, from the ladies' college. She could have married and changed her name. But she was not particularly religious – in fact, we both avoided church whenever we could. Unless she'd had a late conversion, it couldn't be her. This person was mentally unbalanced, but I had to accept that they may not be delusional about the police finding me.

I stared at the envelope and its vivid ink. I was indelibly marked out, stuck.

20

Leon sat at Dorrie's table behind plates of chicken sandwiches and jam scones. He and I were on talking terms again, but there was an edge to our conversation.

'Sybs should be here soon. She tends to be late,' I said. '"Country time", she calls it.'

'Ah.' He nodded with a cough. 'We call it "Hawaiian time".'

He was restless as we chatted, tapping his foot, nudging the bag by his feet. He jumped up when Sybil finally arrived, as if relieved we'd been interrupted.

'Helloooo!' rang her voice, with its inflection of dusty paddocks and tin windmills.

He kissed her on the cheek as she entered, greeting her with a 'Hiya!'

She looked startled. Her dress was a sheer blue, with the sheen of money about it. It was a hand-me-down from the mayor's wife, a co-aficionado of fashion, whose son had been hospitalised with dengue fever. Sybil had received it secretly in a brown paper parcel away from Matron's watch when she, too, was promoted to senior sister. Uncharacteristically shy about taking up Leon's long-ago offer to 'pop over anytime', she eventually asked me to organise a get-together with him. 'Nothing fancy,' she said.

With a slight reluctance I did mention it to Leon, and he responded with a simple, 'Consider me booked'.

I was in Sybil's good books now, at least, I thought I was. 'Where's Tom?' she asked, settling into the chair.

'To be honest, I've found it hard to bring myself to say this, but Tom and I have stopped walking out.'

'Whoah!' she exclaimed with a note of triumph. 'I won't say revenge is sweet, but maybe God's a sheila who's been dumped.'

Leon laughed.

The topic of Tom led to France and war. 'How about you, Leon? Did you serve?' Sybil asked.

He shifted in his seat. 'No, Ma'am. That war was a ridiculous waste.'

'How did you avoid it?' she continued incredulously.

'I had a business to run in Oahu. But, like I said, the war was a big waste.'

Sybil, looking like she'd just discovered mouse droppings in a cake, said, 'So, what would you do? Roll over and let the blighters take you, and the rest of us?'

Leon pushed his teacup aside. 'It's not that simple. I'd defend something worthwhile, like social justice, but I wouldn't get involved in someone else's backyard fight – like this last war. It started with the assassination of some Austrian archduke who most of us didn't know from a bar of soap, and then the bully-boy Europeans ganged up on each other, bringing in their big mates from the States, Australia and elsewhere. Killed millions. You say there's sense in that?'

Realising her gaff, Sybil blurted out, 'Not all bad came from that war you know, especially as we won. It got me out of the bush, got me into nursing. Our house was a shanty out in "Woop Woop", with a roof of tea tree bark and melaleuca. We had old kerosene and Nestles' milk tins for everything – baking, water, washing. Ate a lot of wallaby and bandicoot. We didn't even buy soap – made ours out of caustic soda and leftover fat.' The beads at her collar caught the window light as she leaned in, elbows on table. 'Mind you, my mum made the best galah pie in our ant-bed oven.'

Leon gave her a look of renewed interest. 'That's quite a story.'

'Oh. By the way, I heard the news!' I touched Sybil's arm as a form of congratulations.

'Wha…? Oh, yes!' She sat back in her seat. 'It's official.'

'Oh, yes,' I echoed, maybe too emphatically. 'It's been the best news of nineteen twenty-one. Even though it's just started.'

Only now, she pulled off her gloves and put them on her lap. One slid off her bag and dropped on the floor.

'Here, let me take them for you,' Leon said, putting her gloves and clutch bag on the bureau.

Sybil seemed lost for words. I had never seen her like this, so shy as she thanked him.

'Would you ladies mind telling me what the big secret is?' he asked.

'We've formed a nurses' union. For Queensland,' Sybil announced. 'The Brisbane mob got behind it and I rallied some girls up here, giving it the extra push it needed. First-up, we're going for a rise in wages.'

Leon assessed her with admiration.

'Now maybe we can push the Union to make them remove that stupid ban on married nurses,' I said.

Sybil rubbed her nose self-consciously with the back of her hand. 'Has Leon taken you out for any jaunts in his car? It's the flashest in Cairns.'

'Not since our last jaunt in it,' I said, without thinking.

'I remember *that*.' Leon gave a short laugh.

'Oh.' She blushed and kicked me under the table.

'I've actually brought over some champagne,' he said, producing a canvas cooler from his bag. 'Figured it might fit your afternoon tea protocol. How about we all celebrate with this?'

'Really?' Sybil said this with a look of mock disgust. 'Is this how they do it in Hawaii? Grog with high tea?'

He laughed and poured the champagne into empty teacups. 'Cheers!'

She took a gulp and screwed up her face. 'Ugh. A quart of lemons would taste better!' Sybil's indifference was always meant to impress.

'It's a sparkling wine from South Australia, almost as good as the French. It's hard to get the really decent stuff out here.' Leon was unfazed.

'But I guess this *is* champagne, after all.' Sybil drank the rest of her cup with relish. 'Sorry, I have to go to the loo,' she said after finishing.

'Sybil's a great girl,' I said as Leon and I sat in the awkward quiet. 'She deserves to be treated well.'

'This is just some sort of afternoon tea, isn't it? It's a bit early for your lectures.'

I wished I was away from this matchmaking experiment. Sybil was a smart woman who didn't need a chaperone, but I wanted to show my loyalty. Leon looked so sure of himself as he became engrossed in conversation with her. I hoped he really was a decent man – the attraction between the pair was barely constrained.

Sybil slid purposefully onto her chair, fragrant with freshly dabbed essence of lilac. 'So, Leon, how many wives have you hidden away in Hawaii?'

Leon took a breath as if to laugh but gargled a response, clutched his throat, and made a strangled guttural noise.

'Clever move!' Sybil said at the apparent ploy to avoid her question.

His eyes were wide, his mouth open, gagging for breath. Instinctively we both rose but Sybil got to him first and thumped him several times on the back. We managed to move him into a kneeling position over the chair. Using the heel of my palm I pushed his abdomen into the seat a few times. He exhaled a few sharp breaths but soon turned a light purple shade. He was gagging like a hooked fish out of water when Sybil wrenched open his mouth and poked her finger into his throat. She kept repeating this until he coughed out a mouthful of food and with it, a small sharp bone.

Recovering on the chair, Leon apologised. 'Sorry guys. Don't know how I missed that bone. My throat's been a bit dry this morning.' His voice was husky.

'Well, you should know better than to speak with your mouth full!' Sybil rubbed his back in a familiar way.

When the colour had returned to his face, I said. 'I wasn't trying to kill you, I promise. It's probably the chicken's revenge – Dorrie wrung its neck only yesterday.'

He smiled. 'It's fine. I'm fine. Don't worry about that. But I think it's time for me to head home.'

'I'll go with you to keep an eye on you, in case your throat plays up again. You're only next door and it's on my way back, anyway.'

'It's fine. I'll drive you to the hospital – I owe you that much.' Leon's tone was definite.

'Now you two, stay out of trouble.'

'I know *you* will,' Sybil replied. 'But some of us gotta live a little.'

Leon looked at me with a hint of self-satisfaction. It hit me and I realised just how empty I felt.

'And *you*,' he turned to Sybil, 'there's no wife in Hawaii, or anywhere else.'

Evie thought I wasn't looking, so she scuttled next door into the murky cubby under Leon's house. I followed her and was confronted by Sybil lying on a table draped in sailcloth, hands behind her head, naked breasts and thighs lit and shadowed by a bright lamp. Leon didn't see us at first as he was bent behind a camera on a tripod.

'Oh!' I gasped, grabbing my open-mouthed daughter.

Sybil quickly gathered up the sailcloth to her breasts. 'Hello, loves!' she said as if she'd been expecting us.

Leon groaned. 'I thought the trellis was locked.'

'Oh, that'll be me,' Sybil said, 'I must have left it open after I went upstairs to… oops, children present.'

I pushed my daughter out the door. 'You, young lady, go home now!'

'Before you go off your head, Anna,' Sybil said, 'this is art. And it's private. So, do you mind?'

'Sybil fancies herself as an artist's model. We're reinterpreting Goya's Maja.' His face was hidden in the gloom.

'I'm sorry. It's our fault for intruding.'

'Look at you. You're such an old wowser!' Sybil responded, throwing on a man's dressing gown. 'Want a ciggy?' She went over to the corner where her handbag rested on a trunk. As she fumbled in her bag the handle dropped and caught on the lock. She wrenched it free with such force that it loosened the snib. I wouldn't have noticed if Leon hadn't dashed over to the chest with a thunderous expression and shoved Sybil out of the way.

'Hey!' Sybs yelled at him. 'What's in there, anyway, your grandma's best china?'

Leon stood at the box inspecting it, angrily rattling the loose lock, then fought to recover himself. 'Sorry, gal. This cubby is a bit pokey – not really meant for visitors. How about we all go outside.'

'When I'm dressed,' Sybil said languidly behind us.

Over in my back yard, chickens were scattering, and Evie was clinging to the dunny roof, her face bright red, the ladder having slid out of her reach.

I called out and Leon jumped the fence, charging past me, reaching up, calming her, coaxing her to jump into his arms. The ladder fell with a clatter and a thud, striking his leg on the way down.

'I was only having a little look,' Evie said, as I checked her for injury.

'Here, girl,' Dorrie called. 'Come upstairs for a lemonade and stay out of trouble.'

Leon was already heading back next door with a bloody leg that would be starting to bruise. I followed him. 'Thank you for getting her down.'

'It was nothing.'

'But your leg needs looking at. Let me do something, I'll bandage you up.'

'I don't need a nurse.' He was limping now. 'I've got my own, anyway.'

Leon froze at the door of his cubby. Sybil was at the open trunk, where rows of cans and clay jars were exposed. She was holding a jar in one hand, the beeswax seal broken, the lid in her other.

'What is this, Leon?'

'Jesus Christ, put that back!' He grabbed it from her, closing it quickly.

'It's disgusting, it looks like spew. What is it?'

'Let me see,' I said. I caught a glimpse before he elbowed through us to return it to the trunk.

'Mind your own business,' he snapped. 'C'mon… out!' He gestured towards the door.

'But, Leon,' Sybil said in a whiny voice, 'you mustn't have any secrets from me.'

'It's no secret. It's just some herbal paste. For Chinatown.'

'What for? What are you doing with all this?' Sybil asked.

'Remedies,' he said weakly. 'C'mon, get your clothes on. Party's over.'

21

We sat awkwardly, me thumbing the arm of Tom's sofa, the rattle of eggs boiling in the kitchen. His new rented house was near the mill in Edmonton village, a miscellany of two hundred or so people – cane workers, smithies, and shopkeepers hoping to benefit from the passing trade.

'So. Tell me. What's this important matter you want to discuss?'

I told him about Leon's jars. 'He's a smuggler. Opium. I'm pretty sure of it.'

'That's quite an allegation.'

'Well, it would explain all his midnight trips out to sea, his mysterious visits to joss houses and God knows where else. I've seen too many victims of that trade. But if I report him, I risk the fact that he may be innocent. You know what it's like in these small towns – you don't have to be guilty for people to want you to be.'

'That's what I like about you, Anna, you think about things. You have a solid moral compass.'

'You make me feel like a ship – a dull, lumbering one.'

'No, I mean you're strong. And you know what I mean.'

'You really don't know me, Tom.'

'Piffle.' He drew in a lungful of his cigarette.

I went to the kitchen and took the eggs off the boil. Outside, Evie was bouncing her ball against a mango tree and singing a rhyme, her chin, streaked orange from the fruit.

'Have you read all of these?' I said, looking around the lounge-room. The bookcase was half-filled with an odd assortment of Thackeray, Scott, Chaucer, Plato and Keats, and some Shakespeare editions still in their shipping case.

'Most of them.'

There was a booklet about art. On the cover, a graphic, twisted picture of soldiers invading a home, torturing, raping, abducting. I put it back, turned it face down. 'So, what do you think about Leon?'

'Hmm. Assuming the stuff is what you say it is, and assuming he hasn't moved it somewhere else by now, I think you should report it to the police. All they need to launch an investigation is a reasonable suspicion that he's engaging in a criminal act. Obviously, importing opium is a criminal offence – assuming that's what he's doing. In any case, possession is illegal, too.'

'What's *your* obligation as a lawyer to report him?'

'That's tricky. Short of a confession, I'd need damned good evidence. If he was my client, then that's trickier.'

Short of a confession. 'I also have to consider Sybil, her possibly becoming implicated. She believes his line about "Chinese herbal remedies". If she'd studied medicinal compounds in detail, I'm pretty sure she'd be suspicious, too.'

'And you have? Studied medicinal compounds in detail?'

We were getting onto dangerous ground. 'In my studies, *nursing* studies, I researched opiates, the various stages of production from poppy to medicinal use and its addictive effect on the brain.'

'And Sybil didn't?'

'It's a long story.'

I needed a quick distraction. So, I sat on the arm of the sofa, took his cigarette, stubbed it out in the ashtray, and kissed him. Just like that. I'd forgotten how much I loved the texture of his skin.

I expected him to recoil but he drew me onto his lap, instead. 'I've missed you,' he said. 'As the great bard once wrote: "… what care I who calls me well or ill,… you o'er-green my bad, my good allow… you are my all-the-world…".'

'I get it. Completely. But you don't have to hide behind Shakespeare, Tom.'

'You have no idea, have you? You have no idea how wonderful you are. Truth be told, I'm not good enough for you. Especially after everything I've put you through. But you're still here, forgiving me.' Stroking my cheek, he continued, 'Sorry about the Shakespeare.'

'It may be that you o'er green *my* bad,' I said.

He laughed and held my head against his shoulder, rocking me gently.

'I don't know what to do about Sybil,' I said.

'You have to tell her.'

'I don't know. Doesn't everyone have secrets?'

'Do you?'

'Well, actually, yes.'

'Yes?'

I hesitated while he looked at me, puzzled.

'My secret is you, my wondering about you, your secrets.' It wasn't cowardice that stopped me then, or so I rationalised, even though it made me dislike myself even more.

His eyes widened in surprise. 'Me? Haven't I told you everything?'

'I've never heard you admit your Habsburg ties to anyone else. After all, your lot caused the Great War.'

'Hmm, that's debatable. I guess everyone has to blame someone else. And my "lot" have paid their dues in this country. Anyway, my background is not so much a secret as a fact which is waiting for the right time to be revealed.'

'Yes, you're definitely a lawyer.'

He laced my fingers in his.

'If I did expose Leon, it would be the end of it for Sybil,' I said. 'And I'm already responsible for destroying her last relationship. With you.'

'No, you're not.'

'She did tell me I was like a dingo sniffing around, slinking up on fair game.'

'I think it was the other way around. But she has Leon now, anyway.'

'That's my point. She'd take my exposing his dubious lifestyle as an attempt to break that relationship up.'

'Maybe she really does know, but doesn't want to know – if you get my drift. She never struck me as the innocent type.'

'In a very real way Sybil *is* exactly that – innocent. She puts on this bravado, the *don't cross me, I'm a modern girl* kind of thing, but she's also very sensitive and loyal. I don't want to ruin things for her.'

'But being sensitive also means you can often sense when things aren't true,' he said, thoughtfully.

'Are you speaking from personal experience?'

'Perhaps.'

'So, what untruths do you see?'

He studied my face. 'Ah, that would be telling…'

I looked away and said quickly, 'But what about Sybil?'

'Wouldn't you ruin it by *not* telling her? She has to find out sooner or later, and she might have dug herself in too deep by then.'

'I tried talking to Leon about it, shortly afterwards. It didn't work of course. He denies everything. I was up early for work before light and found him cranking his engine, the car full of boxes. He gave me the "herbal remedy" story again. It's an evil trade, I told him. Opium den outcasts are taking up good beds in our hospital. One died a few weeks ago. You should see them, your clients, in hospital, I said. That stuff sucks out their soul. *Doings? Clients? Gal, you got it wrong,* he says. *Stop before you embarrass yourself.* I wanted to hit him. I told him he had to tell Sybs the truth. He reckoned I didn't know what I was talking about. Then he got up on his moral high horse: *I don't do anything to anyone that they don't want done to them, right?*

Tom burst out into laughter, startling me. 'Nice Hawaiian accent, but I wouldn't give up nursing for the stage.'

'I have to get my daughter away from him.'

'Look, it's not worth trying to sort *him* out. If what you're suggesting is true, you don't know what you're dealing with. God knows who his associates are.'

'He seems to have some rowdy gatherings. But Sybil tells me they're his Communist Party meetings. She seems smitten with the cause as well. Goes to his meetings but ends up doing the snacks and pouring the beer.'

'This is the thing – the war is not really over. Causes like communism exploit people's deep dissatisfaction, give them hope. They're beginning to flourish. But I doubt it will really take off.'

'Leon keeps pretty quiet about it.'

'That's smart. You'd have heard of the Red Riots in Brisbane a couple of years back? Ex-servicemen up against trade union Bolshevists flying those banned red flags. Police used bayonets, the lot.'

'Yes. It was one of the reasons I left the place. Life was getting too militant for Evie and me.'

'At least you'd never be one of those people who shout in the streets, carry banners, go around raging about how badly you're done by.'

He had no idea how uneasy this made me feel. 'What would be wrong with that if it's for a good cause? And how do you know I'm not one of those people?'

'Don't be ridiculous. You're the most strait-laced person I've ever met.'

'That's how I come across. I wish I didn't. But I think you're the one becoming too conservative in your old age.' I was pleased that he trusted me again. For the moment, I'd let the matter of my other rabble-rousing self, rest.

'Maybe so. All that business aside, you should probably report his little herbal industry. You're an eyewitness.'

'Not much of one. I did ask Sybs a few days ago if she's seen any more of his potted remedies. She says the boxes were gone when she last peeked. She's the real witness. I just saw it from a distance.'

'But close enough, obviously. It would be your word against his. Now, who do you think they'll believe?'

'You tell me – you're the lawyer.' I kissed him again. 'I love you, Tom.' There it was, what had to be said. It was the first time without my conscience niggling, without burying it in a mouthful of smaller endearments.

He placed his finger on my heart and said, 'Home of my love.'

'Shakespeare again?'

'Him and me.'

'So… are we officially together again?'

'What do you think?' He ran his hand over my breasts and down to my waist. It felt like relief.

I heard the thwack of Evie coming in the kitchen screen door. 'Later,' I whispered, hoping that maybe this time things could be different. 'But, if we're going to take things further, there's something that's important for me to know.'

'Yes?'

'How is it that you can sleep with Sybil but find it difficult with me?'

His eyes widened in surprise. 'Wha…?'

'She told me.'

'If she told you that, she was only trying to wind you up. It never happened. Trust me.'

'That makes sense.' I wanted to believe him.

A rat run of metal platforms cut through the innards of the mill. We clambered over them for a better view of the rollers, where juice was being squeezed out of cane cuts.

'What's that?' Evie yelled over the hissing boilers.

'It's the bagasse burning,' Tom said. 'It's leftover fibre from the cane. We use it to keep the boilers going.'

With Evie distracted by a piece of sweet cane to chew and a foreman explaining to her about cane trains, rail trains and ships to faraway countries, Tom turned to me. 'I have the answer to your housing problem. I've been thinking about this since you confessed.'

'Confessed?'

'That you really do love me.' He took my hand. 'Come stay here. With me.'

'Goodness. Now who's the *progressive* one? But seriously, Tom, I can't have people thinking I'm a kept woman.'

'It'll help you to save money for your hospital. Make us both a better life.' He paused. 'You could marry me.'

'What?'

He raised his voice over the sudden clank of machinery. 'Marry me! Even though I've been an idiot.'

I stood, confused. 'But we're just finding each other again.'

'It's too hot in here,' he said. His face was a sheen of sweat. He guided me outside and turned me to him, fixing my gaze. 'The point is, we *have* found each other. This is where we're meant to be. I shouldn't have let you go like that. I thought I was saving you somehow.'

'Let's think rationally for a moment,' I said in a mixture of relief and panic. 'If I marry, I'll have to leave the hospital.'

'I could support you while you arrange for your own hospital.'

'Support me? On what? And how can I arrange for my hospital without a job? Besides, if I gave everything up, I'd be the most cranky housewife of the century.'

'We can do this. I'm going back to the law. I've spoken to a solicitor in town who's overburdened with cases right now. This is my point – I can support you now if we marry.'

'This is all unexpected, Tom. I have to think…'

'Don't think! You do too much thinking. Why has it taken you so long to get the hospital going?'

The words hit like a hammer. 'Don't underestimate me. Not ever. These things take time. You know I'm organising finance and…'

'So, find it! Go back to that bank. I'll come with you if you like. And I have some savings. You can have it all.'

'That's very generous, but no. I need to set up the hospital under my own steam.'

'You'll get nowhere at that rate. You're too stubborn, too principled.'

'It *is* what I want, Tom. With all my heart.'

'What? The hospital? Or me?'

'Both, I guess.'

'You guess?' He shifted away.

'I didn't mean it like that.'

'Say it then. What do you want? I'm offering you a solution. I can look after you.'

'I don't need looking after and I don't want anyone's pity. I don't want to be beholden.' As I said this, I realised I couldn't honestly commit to him until he knew the truth.

'Beholden? If we wait for your hospital, we'll both be doddery old buggers — you tripping over your lace and supporting me as I meander down the aisle.'

I had to laugh. And for a moment I felt like ropes had been cut away.

22

Like an overlord, the white house commanded the jungle hill. We swam in its pool, resting occasionally to look out on the careless arrangement of the chamferboard town, the glare of its ocean rim.

'This is the only private swimming pool in Cairns,' Rupert Foster said proudly. His belly protruded from the water like a furry island as he lolled on his back. 'Had a hell of a time getting the pump installed. The men had to adapt a marine motor. We used to go to the floating baths at the end of the esplanade until the last cyclone destroyed them.'

'I used to walk past them,' I said. 'But never got a chance to go in.'

'Tom tells me you're a nurse, Mrs Sinclair.'

'Yes. I'm a senior sis—'

There was a loud thud behind me, and I jumped.

'Oh, never mind that. Just a coconut from one of our imported palms… Helen!' he called, 'another one's down – get Gerry to peel it for us, dear?'

His wife, marcel waves intact, donned a cerise robe which clung where wetness seeped through, and left to find their fifteen-year-old son. The boy appeared with a cane knife, sat on his haunches, and hacked at the fibrous husk.

'Thanks for that knife, Tom – it's been useful around here', Foster said. 'Got to keep the bush from creeping into our back yard – goes like crazy in the wet. Have to get the grass under control to stop feral pigs. They sneak down through it at night and uproot the flower beds.'

'You can thank Captain Cook for those disgusting creatures,' Helen said.

Foster swept his arms in lazy circles in something resembling backstroke, until he reached the side of the pool, where his drink was resting on the edge. 'It's amazing to think Cook saw this coast, sailed right up it well over a hundred years back. Beached his ship just up the road for repairs.'

'In Cooktown,' Tom explained to me, as if I didn't know.

'It's not just one man to blame for bringing vermin into this community,' I said. 'There's all our rats and mice and English roses.'

The cheer of the gathering waned, but the smug grandiosity of this solicitor's lifestyle had brought out the campaigner in me.

'What's wrong with roses?' Helen asked.

'I suppose that's the unavoidable risk of internationalism,' I said quickly, trying to restore the bonhomie. 'We've put our stamp on the place so quickly. The sugar cane, for example. It was Cook who brought it here in the first place.'

'Three cheers for the British!' Foster shouted.

'And for the indentured cane workers – Islanders, Japanese and so on who were used to build this area's economy,' I said, despite myself. 'We all know they had their homes in Malay town burned down. And let's not forget the indigenous groups banished to Yarrabah and beyond. None of them even have the vote.'

'They can't write, let alone read, so why should they vote? All those people you mentioned, they were here exploiting the place before us – no different from any other.' Foster had obviously rationalised all this to himself long ago. 'And Malay town was burnt down because it was a swamp full of bubonic plague. But that hasn't stopped the people returning with their tin rafts and reconstructing their filthy shanties by Alligator Creek.' He looked at Tom, wryly. 'My word, you've got yourself a handful there.'

After an uneasy pause Helen said, 'There's still that mia-mia camp here, down at that end of the esplanade. King what's-his-name's.'

'He's a respected elder,' Tom said. 'But the brass kingplate he wears is no compensation for the way we've enforced our laws upon his people, don't you think? I've heard about the brutality up here in the north.'

'What? The noble savage?' Foster protested, in a tone meant to close the discussion. 'There's been "brutality" from all sides. We're all nature's children. Survival of the fittest. Eat or be eaten. If you check your history books, you'll see that for thousands of years the greatest nations have been built on the backs of others. We've brought civilisation to this country – metal, inventions, technology, the rule of law.' He took a swig of beer, dived under the water and emerged at the steps, the water slicking off his bald pate. 'When's lunch, dear? These good folks must be starving.'

'The girl's getting it now, dear,' Helen replied.

A striking young girl in a loose floral dress and bird's nest curls came out with a tray of sandwiches, ginger beer, and fruit cake. She caught my eye and quickly lowered hers. I didn't think too much of this, knowing how shy she would be of strangers. But as she carefully laid out plates and cutlery, I couldn't help but stare. There was something very familiar about her. She turned hurriedly back into the house to boil water for tea.

'How long has she been working for you?' I asked Helen.

'We've had her for a little while now… can never pronounce her name… we just call her "Mae". She was brought up in a mission. Her mother was a Ja… Jab… what's that word, Rupert?'

'Djabugay, I think.'

'She was a Yid-something-speaking gin and God knows who the father is. The girl's good enough, speaks good English, thanks to her education at the mission on the tablelands, but she's prone to going walkabout. Just takes off for a few days at a time.'

'Is her family close by?'

'I don't know. Possibly.'

'You don't know anything more about her?'

'No. Only that the pastor arrived with her at Rupert's office one day pleading with him to take her in. He said that the mission superintendent had palmed her off onto him and he's given her an exemption to live off the mission. Said she kept running away and was getting herself into "moral danger", whatever that means. Anyway, she's cheap labour, which is hard to find these days.'

The girl with no name came out with the teapot and cups and set them down. As she busied herself, it came to me. A baggy calico dress, red lipstick, arm entwined in Tate the railwayman's. She glanced at me again and I wondered if she recognised me too. Maybe not – I was just another bland member of that white tribe Foster so palpably admired.

'So,' Foster said interrupting my thoughts. 'How does it feel to be the fiancée of my new partner? The *Austen* of Foster and Austen.'

It had been so long since I'd lived with a man that there was fascination in Tom's ordinary rituals. He ironed his own shirts, just so, and polished both shoes to a military gloss. Sometimes I'd stand behind him as he shaved, listening to the rasp of his razor, and watch him methodically clean it then put it back on the highest shelf. His pomade sat next to my rose one in the bathroom cabinet. He'd turn and give me a hug, pleased to have my close attention.

Living a good eight miles away from town gossip had its advantages, but the trek from the village in Tom's sturdy horse and buggy took an hour. I would have ridden the Cairns-Mulgrave tram if it had been less expensive, and more regular. Tom would drive me and Evie in the balmy hours of the morning to the still-closed shops in the centre of town, sometimes stopping at the red bowser to hand-pump petrol into a four-gallon tin. The bowser had become popular due to the town's interest in motor vehicles, which was accelerating at a speed to match Tom's driving (thirty to forty miles per hour).

Of course, the hospital didn't know that I was living in sin with my fiancé. We kept separate bedrooms, in part for Evie's sake, but mostly to avoid the consequences of her loose tongue at school (and with anyone we met). We told her we were lodging with Tom (and his allegedly absent aunt), much the same as with Dorrie. She embraced having a room to herself, and lined up her books on her chest of drawers as the first task of moving in. During that initial week she would open and close her window for no reason at all, do the same with her curtains, and arrange toys and ornaments around her bed like a bowerbird.

It was an improvement from Tom's previous worker's barracks, being snake- and rat-free, but not entirely free from night scavengers – cockroaches, standing stock-still on the sink bench when caught in the lantern's glow.

Tom pressed for a wedding, soon. I suspect he was overly concerned with our scandalous living arrangements – he was now, after all, a respectable solicitor of the town. He was under pressure to start socialising with the 'right' people, and to go back to church, something both he and I had abandoned during the war. But he understood that getting married and quitting work before I'd met the requisites was not worth the risk. Then there was the greater risk of being found 'indecent' by the moral guardians of the town. We might have just come out of a war where unsanctioned lovemaking was forgiven if your man was never to return, but the same censors would never tolerate it in peacetime. I was glad that I had no family close by to monitor my 'undoing'. I relished our audacity, and apart from the practical reasons for holding off on marriage, I was aware that there was something between us that needed testing.

Tom's office was a stuffy room, even with the shutters open, where he was surrounded by rolled up manila files tied with pink ribbon and packed into bookcases until they overflowed onto his desk. Decades of dust mites and silverfish had created a miasma of powdered paper. The building itself was like other brick businesses of the town – a white plastered frontage, with mock urns adding classical gravity and a wooden awning propped up by wooden poles. Freshly painted geometric letters in green and black, *Foster and Austen, Solicitors*, elegantly filled a ten-foot-long sign above the door.

One morning when we arrived outside his office, he said, 'Stay here for a moment,' and dashed inside. He emerged with an invitation addressed to *Tom Austen, Esq., and guest* from Mr and Mrs Albert Clarke to come to their residence for a 'screening' party. There would be cocktails and photographic slides of their latest travels abroad.

'Clarissa Clarke is an old client of Rupert's. Mine now. And you're the "guest".'

'Does she know I'm your fiancée?' I asked in disbelief.

'Of course.'

Our relationship was changing with the upturn in his working life.

'Can I come?' Evie asked.

'No,' I said. 'This one isn't for children, but Dorrie will look after you. You know the rule, right?'

'I'll talk to Leo the Lion from the veranda, then.'

'That's our Evie,' Tom said. 'Determined as her mother.' It was the first time he'd spoken of her as part of us.

The second surprise of that morning came when Matron Chalmers bailed me up outside her office as I arrived, pinning up my car-blown, off-kilter cap. *What was I doing driving around the streets so early in the morning with a man?*

Of course we'd been seen. Cars were not yet numerous in this small town where everybody knew, or knew of, everybody else. I had no idea who'd spotted us and spilled the beans. It wasn't Sybil. She was infatuated with Leon and filled with goodwill towards me for my matchmaking.

'Mr Austen kindly gave us a lift in his car, Matron. Nothing untoward.'

In truth, nothing much 'untoward' happened in that Edmonton house. I slipped into his bed at night where he'd hold me, hugging my back. Sometimes he'd fall into nightmares, his legs jolting, his body tossing with whimpers and calls. I'd almost grown to accept the fact that we might never fully share the conjugal part of a marriage. I was hoping his treatment under Roy Jamieson would help. And it had, in all other respects. His improvement meant, along with a greater cheerfulness, that he could pass a neighing horse or a crashing just-washed plate, without being noticeably startled. But sometimes when he was sitting peacefully, his hand resting on his lap while talking happily, his fingers would tremble.

'This is not the first time, Sister Sinclair. You have your professional standing to maintain. And an example to set for the trainees.'

'My daughter and I are lodging with Mr Austen and his aunt, and he sometimes drives us into town.' I started to colour at this feeble lie.

'He's a single man, is he not?'

'We are engaged.'

'Engaged? And when did you intend to tell the hospital?'

'I'm telling you now, Matron.'

In that second, when her eyes hardened, I realised that my pending unsuitability for employment would be noted at the next board meeting and my resignation expected as a matter of course.

23

The spotted rash spread down Evie's neck, invading her chest, back, and legs; her face burned, her tonsils became streaked in yellowing pus.

Scarlet fever filled the ward, and Evie became even quieter as the days passed. As the miserable faces around her started to brighten, their skin peeling the disease away, I worried about the slowness of her recovery. She'd been one of the last children admitted into the isolation hut. They said she caught it at school, but that didn't stop my added anxiety that I was to blame, that I'd carted the disease around on me like a parasite and given it to her.

I kept trying to remind myself of our success rate with other infections even more deadly, like diphtheria, with the swollen necks and urgent tracheotomies. Von Behring had developed an antitoxin for that disease three decades before and it was being developed into a vaccine. I telephoned city hospitals for advice, but they provided no comfort. Although the cause of scarlet fever was being researched, any breakthrough was a long way off, they said. Medical journals told of European scientists who'd developed a serum from horse blood with some success. But none was available. The fever is rapacious and devours the very young. Fate or bad timing left these children to fight their deadly wars on their own.

With her hollow eyes, her fringe wet with fever, Evie said: 'It's all right, Mum.' A strange husky undertone. 'He'll care for me.'

I'd heard similar declarations many times from hospital beds, and they'd proved baseless. As I watched her weaken, the belief that God had a purpose based on goodness was hard to comprehend. Damp all over, her face set passively, she fell into a doze, with a dangerously contented expression.

'Can you see Him?' I asked.

I'd never raised her to be religious, but she'd received a good dose of Bible study at school.

'No, but He's there.'

I didn't trust my voice enough to ask any more. Most likely, her God had arrived with the minister who did his weekly rounds of the wards, twice weekly with the children. But I couldn't blame him, he'd helped her find some courage.

Matron Chalmers forbad me from nursing my own child. She said I would show Evie favouritism, that I would not give the other patients proper attention. I was allowed in, wearing a mask like any other parent during visiting hours, which formally were in the afternoons. I tried to stay away in the mornings but found myself pacing outside the hut during Sybil's roster so I could snatch a few minutes to wipe Evie down with cool cloths, to rub her aching joints with a foment of washing soda, or to coax water down her pale tongue.

The image of a child with death on her face is something you can't forget, no matter how long you live. In the hours and days of bedside vigil I looked closely for signs of recovery, and marvelled at the tiny pores on her chin, the intricate fold of her ears. Her tiny details that were always present for me.

Those following weeks did seem like years. When I shrugged him off, Tom complained about how incommunicative I'd become.

I couldn't tell him, but the harsh fact was I did not want him then, or our small house at Edmonton. I wanted only my daughter, her lost father. My life then, compared with Evie's, was inconsequential and little more than vanity. If she was taken, there was no point to anything.

△ ◠ △

It was Sybil's expression that told me first. A screen had been pulled up so all that showed was the cotton blanket, its circular embroidered sign, 'Queensland Hospitals', and the shape of small feet underneath.

'She's worse,' Sybil said.

'Oh, I thought… we always pull the screen when…'

'She was wheezing. The other children were becoming concerned.'

'Has she picked up another infection?'

Sybil nodded solemnly. 'Listen.'

Matron made an exception for Tom and me to sit at Evie's bed that evening. She'd been wheeled into the empty Aliens section in the next building, as if allowing her the privacy to die. We watched her small ribcage rise erratically, exhausted lungs fighting for every gasp and sigh. I put my ear to her chest, its vibration.

We took turns to hold her hand, not talking. Then Evie had another breathless spell.

'She mustn't die. Not again,' Tom said.

'Again?'

He composed his face. 'Liese, my sister. It was all my fault. I put a plaster on her thinking that was all that was needed. I never told my parents I deliberately tripped her in a game. And they were certainly looking for something or someone to blame. I'll never forget that shovel flicking up, cutting her, the whack of her body as she hit the ground. This little one mustn't join her.'

An hour later I persuaded Tom to go home. The night nurse came and went quietly, checking pulse and temperature. She did not look at me, but I knew that she too was willing the signs to improve. Around midnight Evie's breathing became slower but more regular. I let hope in for a second. At four in the morning exactly her struggle stopped.

She opened her eyes and begged for water. No sooner had she swallowed than she vomited the whole glass over the bed.

'Sorry, sorry,' she kept saying, not understanding why the nurse and I laughed, or why I then burst into tears.

I'd seen the results of this illness in those who survived – meningitis, paralysis. I still had to be prepared.

I made a silent pact with Evie's God. I had to change, for her sake. With the clarity that only a disaster can bring to our complacent, daily selfishness, I swore that I'd uncomplicate my career. I'd happily settle down with Tom and become Mrs Austen, lawyer's wife. I'd pick Evie up from school, just like she wanted. I'd sew her clothes, have time in the morning to put her hair in ribbons. Little, inconsequential things. Things that mattered in the moment.

24

Clarissa Clarke recognised me immediately. 'I'm so glad you could come today.' She took my hand in hers, not quite a full handshake. Her face beamed charm and welcome. Gone was the haughty stare. Her rounded stomach showed another pregnancy.

Her strata of acknowledged gentry, the respectable inhabitants of Cairns – doctors, lawyers, department store owners, and those aspiring to the tennis and croquet set – were gathered at her 'dusk celebration' and were politely amazed by images of her recent European adventures. It could have been the attractive continuity of Clarissa, posed in front of many different but similar buildings that engaged them. The Eiffel Tower, the Louvre, Big Ben, the Palace of Westminster, all these wonders were gracious enough to stand behind her. This was Europe in cloudy-toned granite, limestone and marble, sanitised of its war, reinvented in Albert Clarke's thirty-five-millimetre rolls of film.

'You're from Edinburgh, are you not?' she asked.

'She is, indeed,' Tom answered on my behalf.

'We absolutely *loved* Edinburgh!' she exclaimed with delight. 'What part are you from?' Her pupils were dilated, either from her state of excitement, or a dose of liniment of belladonna, taken by some ladies for that effect.

'Morningside,' Tom said, before I had a chance to respond. 'Although she never talks about it. Says she barely remembers the place.'

'Ooh! We stayed there. What a perfectly pleasant area. We received quite a few introductions.' Her voice trilled.

I looked across the room, searching for somebody or something that could be my salvation. But she and Tom were now both focussed on me.

'It has far too many cobbles,' I said.

They roared with amusement.

'I much prefer the tropics now. The light… the warmth.'

'Albert thinks Tom's a genius. Your parents must be thrilled at your engagement.' The question was meant for me, but she glanced at Tom with approval.

Whenever he questioned me about my parents, I stuck to my script, making the excuse that I'd had a falling out with my family over my decision to stay in Australia. I'd found this climate was better for my health, which had much improved, of course. When he declared he'd take me back home one day, I said the weather was something I could never handle again. He must have suspected there was more to it. He'd said as much in Roy Jamieson's file.

'Tom has told me that you're a client of his. Although I don't know what exactly he does for you,' I responded.

'Solicitor-client privilege, darling,' Tom said in an unusually condescending way. He had donned his performance clothes – his pale colonial suit, knotted tie, and gallant manner. No one would guess that he could ever possess anything less than equanimity.

'Oh, that's no problem,' Clarissa chirped. 'Tom has done some quite marvellous things for us already. He's saved us from a tricky situation with a hotel in France chasing us for money and refusing to release our trunks. A total misunderstanding, of course. And then, with our neighbours suing us about our trees blowing down onto their house…'

Tom flushed. 'Oh, it's really nothing.'

For Tom, these were minor matters compared to the briefs he'd accepted down south. From his professional perspective, this was a town full of small suburban problems. There could be no specialisation in law, everyone had to be a general practitioner. He'd even started to dabble in criminal law, which he said was easy money.

Clarissa dragged a wandering woman into our circle and introduced her as Mrs Sarah Hartley. She was much younger than Clarissa but wore the same cut of dress and sprinkle of glitter. She held out her gloved hand, holding it limply as I shook it.

'And what do you do?' she asked Tom straight away.

Just at that moment a champagne cork popped across the room.

'Jesus Christ!' Tom yelled as he ducked down, shoulders hunched by his head.

'Well, that would be an exaggeration of your fame,' I said quickly.

His face was deathly pale. 'Sorry, ladies, no offence meant.'

I rested my hand against his back in comfort as he laughed pitifully along with the two women and those closest to us.

'Excuse me,' he said, 'but I must go speak to my partner.' Out of the corner of my eye, I saw Rupert Foster nodding at Tom, who quickly escaped into the party towards him.

'Oh yes, I must also mingle,' Clarissa said.

The man who caused the minor explosion arrived with his bottle, effervescence streaming down its neck onto a linen towel, his face the colour of cooked prawns.

'Here, my love,' he said, handing a glass to Sarah Hartley whose head twitched in a single involuntary tic.

'Oh, Stan, darling, this is Anna. She's getting married to Tom Austen and he is…? Goodness, I don't think he told me.'

'He's a solicitor. Rupert's partner in Foster and Austen.'

She gave a satisfied smile.

I started to explain my own vocation, but she cut me off to enquire which suburb I lived in. When she started to explain her husband's business interests in shipping and fishing, Mr Hartley cut in, talking over his wife and finishing her sentence. Her Tourette's tic appeared again and I felt sorry for her. She was slim, not quite twenty, and was dwarfed by the thick-necked patron at her side, whom she obviously lived for and through. Snobbery, if it was not natural to her, was certainly expected.

Fading with boredom, thinking about what treat I'd bring for Evie the next day, I excused myself after the compulsory polite five minutes. She was out of danger now, free of complications, her body spent, but thankfully whole.

I gathered myself and returned to the party. Tom had lost Foster and was making his way towards us with Roy Jamieson. Just as he reached us, Albert Clarke hurried out of the crowd. He shook Tom and Jamieson's hands but before he could say another word, Clarissa reappeared and whisked Tom away in a trail of chypre – Guerlain. Tom glanced back at us with an apologetic shrug, disguising his gait as well as he could.

'Are you here by yourself?' I asked Jamieson.

'Yes, as always. I heard about your imminent departure from the hospital. I'm sorry. I tried to put in a good word with the board.'

'Nothing will come between Matron and the rules. But I've had more important things to worry about, lately.'

'Yes. Thankfully your little one is doing fine, now.'

Clarke clapped a hand on Jamieson's shoulder. 'God help me,' he said in a lowered voice, but also within my hearing. His face was still that squarish shape, falcon's eyebrows, but there was a puffiness under his eyes and chin.

'Hello, Doctor Clarke,' I said brightly.

He looked startled. 'Ah… Sister Sinclair! I didn't recognise you at first. People always look different out of uniform.'

I'd coiffed my hair into a bob, and wore a long waisted frock of black Fuji silk, shipped up on Tom's insistence from a city department store. It glinted with glass beads, the thin straps revealing more shoulder than I really felt comfortable with. Looking in the mirror before I left for the party, I realised that since Evie's hospitalisation, I'd lost weight, my clavicle now protruding like a coat-hanger.

'Sister Sinclair, your fiancé seems to have become my wife's favourite new pet.' Retirement hadn't dulled Clarke's taste in clothes. He was sporting a cravat and dazzling white trousers, with a Prussian-blue blazer. All that was missing was a yacht.

'Please, call me Anna.'

'And you may call me Albert. Just plain Albert.' He sighed melodramatically.

'Oh, come now, old man,' Jamieson chipped in, 'you don't have to stop practising if it's that bad.'

'No, true. The old life is tacked to you forever. Quite irritating.'

Jamieson slapped him on the back. 'You're looking a tad worn out.'

'Huh! Don't believe what they say about having a young wife. All that traipsing around Europe – could hardly keep up with her. Had to get her pregnant again just to slow her down!'

I admit it gave me pleasure, this new informality, their uninhibited grins.

'You remember Anna and her plans, don't you Albert?' Jamieson gave me a complicit look.

'Er…'

'By the way, how *are* your plans going?' Jamieson asked me pointedly, although he knew.

'Slowly, I'm afraid. I've contacted the local government, worked on the requirements for registration, etcetera. If the support I need comes through, I'm there, but that's not looking likely.'

'What's this?' Clarke asked.

'My hospital. A private hospital, here in Cairns.'

'That's brave of you,' Clarke said. 'I didn't realise you had medical qualifications.' I suspected he used the term *brave* when he meant *stupid*.

I answered the challenge. 'As a Sister I'm able to establish a lying-in hospital similar to other regions.'

'You're right, Albert, she is brave,' Jamieson said. 'But tell him the rest,' he said turning to me.

'Thank you,' I said.

And so, I explained about medical references, board compositions, acquisition of stock, equipment, machinery, leasing and registration of premises, staff requirements and so many other matters that had kept me awake at night and given me groggy mornings. The surprising thing was that Clarke appeared to be interested, occasionally nodding his head, fixing me with his eyes in a curious way. I'd waited for this moment so long that it felt like déjà vu.

'You've certainly been preparing over these last months,' Jamieson said when I'd finished.

'And you've got a good man there for the legals,' Clarke chipped in. 'It'll be a joint venture with Tom, of course?'

'No. It's my own. I'm leading it.'

'Is that wise?' he asked.

'Excuse me?'

'Never underestimate Anna,' Jamieson said.

Clarke was right. He recognised the overconfidence sprung from ignorance. But his reaction stirred something in me.

'I do appreciate your medical support, Roy.' My prompt was aimed at Clarke, of course.

'You just need to attract another medical practitioner, someone like Albert here, for example,' Jamieson said, picking up the cue. 'All he requires is some incentive. Don't you, old man?'

Clarke raised his eyebrows.

'Oh, by the way,' I said to Clarke, 'I think we might have a mutual friend.' I don't know what mischief made me say this, but instinctively I knew it was the only leverage I had.

'Oh, yes?'

'Dorrie Baker. She owns a boarding house further down the esplanade.'

'Catch you later, Roy,' Clarke said as he turned me away by the elbow.

'What makes you think I know her, Sister?' Clarke was looking down at his buffed shoes, averting his face.

'She told me about you… I mean… she remembers you vividly.'

'And your interest with her is?'

'I used to board with her. Me and my daughter. She said you used to visit regularly.'

'Oh, really? And what else did she say about me?'

'We used to talk quite a bit.' I said this too quickly. 'She is quite fond of you.' I didn't even know if this was true, but he was beginning to look like he might panic.

'I think you know more than you are letting on.'

'I…' My silence as he waited for me to reassure him was probably calculated.

'For the record, I think we all have done things in our past of which we are not proud, haven't we?' He looked over to Clarissa who was showing Tom her souvenirs and trinkets, introducing him to people he would be happy never to see again. 'I'm sure that whatever Miss Baker has told you, it's something you'd want to keep to yourself?' He nodded as if inviting me to agree.

'I believe that people who support me deserve all my loyalty. What about you?'

'That's fair, I think.' He looked at me, thoughtfully. 'Now, this hospital of yours. I do think you've got the gumption to make it work. You've got spirit. And I do like spirit in a woman.' He laughed nervously. 'So long as she doesn't turn round and bite me.'

25

Matilda arrived soon after my letter. I'd written to her in a moment of desperation, knowing that she was the only living relative in Australia who'd care. Rather than come to me after leaving the boat, she went directly to the ward where I found her, reading to Evie.

'She's grown,' was all she said.

'Evie, do you remember Aunt Matilda?'

She nodded drowsily. There had been only one quick visit to Brisbane, a few years before, when Matilda had paid for our passage down for her father's – old man Sinclair's – funeral. Apart from Evie, she was the last remaining member of that family now. Andy's father had left an annuity and the decorating business to Matilda in his will, but she sold it and bought a small mansion with the proceeds.

I'd seen little of the old man after Andy was killed. He kept his distance from us. The funeral of Sinclair senior was a strange affair. He'd died by accidental drowning, Matilda told me. But at the wake, a painter now jobless as a result of the sale, whispered to me that one day the old man filled his pockets with tins of white lead, left the workshop, then walked into the Brisbane River.

The service was held in the same church where old man Sinclair had donated a large sum for the construction of a memorial – a stained glass window, featuring Andy in his uniform (his face transposed from his last photograph) standing by Saint Andrew, who looked at him with pride. It was grief over Andy, sole son and heir, the painter said.

'I'm surprised there's even a headstone.' The painter looked at me as if wondering why I had not also filled my pockets.

'Evie would be much better off down here rather than attending that little school in the country,' Matilda had written. 'And when I say *country*, that is a euphemism. There is a particularly splendid girls' school here in the city, it takes boarders as well. You're wasting my niece's potential – all because of your selfishness. Anyway, I'm sure your new fiancé will take up more than enough of your time.' Matilda made little effort to soften her opinions.

I realised then that she was looking for something deserving to spend her lonely fortune on. The thousand-mile sea journey to the north had made her more determined than ever. She set about telling Evie tales of a model school of excellence for girls. It would equip her to do anything she wanted with her life, even become a doctor if she wanted. And there would be such fun and escapades with the other girls – bosom pals forever, just like in the popular children's school stories. Evie absorbed it all, this make-believe life she could never have here with me, in this 'one-horse town'.

I'd put aside the trivial worry about another note from Miss Marchant threatening expulsion just before Evie was hospitalised. I'd left it unanswered. As I saw it then, I had no moral right to deny Evie the support of an upright and sober aunt and a new start.

'She is *my* child,' I whispered, as Matilda, book in hand, savoured the child's face that had so much of Andy in her features.

The plan for Evie, fully recovered, was to stay with Aunt Matilda for a school term and then to reassess the situation at that point. If necessary, she could enrol as a boarder at Brisbane High School for Girls on a more permanent basis, however, what would be the point, Matilda told me. Evie could always stay with her and be given three square meals a day and her own garden to play in. And she would have a bedroom decorated to her own taste. I think it was Evie imagining herself in a house with a panoramic view of the city, and at school, mistresses who immediately recognised she was exemplary among girls, that made her plead with me to allow her to go.

I knew Matilda's arguments had some merit. I couldn't refuse my daughter the opportunity to see if she would thrive in such circumstances. It would give her aunt purpose, someone to dote upon, and fill part of the gap left by Andy. Still, I hated the idea of Evie leaving, and hoped she would be back after finding the reality of the city less fabulous than she imagined.

Evie said her goodbyes at the wharf. She handed me an envelope with her almost neat cursive script. 'Mum, give this to Leon, please. Don't open it.' She already sounded much older than her seven years.

'And this is for you,' I said.

She took the wedding band.

'Your father gave it to me. Here's a chain to wear it with. Now we'll always be connected.' It was tenuous symbolism at best. My daughter was drifting away from me.

26

In the balmy September evening, the Barron River was alight with boats.

'I wonder what the fish will spend it on,' I said, as I cast a pound note and several pork parcels I'd been given into the black water.

'Gourmet crocodiles will do anything for dumplings,' Tom said, and on cue, there was a snap at the river's muddy edge, loud enough to be heard over the ghostly song of zithers and lutes.

We'd sailed to the river mouth from the Cairns wharf in a Chinese junk, a smaller version of the sturdy trading vessels, and crewed by men in long tunics and loose pants. We caught the evening breeze in the large square sails, outrunning the flotilla of tiny sail and rowing boats behind. We were the special guests of Mr Kwong Sue-duc, Tom's client and a husband of four wives, whose latest addition to the family – I believe it was his tenth – I had successfully help deliver.

'Normally,' Mr Kwong said in practised English, 'my wife would have our son at home, helped by our amah nursemaid.' But there'd been trouble with the last few births.

Mrs Kwong's labour had been long and hard, and at one stage her pulse became so high I thought we might lose her. But after an exhausting twenty-three hours of labour, a wonderful, noisy, round little boy arrived. Mrs Kwong settled nicely into the maternity ward with the other mothers, communicating with sign language, sharing baby stories, until her husband appeared, requiring her presence back at home.

Mr Kwong was a hardworking and respected merchant who supplied much-needed fresh fruit and vegetables from his base near the river, but there was a great deal of suspicion surrounding the Chinese in those days. It was partly a hangover from the gold days when they would mine their treasure in large groups of young men, then smuggle it home in funeral urns. There was still a kind of voluntary segregation in Cairns, so that people of the Chinese community wouldn't attend the pictures. They would rather watch films already viewed by the rest of the town in the Masonic Hall in Chinatown, the only large building there at the time.

I thanked Mr Kwong for this rare honour in inviting us to the festival, which was a kind of spiritual celebration.

'It's called the Bar-Lun Sui-Yee Wui,' Mr Kwong said.

He smiled politely when I tried to repeat it.

Hoping not to appear too ignorant, I said, 'I understand it's to appease ghost-devils?'

'Ah yes, the *kwei*, men who capsized here in their banana junk during the floods of eighteen-ninety. My wives have decorated our altar with peacock feathers in their memory.'

I'd heard that the local Chinese sometimes referred to all non-Chinese by that name, *kwei*, and I wondered what the family must think of Tom and me, clearly not used to rolling boats and getting stuck into their sweet, earthy rice wine. I was, by that stage, becoming heady with it.

I looked over to the mudflats where mangrove shadows loomed under the full moon and wondered about the other ghosts here, the older ones; what they would think of all this.

In the solemn atmosphere I thought of my own ghost, Andy, realising I'd known Tom even longer. 'The dead have their place,' I said.

Tom put his arms around me and gently held my head to his heart, swaddling me in a cocoon of music and stars. As the tide carried us toward the harbour light, I said, 'Let's not put it off any longer.'

Tom's parents, Karl Austen, a tall, box-faced man and his wife, Ilsa, her hair as iron-grey as her countenance, arrived two days before our wedding, with marked accents and tins of streusel cake. Tom arranged for them to be put up in the Pacific Hotel, while having to pretend that we did not really live together.

'Sit here, Mutter,' Tom said pulling out a chair in the hotel dining room.

'Don't call me that *here*!' she replied in an urgent whisper.

Mrs Austen turned to me. 'We had a very hard time because of the war, you know. We were lucky not to be put in an internment camp. Lucky we lived out in the desert bush where we were too far away for them to care.'

'Lucky we were farmers, Ilsa,' Mr Austen said.

'The war's over now, Mama,' Tom added.

'Not for us, Tomas. Never for us.'

'And look at what it's done to you,' his father said.

'We're a peaceful family.' Mrs Austen's eyes were fixed on me. 'You know, I made a trip to vote in the anti-conscription line, but they belted and booed me out of it, accusing me of being there for the enemy. And here I was, sending my son to be slaughtered at the hands of cousins, uncles and who-knows-what-else.'

'And I to slaughter them, Mama.'

Her face sank. Karl Austen cleared his throat.

'Now let's not get maudlin,' Tom replied. 'Those days are gone.' He turned to me and took my hand. 'Now, what do you think of my Anna?'

'I hope you've told her, Tomas,' his mother said solemnly.

'What?'

'About Uncle Franz. There's a weakness in the family, Anna. My husband's brother in Austria…'

'You don't visit us enough, son,' Karl said before she could finish her sentence. 'You and Anna must come to see us soon.'

'We live modestly, but you are most welcome.' Ilsa patted my knee, then added as if he were not there at all, 'I only wish Tomas would go back to Brisbane to work with his uncle Max, also a fine lawyer.'

'I have a good business here, Mama. You'll meet my partner at the wedding. Only, please, if you'll forgive the expression, don't mention the war.'

'It's no laughing matter, Tomas.' She sipped her schnapps, recently reintroduced to the local bars. 'Here, Anna, you haven't touched your drink.'

I compliantly took a sip out of my shot glass. It was not a sweet brandy and left a taste of bitter cherries.

'Now, dear Anna,' Ilsa said, 'do tell us about yourself. Tomas has told us only a little. When can we meet your family?'

'Er…'

'I told you they live in Scotland, Mama. Her father is a doctor over there.'

'Yes,' I said, 'it's a long way away, I'm afraid.'

She shuddered. She may just have been thinking of the climate, or the ruins of Europe. 'Oh, that is a pity. What do they think of our Tomas?'

'I'm sure if…when…they meet him they'll approve enormously.' But I wondered what they'd think even if it were possible. Edinburgh had been bombed by raiding zeppelins three years after I left. They came in the dead of night and people sheltered as best they could as the sinister airships rumbled across the city sky. When I heard about it in the news, I wrote to Angus, and he responded that they were safe and that he was going off to war as a medical officer. Our father's colleague's surgery had been bombed, he said, along with other random buildings around the port. In my bitterness, or in fear, I asked Angus not to tell anyone, not even Malcolm, about my letter to him. I was a widow in Brisbane then, but they didn't know that. They knew very little about my new life. It's a platitude, I know, but pride really is a self-destructive thing. Angus's letter was the last I received from Edinburgh before my father's response.

'Tomas tells me you've married before.' This was Ilsa.

'I'm a widow. My husband… first husband… was killed in the war.'

'Yes, that is very sad.'

'And I have a daughter, Evelyn. Tom has no doubt mentioned her to you?'

Her face blanched. 'Goodness, no! Tomas! Why do I hear this now?'

'Mama, she's the best little girl in the world. I wanted to surprise you.'

'So! Where is she? Where is this girl?' Ilsa asked, looking around.

'She's at school down in Brisbane, Mrs Austen, but both she and her aunt will arrive tomorrow. She's very excited about meeting you.' A small lie in the larger scheme of things.

It was October 1921, and the day was bright and green.

'You look gorgeous,' Sybil said, straightening my skirt.

I checked myself in the guest room mirror – marcel waves, cupid lips. Tom had persuaded me that we should accept the kind invitation of Rupert and Helen Foster to hold our wedding reception at their house. It would save 'loads of money', he said, and more importantly, make his partner happy.

'Is it ridiculous to wear ivory, Sybs – and am I showing too much cleavage?'

'You look terrific. Truly.'

'I'm a collector of husbands. Two times a fool.'

She took a bottle of perfume from the dresser, spraying it in a halo around my head. 'There. You are positively angelic.' She steered me to the door. 'C'mon, it's time to get married.'

I got to the door and stalled. 'But, seriously, Sybs. This isn't right. It's not right at all.'

'What's the problem?'

'I think maybe I'm just scared of dying alone.'

'Are you kidding? Death will come whether you've got company or not.' She gave me a push towards the threshold.

'I just can't.' I'd held back the truth from Tom, and the longer I did so, the greater was the urge to tell it. But with that, the urge to withhold it intensified, now creating something twisted inside, like a bitter narcotic.

'Dear lord, give me strength! He's a handsome fox and he adores you. So why the hell not?'

'I'm sorry, Sybil.' I started to rip the flowers out of my hair. 'Sorry I asked you to do this.'

'You're a ratbag. And so bloody frustrating. He's always been yours, really. Besides, it's time you had some happiness, my love. Even if it is with my stolen boyfriend.' She raised her eyebrows in mock disapproval and guided me to the dresser chair. She fixed my hair. 'Now,' she said, squeezing my shoulders and meeting my eyes in the mirror, 'show some of that grit that just barely makes you worth putting up with. Pull yourself together!'

Helen Foster knocked and swept in with Evie. 'They're all waiting, girls, including the harpist. Oh my, you do look chic.'

'Mum, you're so pretty! Wait till Tom sees you.' Evie looked at me in a way I'd never seen before, then gave me a crushing hug. 'Now there will be three of us.' She sounded older than her years.

We were married by a justice of the peace. It was an afternoon tea event, with dessert fully catered for by the array of Gugelhupfs, streusel cakes and other delicacies brought in by Tom's parents. Wedding presents largely consisted of crockery and crystal unwrapped and displayed on tables by the cake, as well as a bright embroidered quilt made by Ilsa Austen.

Doctors Clarke and Jamieson were there with Clarissa Clarke, looking tired from her pregnancy. Dorrie arrived in her new car, her hair more windblown and orange than usual. I'd invited Matilda who was happy to chaperone Evie over a thousand miles to the wedding, but said she couldn't attend the wedding itself, without providing any excuse. I understood it was out of loyalty to her brother, but her refusal only deepened the unease in me.

Leon loitered at the fringe of our party, as if unsure of his welcome. Sybil whispered in his ear and having received this call to arms, he followed Rupert Foster's lead and eloquently made the second toast to our health and happiness.

Sybil took me aside and said that if the bouquet were thrown in her direction, it would be worth a whole day's pay. Sybil was at the stage with Leon where a girl might expect her beau to propose. He was setting up his own jewellery store, a fact which Sybil decided made Leon even more eligible, but also appeared to be the reason for him to delay any nuptials.

Among the caterers hired for the day, there was no sign of Mae. When I asked where she was, Helen told me the pastor had found a husband for her in Yarrabah mission. I asked if that was what Mae wanted, but Helen shrugged and gave a little laugh as if I'd said something ridiculous.

Evie was refreshingly cheerful as she passed around the sandwiches. When she was introduced to Ilsa, the woman touched her plaits, a tremble on her lips and whispered something about her 'own Liese'. It was then I understood why Tom had not already mentioned Evie to his mother. I took Ilsa to the pool to recover and together we stood at its rippled edge. The ferns moved as if someone had just brushed them.

Our honeymoon was a few days' stay at Kuranda, the place where Tom said he fell in love with me. But we spent that night at a hotel in town, our suite laid out with a lace bedcover, lavender pillows, mosquito netting, small handmade chocolates in crystal bowls and champagne in an ice-bucket. Our first night as husband and wife was more than mere ritual. We shed our ghosts, at least temporarily, and revealed ourselves to each other, physically and lovingly. His hands lifted the small of my back, lips grazing my stomach, my neck.

I woke, captured by him, his body pressed close. I traced a finger down his scar, now paled into a benign keloid.

PART THREE

1922–1923

27

It made people stop and stare. A weatherboard building capped off by a red tin roof, ploughing towards the inlet. That was my new hospital, a once-roomy fashion house from Cooktown's heyday of goldfield money, carved up and loaded onto a steamer.

I leased a plot of land for my building near the centre of Cairns, across the road from the cemetery, and not far from the site of the temporary plague station set up a decade before. Just before the wet onset of 1921, I registered the property with the town council as Huntly Private Hospital, perhaps too bravely reclaiming something of my lost self.

Tom and I moved in downstairs to the parlour beside the kitchen, sleeping in a small bedroom (another, the size of a cupboard, was for Evie whenever she came back north). There was also a room downstairs for live-in nurses (required by regulation) and a laundry with a side room, leaving upstairs for the wards, enough for nine or ten patients, and an operating room.

We stood at the doorway of the operating theatre, bright with natural light from large windows illuminating linen-covered trolleys and trestle tables, rolled up towels and large shining sinks, and admired the rows of forceps and other medical instruments, sterilisation trays, locked glass cabinets packed with bottled medications, jars filled with swabs, enamelled bowls stacked and ready, the empty linen bins, and of course, a mop in the corner.

'I'm proud of you,' Tom said simply.

In my last appeal to the bank manager, I was more than determined. I sat tall, opposite his picture in uniform, and described to him in a congenial manner (and without drawing a breath), injuries I'd tended, of returned soldiers, broken in body and mind, providing graphic, gory detail. I swear he winced. I think I even quoted President Teddy Roosevelt's saying about mothers being far more important than any businessman, artist or scientist and that I, such a mother and a businesswoman, deserved all his support. I thrust my two references, stock list and budget at him and suggested he refer to my most recent bank balance, which was still not impressive, but had grown. Then I produced the fruit of Albert Clarke's shame, and perhaps his powers of persuasion – a promissory note from Mrs Clarissa Clarke, would-be investor in this 'extremely worthy' project. Hall didn't give me an answer straight away.

And now I had my board. I was Chairman, not that an outsider looking in at our meetings around my parlour table would guess, with the robust personalities of Clarke, Jamieson and our accountant, Peter Corrin, contesting points of view over tea and biscuits. Jamieson had obtained special permission from the Cairns District Hospital Board to assist at my hospital after his persistence that they lacked space and resources.

I employed two live-in nurses – Lillian Wilson for the night shift, and a registered day nurse, Hazel Gregory, who'd applied for a job at the District without success. The indomitable Hazel had arrived from Townsville, newly qualified as an RN, while Lillian, whose serious expression hardened an otherwise pretty face, had worked as a nurses' helper at a mental asylum in Brisbane. They shared a room on the ground floor, decorated to their own taste.

I wrote to Evie every week and imagined her every day. I kept her small room dusted and ready. I arranged her books in tidy piles, waiting for her. In her bedroom at Edmonton, she'd started strewing them around. I'd find bunched vests and socks, lost for weeks, under her bed. But in this new room it was as if I'd tidied her away too. She'd left behind her stuffed felt wombat, asking me to give it to a 'poor' child because she was too grown up for it now. Every night I'd hold it to my cheek before I went to bed.

'I miss her, too,' Tom said, holding me in our cool quarters, windows open to let out the smell of fresh paint.

These moments – the caring, the tender way he looked at me, the joy of building something together – were all that mattered. Not the other things, the things I assumed would resolve with time – his fright at a clattering cup, his irritated outbursts followed by quick apologies, the slamming of hands on the wall when we sometimes argued. In those angry moments, I decided that if there was such a thing as complete marital happiness, I didn't really deserve it.

The patients came one or two at a time as many women still gave birth at home. My Visitor's Book began with entries from Mrs Starr, Mrs Cotter, Mrs Flaherty, and Mrs Murray. I remember these women to this day, miners' and farmers' wives from the tablelands and outlying areas, women who needed longer lying-in care.

'I don't believe in hospitals, but anything's better than delivering at home. I've lost my last two, you see.' This was Mrs Flaherty, who was admitted with third trimester Braxton-Hicks. 'And your fees are low enough.'

I mentioned this to Tom as he stacked some books.

'My mother hates hospitals, too. She wants to know why we have to live here. She seems to think I'm looking for new clients a bit too assiduously,' he said.

We both laughed.

Mrs Murray's labour was not easy. Albert Clarke attended, and I was grateful for his experience. 'She'll wake the dead across the road,' Albert said of her screams. I focussed on the baby girl trapped in the forceps, rupturing her way into the world. Clarke prided himself on his neat sutures, and as soon as the afterbirth passed, he deftly stitched Mrs Murray to her pre-birth state. *Even tighter than she was before*, he boasted.

I soon realised I'd not thought through all the necessities, which left me, Lillian and Hazel also in the position of housemaids and cook, so I placed an advertisement in the local newspaper for help. There was no shortage of war widows with rough, cracked hands and worn faces applying.

Jean, wild-haired, eighteen, and recently arrived by assisted passage from Ireland, was employed as the new housemaid.

'It's a cosy wee place,' she said of her cabinet room beside the laundry. 'A fairy couldn't dance in here, but I'm not complaining, mind.'

She closely supervised the area prescribed for laundry and drying, and religiously followed her own god of cleanliness. Bed bugs and fleas brought in by a patient were quickly eradicated with swathes of disinfectant, and nightgowns and sheets changed every day. She would occasionally look at me as if I were a murderer, appalled at the amount of blood that had to be boiled out of hospital sheets and scrubbed from trolley wheels.

As my hospital became busy and Jean was required as a full-time laundry maid, I also took on a live-out housemaid, the spry Gillian Herd.

My cook, the sun-cracked Mary Sheehan, was a woman with impeccable references who'd left the rough and tumble of a cattle station out in the dry arid country.

'I'm getting on a bit, now,' she said. 'I need a position in town, and this hospital will do very well, indeed.'

Mostly, the days brought healthy births and quick recoveries, including Albert and Clarissa Clarke's second child, another boy, delivered this time by myself and Roy Jamieson. Albert said it wasn't ethical to undertake surgery on his own family, but according to Jamieson it was more about his nerves.

During that first autumn and summer, nine months on from Christmas and Easter indulgence, my hospital became a birth factory. The full-term squealers, six, seven, eight pounders, slid into the world in their cheesy vernix wrapping, puffy-eyed, wriggling, beautiful. We clamped and cut umbilical cords, checked tiny racing hearts, inspected feet and hands, cleaned eyes and noses, weighed the newborns wailing at the world and I prayed silently that they'd never have to see a war. We checked the boys' testicles were descended, and for girls, we looked for signs of discharge. The early-termers received cotton wool beds, fluids by pipette, no baths but a wipe-down with olive oil and boracic lotion and plenty of prayers.

But not everything was perfect. There was the odd harelip, requiring post-birth paring and stitching under anaesthetic, or a cleft palate, to be repaired in two or three years' time, with the child fed by a large-teated bottle, or by spoon or pipette. We nursed these ones continually to prevent them crying and splinted their tiny arms to stop stray fists and nails pushing into the mouth.

Working with new life is a good way to distract yourself from the old. My hospital was growing. It was a big breathing organism, and every morning I'd wake, renewed and happier than I'd been in years. I almost dared to think I was free.

28

Dorrie ploughed her imported car into the window of a clothing store, missing a pedestrian and her pram by inches, propelling shattered glass everywhere, and her two dogs towards the crocodile swamps by the inlet. Her smiling photo, taken at a function many years before, was featured on the front page of the local newspaper. There was also a photo of her car, half-interred in the shop. It featured a policeman inspecting the leather upholstery to no apparent purpose. I recognised him when he came to interview her at my hospital.

They'd taken her off to the District at first, but on regaining consciousness in the accident ward she discovered her bed was next to the shopkeeper's. He'd been admitted for shock and decided his recovery would be hastened by threatening Dorrie with legal action, augmented by as many abusive nouns and adjectives as he could muster. She discharged herself into my care, flouting the obvious – that she could never be considered pre or antenatal.

Her head was a mess of contusions from striking the steering wheel. Though in pain from a badly bruised chest, she hadn't lost her humour, laughing at the streaks of dried blood in her hair: 'I look like a dazed tiger. How fitting.' Bed rest was ordered, and she was monitored for signs of brain damage. She refused laudanum. 'I touch nothing that lets down my guard.' Her main concern was her lost dogs. 'They'll be curry if I don't get them back soon.'

Leon arrived with paw-paws. 'Aloha, gorgeous lady.' He laid the fruit on her bed. 'They're from my back yard. I thought you could do with something sweet.'

'Ah, you're a darling.' She patted his hand.

I took the fruit and went to get a bowl for them. When I came back, Dorrie and all the other ladies in the ward were laughing at something Leon had said.

'I must go,' he said and kissed Dorrie on the forehead. In that instant her face softened.

On his way to the door I asked, 'How's Sybil?'

'I don't think she's talking to me. I've no idea what I've done wrong.'

'I can't imagine.'

He ignored my sarcasm. 'And how's Evie going in her new school?'

'She's fine.' I remembered her manila envelope which still sat in my drawer. 'She left something for you… a while ago, sorry.'

Leon read out the letter and smiled.

A photo was tucked into it. She was in a boat – Leon's – and behind it, mangroves. In a triumphant pose among crab-pots she held the pincers of a mud crab, its body dangling below. Her teeth shone, the sun whitening her nose and fair brows. On the back, Evie had written, 'Me and the enormous crab'.

'What is this adventure she's thanking you for?' I guessed the answer, but needed to hear it from him.

'I took her crabbing in the inlet near the esplanade, not far from Dorrie's. That's where I took this photo. I had to take a few before I captured this clear one. The boat was swaying in the waves so…'

'Why didn't you ask me for permission?'

'She said it was fine by you so I assumed everything was okay. She was very persuasive. Had to catch that tide and you were always at work.'

Leon was irritatingly blasé, but I couldn't deny he was right. I put myself in the picture beside her, laughing too. I imagined her framed by the Bakelite-green leaves, the olive brown water over the mudflats. I still imagine it to this day.

'It was dangerous,' I said. 'There are crocodiles in that inlet.' I tried to sound stern.

He shrugged. 'Evie was safe with me. And look at that face. Here, you keep it. I can see that you'd like to.' He fixed me with his intense stare.

He came back again two days later with Dorrie's fox terriers, one animal under each arm, ignoring the hospital rules of hygiene.

Having sunk into a midden of dolefulness, Dorrie was under the covers pretending to sleep. She was already in mourning for her pets. One gave a piercing whine and immediately she sat up.

'A little kid in Malay town found them,' Leon said. 'They're getting sick of living off porridge and carrot-tops though.' As soon as the animals saw Dorrie, they wriggled in his arms, licking the air violently.

She hauled her varicosed legs from under the sheet and stood. 'That's it. I'm taking them home.'

'Not without a doctor's inspection,' I said.

'Bugger that. Anyway, the babies here keep me awake at night.' She shooed us into the hall while she threw on some clothes.

Leon shrugged and said, 'I'd like to see you try and stop her.'

'Just send me the bill,' she shouted from the stairs. 'And tell the police they can find me at home.'

'There's no charge, Dorrie,' I said to the echoing footsteps. 'I'll call on you tomorrow.'

She was suspended from driving.

'I don't know what good they think that'll do me,' she said. 'Contemplating my belly for three months won't change anything. And from now on I'm buying my bloomers elsewhere. That shopkeeper's has enough of my savings to stock a hundred years' worth of cottons.'

'Where in God's name have you been hiding?' Sybil found me on the post office steps with my mail.

'I could say the same about you.'

'C'mon, let's pop over there.' She pointed at a low building with plate glass windows, the only tea shop in the street.

A horse towing a cartload of barrels and packages pulled out from the side of the kerb and dropped a pile of dung in front of us.

'Phew!' I waved away the smell. 'It's too hot for tea.'

'Well, have a bloody lemonade then. Or, how about a beer?'

'Have you forgotten they don't serve women in pubs?'

'Yeah, I know, stupid men, I think deep down they're scared of us.'

'Not that deep, Sybs,' I said, veering around the dung into the sun-blasted street.

We found a seat by the counter which was covered in fly-net serves of scones, pikelets, and cakes.

'What's your news?' She fanned herself to no effect with a serviette.

'None. I'm busy. As usual. Luckily, I have Hazel and Lillian full-time – I had a contract nurse but she moved up the tablelands to get married.'

'Lucky her!'

'Don't you be so sure.'

'What do you mean?'

'Never mind.'

'Why is it so bloody hard to get a man to put a diamond on this, eh?' She made a fist with her left hand.

'Talking of which, I saw Leon the other day. He was visiting Dorrie.'

'Poor old dear. Yes, I saw her at the District.'

'He says you're not talking to him.'

'He should bloody well know why not! I put the hard word on him about getting married. I'm getting sick of all this *coitus interruptus*.'

An elderly man at the next table shot Sybil a glance and quickly shifted his newspaper away from us.

'The Stopes bible?' I said, controlling a laugh.

'I want it all, Anna. The whole marriage thing. But he said he wasn't the marrying kind. I told him he was a jerk, leading me on. He said he didn't mean to, that I was the best girl in the world and if he did ever marry, it would be to me.' She bent her head and smoothed her hair with both palms.

'Has he explained why not?'

'Nope. I don't believe him, of course, about this *best girl* business. But I'm crazy about him, Anna. What does he see in a bushie like me?'

'I'd say that's something he does mean. You're gorgeous and you can't see it.' Her turquoise eyes blinked. 'Truly, Sybs, I don't mean to be cruel, but look at the facts. He would've moved on by now if he didn't. He would have found someone else.'

'Sometimes I do get the impression he's waiting for someone else. I mean, Tom was, wasn't he? And I didn't have a clue.'

'Oh, Sybs. I'm sure that isn't true.' I coloured, remembering that night with Leon, but she was too busy eyeing a Neenish tart to notice.

'He's obsessed with his shop, you know. And his communist mates.'

'I wouldn't say that too loud around here.'

'I mean, how does he justify that?' she said. 'He's a commo but he's running a capitalist business.'

'So, he *has* stopped importing herbal remedies?'

'He says that's done its bit for him. Said he made quite a bit of dosh from it.' She took a bite of tart, a crumb settling on her lip. 'Oh, but he did give me this.' She pulled out a fine chain necklace from under her blouse and dangled a large drop pearl. 'It's compensation, I'd say. He told me to shut my eyes and open my hand. I thought it was a joke. We were on the beach, and I thought he'd just picked up a pebble.'

'It's exquisite.'

'I once had a bloke give me a box with my name on it and I got all excited. He pretended the brooch was an aquamarine. Turned out it was paste. He was a bit of a lair, anyway. At least Leon doesn't pretend with me. I know he has a history with women. I never ask for the details, of course. But I think it's time *I* started playing hard to get.' She stuffed the rest of the cake into her mouth, chocolate icing on her lips. 'But tell me, why do I always get the difficult ones?'

'It's not just you. I'd like the whole marriage thing myself. I'd like more children, but...'

'Oh? What's Tom up to, then?'

'Can I ask you a personal question, Sybs?'

'Go ahead, I'm all yours.'

'When you were with Tom, did you... did you... did you really...'

'What?'

I took a large sip of water. 'Er… compound your alchemy?'

'Crikey, love, that *is* personal.'

'You told me once before that you did. But I wasn't sure if that was just to make me jealous. Tom denied it ever happened, and I believed him then, but lately I'm not so sure about anything he says.'

'He's the best kisser I've ever met. We did everything…' She licked her fingers as if relishing a memory.

'Really?'

'… but that! If you must know, I was a virgin until I met Leon. Did you really think I was that quick off the mark?'

'No Sybs,' I said with affection. 'But I think your mouth betrays your heart.'

'So, why is this old Tom stuff so important to you now? Crikey, you've got to get over it.'

'It's not what you think.'

'Tell me. Don't bottle it up, whatever it is.'

I lowered my voice to a whisper. 'You know he's been affected by the war. With his neurasthenia?'

'Oh, I see.'

'It's not that he can't… you know… at all. But, let's see, I can count the number of times on one hand. He's getting treatment from Doctor Jamieson, but things haven't improved much lately.'

'I think you need to talk to the good old doctor.'

'Done that.'

'He's made quite a name for himself, Jamieson. I wouldn't be surprised if he becomes the next superintendent. But it's weird, you know. He's the only one who doesn't chase the nurses. I reckon my theory…'

'Tom and me… we've started arguing a lot. It started after I became busy with the hospital. He says he needs me to be available for his client functions, and so on, and I'm not always free. But when I do make time for him, he's full of moody silences. I can't win, these days. He's getting worse and I feel helpless.'

'Helpless? That's not like you, at all.'

'He put a boot-sized dent in the bathroom door, yesterday.'

'My dear, I think you two need a holiday together.'

29

W hen I woke the next morning, Tom appeared with a tray holding a boiled egg, toast, and tea.

'Where were you last night?' A sharp pain sliced across my head. I'd stayed up till midnight worrying about him.

'Had a long session with Roy then went for a walk. Didn't want to wake you when I came home.' I recognised the remote tone.

'What time was that?'

'Can't remember.'

'Are you avoiding me?'

'No, no. I'm just tired.' The subject was closed for discussion.

I put the tray on the bedside table. 'Come and lie by me for a while.'

'Anna, I'm due in court this morning.'

'Just a short while.'

'Isn't Lillian due to knock off night duty soon?' he asked.

'I have at least thirty minutes. Don't leave just yet.'

He continued knotting his tie.

'Tom, do you still love me?'

'Always. Tonight. I promise.'

With a peck to the cheek, he left me alone with my useless naked body. I lay on the quilt which his mother had padded optimistically with duck down, soft enough to cradle a baby.

'Tonight' never happened because of the emergency admission of Alice Matthews, an assistant seamstress, aged sixteen, haemorrhaging violently. There were signs of an attempted termination with a knitting needle or the like. When I asked where the father of the child was, she looked at her own father who had brought her.

'Never you mind about that,' he said.

With blood soaking her clothes, the bed, the operating table, we were unable to save the foetus, which had to be aborted by curettage, and we nearly lost Alice herself.

'It's just as well,' she said when she came round. 'I couldn't have liked it.'

'Don't you go telling anyone about this, you hear?' Matthews said, as he paid her bill.

'You're aware that any attempt to abort a child is a criminal offence?' I said, avoiding the other question of paternity.

He replied, unconvincingly, 'Don't know what you're talking about.'

'Alice's "accident" should be a warning, don't you think?'

Matthews blanched.

I'd already mulled over the quandary of reporting it, bitingly aware that it was suspicion only, that I had no right to sit in moral judgement, especially with this hapless girl, who I reasoned was still a child and a victim of her circumstances.

'The officer says to the new recruit: *Have you come here to die?* Recruit answers: *Nah, I came here yester-die.*'

Tom laughed, but the beer-soaked joker – the client who'd invited us on his yacht trip to Green Island – didn't notice its hollowness. The joker and his group of friends would not realise how Tom behaved so differently with them, as if concealing himself, as if lacking spontaneous charm.

I jumped into the ocean to snorkel around the colourful corals and called to him. But he stayed on board, his shirt unbuttoned, deck shoes still on, tattoo and toes covered, 'to guard the yacht,' he said.

I'd been looking forward to the day, to spending time with him and re-connecting, mistaken that the distance between us was brought on by the bustle of our lives. That night at home, I tried, again.

'Sorry, Anna, I'm too tired.' He shifted out of my embrace and turned his back to me.

'That's supposed to be the wife's excuse,' I said.

'You're red-raw with sunburn, darling. It's not a good idea.'

In this uncertain, condensed version of Tom I'm still confused about that series of silences. Our relationship had become marked by his preoccupied 'hmms', his eyes wandering to any distraction outside when I had something important to say; the silences when he was deep in thought, eyes down, not meeting mine. He started apologising for little things, or nothing in particular. Whenever I tried to get him to talk about it, he became irritated. Once, he stopped his open hand, about to slap me. He looked mortified and apologised. Regardless, I held my conviction that people can be changed, rescued, through sheer will and belief. But he was struggling, and I was helpless.

A light wind rattled the blind, tat-tat-tat. He started moaning in his sleep, wrestling the sheets.

'Darling,' I whispered, stroking his head. I was already exhausted from a long day.

He let out a yell and sat upright. I lit the lamp. His singlet was damp with sweat.

'Tom?'

He turned and took a moment before recognising me.

'Lie back down. It's all right now.'

He lay back with a glazed expression. I helped him out of the singlet.

'If it would just stay in my dreams, I might be able to handle it.'

'Did you take your sedatives? What does Roy say?'

'We keep going over the same old thing. I feel like a caged mouse scrambling on its wheel, going nowhere.'

'What about a change? How about we take a holiday? I'll find someone to manage the hospital.'

'The cage would come too.'

'But we'll be together, just the two of us. No cages.'

He sat up, rested his forearms on bent knees. 'I thought being back in practice would help. I was going okay for a while.'

'Do you want to talk about it?'

'No.'

'I wish you would. But I understand. The important thing is that you survived. You're alive and are dealing with it.'

'Am I?'

'You're alive and you're here with me, in our bed, in our own hospital. Tomorrow you'll go to work in your office and life will go on, just like it always does.'

'Have you seen that grotesque painting by Max Beckman called *Die Nacht?*' he said.

I nodded, remembering the cover of one of Tom's magazines.

'When you woke me, I was having this dream. It was like I was in that painting. In France, we lodged with a civilian in the hedgerows beyond No Man's Land. Her three kids were hungry, but we took her food anyway. I dreamt I was chasing that woman's kids; I don't know whether it was to catch them or save them. I shot them in the back, and they tumbled down, and I slipped on their blood.'

He paused and was about to say more when, outside, a lone night bird called.

'Damn this.' He threw off the sheets, went over to the window and slid it down with a scraping thud. 'Damn this pokey place. Damn this hospital!'

'Come back to bed. Let's talk some more.'

'I've talked and talked till the cows come home.'

'You can do this, Tom.'

'Don't say that. You've no idea…'

'If we're to get anywhere in this marriage, we have to start being frank with each other. I understand how you're trying to be strong by keeping the worst from me. Maybe we've both tried too hard.' I pointed to the mark on his neck. 'This. Let's start here.'

He sighed and pulled the sheets up. 'Go to sleep, Anna.' He put out the lamp.

I propped myself up on an elbow and shook him. 'Tell me. I'm serious. What's going on? Tell me!'

He turned and grabbed me hard by the shoulders. 'Is this what you want? Is this what you want from me?'

He started shaking me, not releasing his hold. I clawed at his face and tried to push him away. His hands went to my throat, and I tried to prise them apart. I screamed but no sound came, and I felt my heart's erratic thump. Just as I was about to pass out, I heard the hallway clock echo three times. Suddenly he released me.

This was the change. How quickly it happened.

I lay sobbing and after what seemed many minutes, he said quietly, 'Jesus. Sorry. I'm so very sorry. I didn't mean to hurt you.' He put his hand on me and I flinched. 'Shh, Anna. Shh. I don't know what came over me. I'm scum of the earth. Lame, cowardly, scum.'

He stroked my arm.

'Don't. Don't touch me.'

As we lay silently awake, I could hear his breathing, still erratic.

'It's getting worse again. I don't know what I'll do next.'

'I need to feel safe with you, Tom.'

'Did Andy ever hurt you?' The question took me by surprise. It was the first time he'd ever spoken his name, rather than 'your first husband'. It sounded odd, as if he and Andy were one.

'Not physically.'

'At least you had reason to grieve over him. I shouldn't have lived.'

'Don't you ever say that again.'

Tom slept on the sofa that night, in the sitting-room. I locked the bedroom door.

A few days later, he came back before lunch and started packing his suitcase.

'What's happening?' I asked.

'I'm checking myself into a sanatorium. In Sydney.' He came over to me. 'Permission to touch?' he asked.

I let him hug me, but the glow about him had dimmed, perhaps because I feared him a little, or because his wounds no longer seemed so benign.

'I love you so much.'

'We have things to talk about, Tom. Is running away really the answer?'

'I don't know what I'll end up doing if I stay. I can't share your bed while I'm like this. And the sofa is giving me neck ache.' A smile.

'Have you spoken to Roy Jamieson?'

'Yes. He recommended it. It's voluntary. Roy knows this fellow down there who has a centre treating shell shock with psychoanalysis, similar concepts to Freud. He describes it as a "kinder" treatment, whatever that means.'

Keeping my tone light, I said, 'Although one of Freud's theories is that the war problems come from men being cooped up together, with their repressed sexual emotions.'

Tom laughed softly. 'Maybe he has a point.'

'So, what about work?'

'They'll get a locum in. They've done it before.'

'Have you told them?'

'Not the truth, of course. I've told them my parents are ill.'

'You know I'm setting up something right here that could help you.'

'If I stay here, I'll make your life hell. Anyway, Cairns is too small, and I'm worried I'll do something unstable that loses me my job.'

'But what if you *can't* sort it out down there?'

'We'll worry about that if or when we come to it.'

Those were his last glib words before leaving.

30

'Put some muscle into it.' Leon pushed me away from the handle and gave it a robust turn. The engine chugged into life. 'Did you notice how my thumb was wrapped under the handle and over the fingers? And use your left hand. It's the best way to avoid kickback. Remember. Clutch, reverse brake – left to right.'

'Just keep practising,' Sybil yelled from the kerb. 'If I can do it, so can you.'

'You never start the car unless the handbrake is on and the shifter is in neutral,' Leon said. 'Key must be on. Retard the spark. Lower the throttle lever. You can pull the choke out – but be careful not to flood the engine. That's it.'

I went through numerous cranks of the lever until I was eventually able to start Tom's Model T Ford. It had been sitting out the front since his departure for Broughton Hall and Sybil had shamed me into learning how to drive, telling me I'd soon be the only horse and buggy driver left in the town.

I'd opened up my parlour for her during her cyclical fights with Leon, told her that I missed the old carefree Sybs, then watched her return to him. I soon realised that my role was not adviser, but listener, nodder, agreer. Today was obviously a time of détente, but

I was concerned she'd fallen into a pattern of prickly acceptance, that her spirit was being doused by him.

'Now, hop in and go through the gears I showed you. She sounds a bit out of whack – may need tuning. And you don't need to crank the engine if it's already primed – you can just use your key. You're lucky – this is a newer model than mine.'

And so, I learnt how to drive, how to use gears to slow down, braking without stalling, keeping my eye on the middle distance while negotiating a close turn, accelerating out of corners, becoming part of a machine. I explored tracks and roads I'd never realised existed. I went to Redlynch and trekked up to Crystal Cascades where I stripped down to my underwear and dived in. I slid like an eel down the rock waterfall and floated in the soft pool, staring up at the rainforest canopy, listening to whip bird echoes and frog stutter. I felt watched but could not see the watchers. Here was a white-stomached woman, a bag of bones, muscle and fat, sharing their water, those watchers, their same contentment, and I felt that judgement was being passed.

I saw Tom's hat forming in the sky, the squashed one he'd worn at the cane. He wrote sometimes. I imagined him in the gloom of a consultation room, the barred light illuminating his face, or lying in an institution's bare ward of forty beds and thick walls. Straightjackets, multiple medications, indifferent staff dealing with the screams, bangs and demands of his fellow inmates. Not even his family knew he was in Sydney.

The Huntly didn't allow the luxury of escape to visit him. It now financed a contract cleaner who assisted Gillian Herd, two cooks including a junior and Mary Sheehan, Lillian, Hazel, and occasional contract nurses (all decked out in their grey striped nurses' zephyr), and Jean, laundry mistress. There was also equipment I could now afford, selected from the catalogue.

As I floated and dipped and rolled, the water dissolved everything, the good and the bad.

◠ ◠ ◠

The members attending our board meetings had increased, including some from the town council, but retained the core of Corrin the accountant, Jamieson, Clarke and myself.

'We have the capacity to expand,' I said with a note of satisfaction. 'We now have the resources to take in war veterans.'

'What for?' said the board secretary – a retired police superintendent.

'It was a founding goal of my hospital. I discussed it with the medical practitioners, right at the start. As you may be aware, Doctor Jamieson has expertise in counselling and treating neurasthenia and other effects of the war.'

Roy Jamieson nodded.

Clarke spoke. 'Quite a few diggers have ended up here, in the north.'

'Can they pay?' Peter Corrin, the stereotypical accountant.

'If Matron Austen is prepared to provide the room and resources, I'm happy to attend to patients, pro bono at first,' Jamieson said. 'Once I've confirmed this practice with the Medical Practitioner's Board.'

'The war finished over four years ago. Is there any point?' Corrin again.

'Yes, fair comment. It's a waste of time. It's just bloody cowardice, anyway,' the policeman said.

'War-related neurasthenia is an enduring and insidious condition, which is now beginning to be recognised. Numerous worldwide medical publications have advocated various treatments.

I've made headway with *some* of my own experiments.' Roy was barely able to keep the contempt from his voice.

He knew more about Tom than he would let on. After Tom's disappearance to Broughton Hall, Roy had been supportive, but was more affected by it than he should be. I had, at first, assumed it was from a sense of professional failure. But doubts began to set in. I knew what I shouldn't know about him, and also realised how lonely it had made him. His relationship with Tom was close, closer than most professional relationships. It was as if there was a silent pact between them, another secret. Their sessions always seemed to take longer than the normal one-hour allotment and I had begun to wonder again about Tom and our many unconsummated nights.

'I currently provide general consultations with returned soldiers at the District Hospital clinic,' Roy continued. 'But I intend to get authority for my own practice and to assist the local hospitals, including the Huntly of course.' He said this casually, as if he were not already treating patients informally.

I looked pointedly at the council member. 'I'm sure the local authority would have no objection issuing a licence to the Huntly for use as a general private hospital?'

'Judging by your management to date, the exemplary health inspections, I'm sure there'd be no problem. Subject to all official requirements being met, of course,' he replied.

'And how do you think they'll mix with all your pregnancies and births, Matron?' the policeman said through his cigarette smoke.

I drew a line across my notepad with my pen, slowly and steadily. 'I am sure like any other hospital.'

Tom's absence grew from weeks to months. During that time, Dorrie would turn up with eggs, chokos or tomatoes from her garden and ply me with sympathy and tea, indulgently turning the pot three times. It was as if she guessed that something had happened between Tom and me.

On the day she received her licence back, she insisted on driving me to Ellis Beach. Each time she negotiated a cliff corner I closed my eyes, despite the spectacular view of a sparkling coastline. We swam and lay among the beach vines and almond trees. While she talked about her guests, more upmarket these days she said, I daydreamed about Brisbane, the decorator's shop where Andy listened so keenly, arms around me, while I told him I was pregnant. I imagined the scene again, with Tom. As I felt the sunshine, pink through closed eyes, letting the sound of the surf hush away my loneliness, I could hear his voice in the breaking waves.

When I arrived home from the beach, the envelope was waiting, redirected from the post office. I threw it in my dresser drawer, unopened. But hiding that third letter didn't dispel the prospect of policemen at my door whenever the knocker went. I'd once asked Tom, trying to appear disinterested, about case scenarios involving escapees from British justice, only to be 'assured' that mutual Commonwealth interest was well served when it came to the law.

As we started to receive patients with general illnesses, the new Huntly kept me in the urgent present. Our small hospital wasn't allowed to admit infectious disease cases, by regulation. The District was far better equipped, with special calico walls and steam pipes around diphtheria beds in the isolation hut.

I distracted myself from that drawer by reading widely – medical journals and university articles which I discussed with the board. As a result, our practices differed in useful ways from some of the less inventive, outdated ones at the District. No blood-letting leeches or wound-eating maggots, not even a fly which might carry typhoid, was permitted in our hospital.

Increasingly, we received intakes of prenatal women from the railway camps and mining towns; arrived from cramped cottages with no water or ice chests, and the only shelter of undernourished children. Some women were already stressed from overwork and illness, and infection was a nagging risk with every birth. City medical specialists wrote that European women (their smugly described 'white race'), did not belong in the alien landscape of the tropics. It was a view I occasionally was tempted to agree with, especially after delivering a child to an exhausted outback wife teetering on the brink of death. They would be sent home to their shacks, restored by our kitchen roasts only to return within the year in their original gaunt state.

My readiness to accept the poor caused tension in board meetings. 'This hospital is a commercial enterprise, not a pauper's home.' This was Peter Corrin, the overweight accountant.

He was referring to Janet Affleck, a young widow. She'd woken from a brain operation unable to speak, with her dominant arm paralysed, fingers as fixed and curled as a fallen leaf. It was a tumour, they said. Brain surgery in those days was still experimental. She was sent back home from the city and referred to me by the District. For a long time, she would jumble words and stare. I didn't charge her for those many months she stayed with us. With sheer determination she overcame her dysphasia and learnt to use her left hand in place of her now uncompliant right.

When I advised the board that Janet had returned to her occupation as a tailor, still the most deft in town, Corrin said, 'That's well and good. But you mustn't wallow in self-indulgent deeds of heroism. Charity does not keep a business running.'

We purged twin boys with salts who'd decided the plump tubular berries growing across the road from their bush home would make an excellent breakfast. One of the boys had eaten more than the other and we were unable to save his sight.

'But we saw an Aboriginal on walkabout eat them,' they said. 'They're not poisonous.' In those days, not too many people knew about the finger cherry, how it could make you go blind if you picked it at the wrong season.

Sister Hazel and Lillian were meticulous. Although Lillian was unregistered, she was a quick learner. It was during a quiet nightshift that she confided her struggle to leave behind a past of poverty and prostitution to become a maid, then a nurses' helper in a mental asylum.

'You make your own future,' I told her, sounding more confident than I felt.

⌒ ⌒ ⌒

When he returned from a medical course in brain disorders, Roy Jamieson left the District and started his own general practice. He also consulted at the Huntly in our new Returned Soldiers' Clinic, holding his auxiliary practice from a cane chair in a corner of the veranda, and well away from inquisitive ears in the wards.

His manner made everyone feel at ease and it was during this time that I felt I could ask him anything. So, one afternoon, when his sessions were over and I had plied him with some of Tom's whisky, I unravelled my doubts. I didn't try to soften the question; I just blurted it out.

His face grew pale and he cleared his throat and I immediately regretted asking. But he recovered quickly. 'I understand your concern,' he said thoughtfully, as if I had not deeply embarrassed him. 'It's natural for any wife to feel that way when their husband is having sexual difficulties. But I cannot divulge what passes between Tom and me in the clinic. You know that.'

'I already feel like an idiot for asking,' I said.

He lowered his voice to a whisper. 'You asked for my complete honesty, and I can tell you that your husband is not a lover of men. He loves you, above and beyond. Do you understand?' He wiped his glass with his thumb as if clearing a smudge, and stood to leave.

'Please forgive me, Roy. I'm sorry for implicating you like that.' I wished at that moment for the floor to engulf me.

But his expression softened, and he held out his hand for me to take. He pulled me gently from the chair. He drew me into a long and friendly hug. 'Shall we leave it at that?'

'I guess I just have to learn to trust,' I said. 'But I wouldn't blame him. You are perfect.'

'Not quite,' he replied with a half-smile.

I made jokes at first about his cure for neurasthenia being a cane chair and a veranda, but the more I read about the treatments, the more I understood his method. British psychiatrists such as W. H. R. Rivers, had developed treatments for war neuroses by methods other than the orthodox brutality of electric shocks, or subcutaneous injections of ether. They were exponents of the 'talking cure'. Jamieson would take groups of men together, some scarred and disfigured, and there would be low, serious discussions. I was allowed to sit in and listen to their traumas, small to major: a man's boot going through a corpse's ribcage and becoming stuck; being trapped in trenches for days with dead mates; becoming frozen with fear in front of the officers.

Roy said, 'It's the ones who've lived through the worst who never talk about it; the damaged ones who never claim their status as war hero. They're often the least likely to show their medals in the Anzac parade.'

Not only veterans attended, but also hardened men who'd suffered industrial accidents in the tin and wolfram mines, their lungs destroyed by poor ventilation and steaming heat. But, in spite of the satisfaction I gained from seeing broken men improve, the faceless man still accused me in nightmares, my heart protested with its erratic beat, and the third letter burned in the drawer like a hex.

31

Leon's shop sat between a tobacconist and a men's outfitter. At the front, *Pacific Pearls* was printed above a painting of a pink oyster containing an impossibly large white pearl. But it backed up its promise with shelves of beaded pearls, opals, pearl rings and earrings on velvet beds of black, green and navy under a single glass counter.

He surfaced from his cubicle at the back, wearing a jeweller's loupe around his neck.

'Your display is lovely. But I wouldn't have thought there were enough people living up here to afford this kind of jewellery,' I said.

'And good morning to you, Matron.'

'I'm not on duty, Leon.'

'So, what can I do for you?'

'Your displays are pretty impressive.'

'This is my trade, you know.'

'Oh, yes. Your family in Hawaii. Are they involved?'

'They have connections in the pearl trade. I get mine and the mother-of-pearl from Thursday Island luggers, amongst others. I can see a market here for making pearl buttons too, but that's down the track. As you can see, my shop offers variety. You can never go wrong with mantelpiece and travelling clocks.' He indicated the gold array above him on high shelves. 'I do most of my sales by mail order – through advertisements in the national papers.'

'I have to congratulate you,' I said sincerely.

'Would you like to buy something?'

'No, thank you.' I had my nurse's watch and badge, that was enough. I kept my mother's silver earrings locked away in a suitcase, thinking irrationally that one day I'd be able to return them.

'You know, Leon, despite everything, I think you make a very respectable capitalist.'

'What d'ya mean?'

'Your Bolshevik meetings? Sybil told me.' A slight exaggeration.

He blinked in irritation, missing my clumsy attempt at light-heartedness. 'Bolshevik? Sybil's got it screwed up. If you insist on putting me in some pigeonhole, I'm a socialist. I sympathise with the Soviets – some of them, not the White faction, and not all of the Red. I didn't condone the assassination of the emperor's family, in case that's what you're thinking.'

'But why care? The USSR is miles away from us here, miles away from your Pacific Pearls.'

'It's obviously escaped your notice, but there are enough jacked around people in this country who do care. And, apart from the fact that anyone who *reads* should be aware of the Soviets' shitty situation, my mother came from there, if you must know.'

'I thought you were from Hawaii?'

'Yep, Oahu. That's where I was born. My father was too. He met my mother when he was travelling and took her back with him. When I was older, me and my father spent more time in the mainland States selling our pearls than back home in the shop. While we were away my mother died suddenly. He's dead, too.' He delivered the last words like a counterpunch.

'I'm sorry, Leon.'

'I don't need your sympathy.'

'Do you still have your shop in Hawaii?'

'My uncle took over the business. For a song. I'm out of it over there.' He gave me a look as if to say: *Leave it.*

'Well, you look very much at home here.' Everything was pristine – including him, from an uncharacteristic white collar and sea-grey tie to closely shaved chin.

'Let's start again. What can I do for you today?' he said.

I placed my handbag emphatically on the counter. 'There *is* something I'd like to talk to you about.'

He started to shift jewellery around in the shelf. 'I don't have time for any chit-chat.'

'I'm not here to talk about herbal remedies, Leon. I'll get straight to the point. Sybil. She's mixed up. It looks to me like you're just toying with her.'

His dark tan coloured. 'Anna.' He wiped away invisible dust from the counter, accidentally knocking my bag in his irritation. '*We* are none of your business.'

'Sybil's my best friend. So, what's going on?'

'Sybil and I have an arrangement. It works. Bugger off.'

'Excuse me?'

'I said, *bugger off.*' He mimicked an Australian accent.

'Look, I got you two together. I'm responsible.'

'You had nothing to do with it. And you keep sticking your nose into things that aren't your business.'

'Sybs deserves happiness.'

'Oh, don't you think she's happy?'

A customer hovered on the threshold, looking at us. 'Come in!' Leon said with the broadest smile. 'What can I do for you, sir?' He showed him a range of jewels, and the man peered at the nacre and fire of opal through a magnifying loupe.

While I waited, leaning on the wall, something was said, or exclaimed, about 'filthy felons', and I was jolted to another place. Pain, shock, noise, gore, the faceless man. The world became weirdly faded as I stood there swaying, with a rush of chill and sweat. I concentrated on looking at my shoes, holding my breath, waiting for the panic to settle.

Finally, the man put a down payment on 'an even better replacement', a necklace for his wife, and left.

'Are you still here?' Leon asked, as if I had not been just ten feet away for the last few minutes. 'You look peaky. I think you should go home.'

I took up my bag but remained, gathering myself.

'I'll take you home,' he said.

'No.'

He shrugged as if to suggest the common sense of his advice and the stupidity of my failure to take it.

I wiped my face. 'We haven't finished our conversation.'

He shook his head. 'Whatever it is you want me to say about Sybil, you're not going to hear it.'

'You're a hard man, Leon.'

'Only to those who cross me. Look, I know Tom's away with his parents an' all, but if you're looking for something to fill your life, you're not going to find it interfering with mine. You had your chance.'

I ignored his taunt. 'Look, you need to hear this. You know what Sybs wants. You're making her miserable, dangling her on a string, neither telling her to stay or go.' As I said this, I realised that I'd once been guilty of doing the same thing to Tom.

'Sybil's a big girl. Like I said...'

'Bugger *you*, Leon!'

'Lookie here, Matron. Why don't you go and look after your own stuff. How about your daughter? Seems you've forgotten about her already.'

He had hit a nerve and for a moment I was speechless. 'Well, you don't give a *shit* about anyone except yourself.'

He may have been shocked; I was too unsettled to notice. I had no other option than to walk out while I still had some dignity left. But he'd made me realise there was something long overdue that I had to do.

◠ ◠ ◠

The wedding-cake confidence of Cumbooquepa made a promise to all students within its walls. The confetti-covered red bricks had charmed Evie. Here, she was no longer the daughter of awkward difference.

She was so engrossed in talking to her friends in crisp blazers and glossy shoes that she almost walked past me at the gate.

'Mum!' she cried, and thudded into my arms.

It was meant to be a surprise. I'd told Matilda of course, and she'd graciously kept it to herself while I negotiated the trip down to Brisbane by steamer and train. She insisted I stay in one of her rooms, not a hotel. Displayed around her large house were photographs of the Sinclair family, including a studio portrait of Evie sitting prominently on the white mantelpiece, as if in warning.

Matilda was superb in masking her resentment at my intrusion. She was a gracious host – waved happily in her mothball scented cardigan as Evie and I left in her car for a day at McWhirters department store in the Fortitude Valley; admired our purchases of girls' dresses and hankies initialled in 'E', for Evie, and 'M', for herself.

Evie absorbed the city, wanting to understand everything about it, the way it worked, the people who worked it. She showed off her urbane mastery of the public transport system – a ferry trip up the river, now trimmed compactly with motley roofs of red tiles and red-painted tin, and airy tram trips to the end of the line and back. I met her best friend from school, a close neighbour and merchant's daughter. That was the only day Evie did not give her free time to me.

If it hadn't been for her, I doubt I could have stayed those two weeks in the city. There were too many memories. The house Andy and I used to live in, and the streets where I'd protested. The building that was once to be my hospital was now refurbished as a residence much grander than the Huntly. All this helped me take stock.

I dropped my card at the brown-and-cream brick chambers of Tom's uncle, Mr Maximillian Augstein, with a note to say I'd call during the week, if convenient.

Max was a taller, bearded version of Tom's father. He greeted me warmly, apologising for his inability to attend our wedding. At his club, where he signed me in as a special guest, we sat on leather chairs. He asked me questions, but it was clear from his distracted eyes, his nodding at old chums, that he was not really curious. I told him Tom was in Sydney on a case (in keeping with Tom's version to his parents) and when he said, 'Oh? *That's* interesting', I created a flustered story stitched together with adjectives like 'big' and 'complicated'. He didn't seem convinced.

'I'm glad he's back in practice. I had to retrain when I arrived in this country. Such a hard-earned qualification should never be squandered.'

It was Uncle Franz, Max and Karl's younger brother back in Austria, I wanted to find out about. I had to approach it obliquely. 'Has Tom told you much about my hospital?'

'Not much, but my brother Karl has told me you have a successful lying-in hospital.'

'That's kind of him to say so. I've now expanded. I cater for returned soldiers as well. I'm particularly interested in diseases of the mind, which many of our patients suffer as a result of the war.'

'I've defended a few returned soldiers who've taken to a life of crime. Perhaps they had a disease of the mind also?' He was mocking me.

'But seriously, it may be related. I believe these health problems are not only a result of war. Some may be inherited or exacerbated by environment and upbringing. No one really has the answers yet.'

'Perhaps. But tell me, have you seen Frank and Ilsa recently?'

I avoided his obvious attempt to steer me away from the topic. 'Oh, yes. In fact, Ilsa is concerned about your brother, Franz.'

On the passage down to Brisbane when the steamer docked at Yepoon, I enjoyed the novelty of brown dry country through the train's open windows. I met my parents-in-law at Rockhampton as arranged, and avoided cross-examination about Tom, who'd already decided his mother wouldn't handle the truth. *You will give me a granddaughter, yes?* These had been Ilsa's parting words to me. My own daughter simply did not count.

'Ilsa says they haven't heard from him. As I understand it, the institution Uncle Franz was held in was demolished and the patients taken elsewhere. He wasn't doing well when she last heard. She says communications have deteriorated since the war.'

'I have heard about him lately, and I've told Karl what I know. He's obviously keeping it from Ilsa. I'm afraid she can be rather a gossip,' Max said.

'I know it's none of my business, so my interest is purely professional. Can you tell me more about his illness? Do you know how this has affected him?'

He looked uncomfortable, but to give him his due, he told me what I wanted to know.

⌒⌒⌒

I walked past the closed theatre and its posters advertising a 'jazz club dance' with bold drawings of colourful flappers in red stockings and men in black tails, proof of a secret dynamic that had reached this complacent city. Motorcycles chugged past and cars flew along, blowing horns at anything that got in their way, impatient with blinkered carthorses sharing the street. I knew I could never live here again. I belonged to an in-between place where opera societies practised next to miners' pubs, where ladies shopped a block away from red-lit shacks, where boundaries jostled in full view, as if the dusty road was a narrow ocean.

I took Evie down the hill to the river, ostensibly to admire the cluster of yachts moored there. 'You've asked about Leon at least twice, but haven't mentioned Tom,' I said.

'Mum. He's my stepfather and I love him. But he's all yours.'

'And Leon is *yours*?'

'Don't be silly! He was just more fun. That's all.'

Past tense. The jazz-sharp city already had her in its grip, as did her aunt. Matilda was watchful and according to Evie, 'didn't scold much'. She'd suggested Evie call her 'Mater'. She settled for 'Aunt'. I wondered if the two personalities would eventually clash.

Nevertheless, I had to ask: 'How would you like to come back with me to Cairns?'

'What about school? Up there, I mean. They won't have me!'

'I'm sure everything has been forgotten.'

'But you'll just waste your money looking after me.'

'Evie, I don't know where you got that idea from, but I'll support you no matter where you live, and it is not a *waste* of money, here or in Cairns. Your school fees come out of your trust fund, if you understand that. You're my daughter, always.'

'But I hate it up there. I really do miss you, Mum, but I don't want to go back.'

'Goodness, I wasn't expecting you to be so adamant. This is the reason I came down here. I was hoping you'd want to come home with me. Your room is waiting.'

'Why don't you move down to Brisbane instead?'

'I miss you every single day, but you know I'm committed to the hospital. And Tom has his practice now. But if you come back with me, we won't have to miss each other.'

'Mum, I think we both have to broaden our horizons.' This piece of glib wisdom was probably a phrase picked up from school. A place from where she could be proud that her mother was champion of a private hospital and where the memory of her gallant father would remain unchanging. It gave her expectations, 'like Dickens' ambitious Pip', Tom would say.

'I could make you come home if I chose to, Evie. But you know what?' I drew her close and kissed the top of her head. 'Regardless of where you live, you'll always be my daughter.'

I dug around in my bag and took out a small envelope.

'Earrings!' she said with delight when she opened it.

'Yes. Silver acorns, see?'

'I've never seen a real acorn.'

'An oak tree grew in the garden of the house where I was born. It was very sturdy, just like its little acorns.' I helped her attach the earrings. 'These were my mother's.'

And so, I left Matilda with her smile and Evie with her horizons, praying that one day, they would focus northwards.

32

'Don't you *ever* get ahead of yourself,' my parents would say. Their warning should have been uppermost in my mind when I so confidently met the uncertain smile of Sarah Hartley, wife of the wealthy proprietor of Hartley's Shipping Co, as she arrived with oedema, hypertension, and a baby wanting to be born.

Doctor Clarke came immediately. We settled Sarah through three, four fingers dilation, the baby's head promising a show, still coaxing her at dawn, hair plastered to her forehead, until there was no other choice. Clarke sliced a transverse incision into her lower abdomen and drew up her uterus to the anterior. *Liquor amnii* gushed out as he inserted his hands into her womb, took hold of the baby's leg and delivered it. I clamped and divided the umbilical cord to separate the infant boy. Her heart rate settled as we propped her into a standard Fowler's position, padded her, and Lillian took the child away to weigh and sponge.

The grateful father, the bluff bow-tied man I had seen at Clarissa Clarke's party, came to my hospital and shook Doctor Clarke's hand heartily, giving him a cigar.

Two days later Sarah's face became drawn, her pulse thready and she became too weak to hold her crying son. We drew up her knees, arms above her head, to assist breathing. I did not see much of my own bed during those next few days as we witnessed Sarah helplessly vomit then become cyanosed. Peritonitis had taken hold. We gave her laudanum and swabbed her in bandages soaked with disinfectant.

Clarke decided the only solution was to open her up again, first thing in the morning. Lillian and I took turns to sit through the night with Sarah, holding her hand, soothing her through bouts of delirium. She'd toss her head, saying, 'No, no!' as if someone was about to strike her. She'd cry and call for water and her mother. Then she slumped into a kind of peacefulness. When Clarke arrived the next morning for theatre, I had to tell him, my heart trying not to break, that she'd died in the night.

When Stanley Hartley came with a grey face to collect his wife's body, he left the baby with us, saying he had to sort things out, find a nanny.

There were no wet nurses available, so we fed Baby Hartley a powdered milk formula. He was frail as he had been stressed in the womb, with his heart rate down and a good dose of foul meconium liquor aspirated from his nose and mouth after birth. He started to gain health, but then, too quickly, he developed meningitis. He, too, passed away, with a fever.

Death in hospital is something every medical practitioner is used to, but these were the first in my own practice. Nursing school seemed far away now: *It is the right of every child to be well born.*

I was still in shock when a man in a suit and hat came to the hospital and handed me a large brown envelope, stamped with a local solicitor's name. It was a writ against me brought by Stanley

Hartley, trustee and executor of his wife's estate, claiming damages for breach of contract, and, or alternatively, 'trespass on the case', causing the death of his wife and son.

'Bloody hell!' Sybil said when I told her. 'I've never heard of such a thing! Patients die all the time at the District.'

'But no one has ever sued Matron Chalmers. Maybe because she is such a stickler for her rules.'

'Rules, blow that. Everyone is just too scared of her.'

'We did all we could. I was assiduous with Sarah's dressings. But, to tell the truth, I was exhausted much of the time and it's possible I missed something. I just wish I could remember what.'

'Exhaustion? You and every bloody nurse who has ever lived! And what the hell can you do against infection once it's set in? Why is he picking on you, not Doctor Clarke? Is he insane?'

'For a start, the hospital's registered in my name, which means I'm responsible. And he's saying she died because of my treatment after the birth. The baby also. He claims I should pay him an inordinate amount of money. Exceeds the worth of everything I own. I don't know what to do, Sybs.'

'Won't you lose your licence for the hospital if he wins?'

'Very likely.'

'When is your husband coming back? Surely your need is greater than his parents'.'

'His issues are more important than this.'

'More important! For God's sake Anna, look at yourself. You're stick-thin with worry and you've started smoking. Talking of which, can I have another?'

Leon took out his tobacco pouch. 'What did you say the fellow's name is?' He rolled a cigarette. There was a kind of ceasefire between us now, with neither of us willing to be the first to call a complete truce.

'Stanley Hartley, of Hartley's Shipping Co.'

'He must think you have tons of money,' Sybil said. 'I mean, he's loaded, isn't he? What does he want with *your* money?'

'I think he wants to prove a point of some sort. I wonder if it's fired by guilt. You know, he just dumped Sarah with us that day, didn't bother visiting her until she had actually produced his son, then he was all: *Hey-ho, jolly-fellow-well-met.*'

'Can't you just find a way to pay and make him go away? You know·what'll happen if people start to hear about this?'

'The hospital is doing well, I have to admit. But I'd have to sack all my staff and sell the hospital to support his claim. I'm sure he has enough resources to pursue this until he bankrupts me,' I said.

Leon went off to his kitchen to make coffee. I noticed a new photo on his wall – Sybil, sitting against a tree gazing seaward with a quiet smile, wearing a man's shirt which had blown open and exposed her cleavage.

'How are his political meetings going?' I said under the clatter of the coffee grinder.

'According to Leon, he's left the Party. Reckons he agrees with the idea, but they were too hard line on working class centralism, something like that. Those meetings he had – he said those guys had some crazy suspicions about governments and petty officials. Said they were not up to it, all mouth and no brains. Don't ask me. I think it's got more to do with his bloody pearls than his principles. He adores that shop.'

'And you two?'

'It's strange, you know. Since I've graduated to Deputy Matron, he's started wanting to see me more. But I'm so busy I don't care if I only see him every so often.'

'You've been playing "hard to get" without realising it.'

She laughed. 'Can't be bothered with games now. Life's too short.'

As Leon came in with the tray of coffee, she said, 'But seriously, Anna, write to Tom. Tell him to come home.'

He arrived at the wharf two weeks after my letter.

When he stepped off the gang plank, I took his arms and squeezed them. 'You're real,' I said.

He kissed me softly, as if to demonstrate his love no longer carried a threat.

When we got home, I said, 'You're tanned. I didn't expect that.'

'I was outside a lot. Helped build their gardens – little mounds, bridges, streams. It was part of my therapy. They were mostly men like me. There's more of us than you could imagine.'

'Did they prescribe anything?' I asked.

'It was mainly meetings. We were free to discuss anything – our worst deeds and fears – without judgement. Doctor Jones – he runs the clinic – discouraged us from repressing painful memories, though we were also warned not to obsess over them. If we did, he taught us how to shift the focus elsewhere, to something simple and meaningful.'

'That can't have been easy.'

'Some of the men were in a very bad way. But it was a relief to be able to talk with them. They're not all down-and-outs, you know. Some have high-level jobs, but they keep their condition pretty quiet. I had some bad nights, and the doctor gave me something for that. It was voluntary, I didn't have to take it. And now I have something they don't have. The secret cure.'

'What's that?'

'You.' A crushing hug.

'So,' I asked cautiously, 'you're cured then?'

'I'll never be cured, Anna. I think you know that. But I'm beginning to manage myself better, now.'

He unpacked and took out a bundle wrapped in cloth. 'This is for you.'

It was a watercolour, amateurish but intriguing.

'What is it?' I asked.

'I've been painting. Writing poetry, listening to music, anything we felt like. At first, I thought Doctor Jones must be a charlatan, sending us out to play like kids. But Roy was right, he's a real pioneer. Everything he prescribed was meticulously planned. His garden has all sorts of interesting twists and turns which we helped create. I'd sit for hours by a fountain and contemplate the ferns. Sounds like a holiday – it's hard to explain. It was more like mountaineering for the mind.'

'That's different from the rugged methods used in other clinics.'

'None of us were certified, which helped. Although some were teetering on the edge, including me, by the time I got there.'

'Even so.' I held the painting against the wall. '*You* did this?' There was a white building with slatted verandas, floating in an opal sky. The picture reminded me of the French impressionists – an intermingling haze of pinks, blues, lemons and greens.

'Those things around the building – they're clouds. It originally wasn't meant to be like that. I was dabbing away and had put too much water onto the brush and the clouds started running down the paper.' He laughed. 'I won't be giving up my day job.'

'I think it's excellent.' I was thrilled by it.

'I was thinking of you when I did it. Of us. And every colour in the rainforest.'

'We'll get it framed. What shall we call it?'

'Hmm. How about "A Hospital in the Clouds"?'

It took only a few weeks for word of my 'negligence' to spread throughout the town. My patient numbers dwindled. The mothers' ward was now only one third full, mostly with regular patients for their second, third or fourth births.

Tom returned to practice at Foster and Austen shortly after he arrived. He continued to see Doctor Jamieson at my clinic as the last patient of the day. By agreement with Jamieson, I suggested to Tom that this be a private affair, not recorded on the hospital books.

'I'll pay like any other patient. The hospital needs the income,' he said.

'But you're only putting into our pockets what we take out.' I thought this would be obvious to him.

'I will do what is right, and importantly, be seen doing it,' he insisted.

He drafted and filed a legal response to Hartley's claim, arguing no connection could be made, either directly or indirectly, relating to my treatment of Mrs Hartley, or her baby, and their deaths. Neither was there a breach of contract, as the contract had been satisfied on successful delivery of the child, and that all treatments were by consent. The statement outlined how I'd followed all proper medical procedures. It counterclaimed that there was no relevant legal precedent which would support Hartley's claim; alternatively, that there was no known legal principle which supported a direct claim of negligence against my actions. Tom was unsure how the counterclaim would go, but told me there'd been some very old cases in England which Hartley's lawyer might rely on.

At the next board meeting, there were raised voices and threats:

On the figures, at this rate we can only keep in business for another few months. That was Peter Corrin, mumbling into the ledger before him on the table.

How in God's name did you let something like this happen! The motor shop proprietor, slamming down the financial report as if swatting a fly.

If you hadn't provided all those free services, you'd be in a much better position by now. You have to start planning a reduction in staff. Don't leave it too long. Corrin again, his face dark with condemnation.

Why is your husband being treated in-house by Doctor Jamieson? The ex-police superintendent with his interrogating stare.

I could barely draw breath between answers. I didn't respond to the question about Tom.

◠ ◠ ◠

'People will always kick a man when he's down', Tom said. He was losing clients too, a fact which Rupert Foster pressed on him.

Tom had now been swept into the current of rumours surrounding me. Somehow, his treatment at Broughton Hall became widely known. Jean whispered to me that the gaslight man had told her Mr Austen was a loony, and she'd given him a bawling out in return. When he'd told her she had a filthy Irish mouth, she pointed out that he was dirtier than a pig and should come to her laundry for a good scrubbing.

My sleep, when I was not on night duty, was so disturbed by Tom's restlessness that I'd creep out of the bedroom to bunk down in Evie's small bed.

I had to dismiss the contract staff and reduce the hours of a disgusted Hazel Gregory, a teary Lillian Wilson, an angry Mary Sheehan ('I'm not going back to that bloody cattle station!') and shoulder-shrugging Gillian Herd. My headaches returned as the workload increased and Jean, sweating and complaining, took on extra jobs, too.

During one night of insomnia, I drew out some books from the bookshelf. They'd become an incubator for cockroach eggs, except one pristine volume of Shakespeare's sonnets. It showed signs of recent leafing through. As I lined it up to put it back in the bookcase, a piece of paper fell out. Tom's handwriting was scrawled across it with stanzas of poetry.

One, I recognised:

No longer mourn for me when I am dead

Than you shall hear the surly sullen bell

Give warning to the world that I am fled

From this vile world with vilest worms to dwell...

And so on. Tom's version of the sonnet had obliterations and revisions, as if struggling to recite it. And there were blotched ink marks, as if water or tears had fallen on the words.

I realised as I curled in next to him that he'd come back too soon.

The next morning, I went to Roy Jamieson's consultation rooms at his general practice without appointment and startled his receptionist by insisting I see him immediately.

'It's about Tom,' I said, when we were alone.

'I'm happy to talk about your concerns, of course. There's a patient due, but I have fifteen minutes.'

'That should be enough.'

His expression as he waited for me to speak was warm. I was reluctant to disturb the serenity he projected, and I felt foolish.

'I don't think I'm over-reacting here, but I think Tom's in danger. I need your help.'

'Tell him to come and see me as soon as possible,' he said calmly.

'*I* need to speak to you. I need to know what is really going on with him. What he won't tell me. Here, look.' I handed him Tom's poems and he read them quickly.

'Anna, you know I can't talk about a patient's confidential medical condition with anyone else. On that point, I do recall you launching your own investigation into my filing cabinet over there.' It was a declaration of truth rather than accusation.

I blushed. 'I'm sorry. Tom is such a puzzle – I hate puzzles I can't solve. Anyway,' I said, trying to make light of it, 'you fooled me with your cryptic doctor's writing.'

He frowned. 'I decided to let you off with it a long time ago.'

'I'm worried about what could have driven him to think about suicide again. He's hurting. He's fragile.' I told Jamieson about the series of silences, the new set of nightmares, how at first I thought Tom was just depressed about the hospital, that the weight of public opinion against us seemed more than he could carry.

'I can consult with both of you together if Tom agrees.'

'He will never tell me what he tells you. Look, Roy, I'm falling apart here.'

He passed me a laundered hankie from a reticule on his desk.

'I think you have to respect the fact that I'm a medical professional, also. I'm not simply an overwrought wife demanding confidential information about my husband. We should be working as a team, you and I. Nobody, no specialists in their research hospitals, no writers of scholarly articles, know the cure for neurasthenia, do they? Maybe if *we* put our heads together, we might be able to really help Tom.'

He smiled. I have no idea why. He got up and walked over to the window, hands in his pockets and stood pensively for a while. After what seemed like an interminable amount of time he said, 'What is it? What do you want to know?'

'You know everything about him, I'm pretty sure of that.'

'Look, Anna… he's a disturbed man.'

'You know he attacked me?'

'Yes.'

'Now, he's turning on himself. Has he told you his uncle in Austria suicided? And *he* wasn't involved in fighting any war. Perhaps you're missing something?'

Jamieson closed his eyes tightly as if keeping out the sight of me. 'I can't justify what he did to you, Anna, but he loves you. He's confused, desperate even, but he *loves* you.'

'But that's not the point!'

'He was a brave soldier. You must never forget that. You can't imagine what he went through.'

'That's why I need to know. Please.'

'First, I need to know what your understanding is.'

'From your notes – that he got that mysterious scar on his neck because he was hit by a sniper. That for some reason a lot of his problems relate to that event. And he's told me about his little sister. I know that's been eating away at him.'

'I have to trust you on this, Anna, because Tom trusts me. So, given the circumstances, I can tell you something that should help.'

And so, Roy Jamieson informed me that Tom had previously tried to commit suicide at the Front. At the time it was a serious offence under military law, and Tom had never brought himself to confess.

'I would never have guessed it was Tom who pulled the trigger. I always assumed it was the enemy.'

'Strictly speaking, it was. Most trench suicides happened when they shot themselves with their Lee Enfields. Usually, they put the barrel under their chin, took off a boot and pushed the trigger with their foot. But some chose what Tom did. It was during an exchange of fire. He took off his helmet and stood up on the fire-step above the sandbags. It wasn't long before he copped an enemy bullet. It went clean through his neck, just missing his hypoglossal nerve. There's an exit wound under his hairline which you've probably never noticed.'

'I assumed it was part of his alopecia,' I said.

'Even though he narrowly missed injury to the nerve, which would mean constant drooling and inability to speak, he doesn't think himself fortunate at all. He said he was hoping for a straight shot to the brain. He was seen by another officer who dragged him away and sent him down the line. But he wasn't reported. There was suspicion, but because the bullet hadn't come from his own rifle, and maybe because he was an officer, he was quietly sent away. If he'd confessed, he would've been court-martialed and given the death penalty. The AIF did eventually reduce the penalty for attempted suicide to life imprisonment, but he still thinks he deserved a coward's death. Apart from the daily trauma of memory, he thinks he's let his men, everyone, down, that he's somehow not worthy, and hasn't forgiven himself.'

I'd distractedly folded the hankie into a tight square. I put it back on his desk. 'He once told me it was part of the shrapnel scatter, but it looked very different from the scars on his chest. I never believed him, and I wish he'd told me the truth. I would have understood.'

'Tom is a complex case. There are other issues, too. Deeper, older ones – his sister for example – which have been exacerbated by his war experience. He's made so much progress that I'm hopeful one day he'll be completely stable, nightmares aside. But you're right – we can't ignore what this note is trying to say. I'll contact him today to get him in.'

I imagined Tom sitting where I was now, Tom trusting Jamieson. It took courage for Tom to admit it to him. If only he'd been able to tell me, too. It wasn't only neurasthenia he was suffering from. It was stubborn self-hatred.

'And you, Anna,' Jamieson said in his doctor's voice, 'you must take care of yourself, too. Feel free to come back and see me anytime.'

33

Hazel was the first to leave. Within a few weeks of having her hours reduced she found a full-time position at the District, giving me a day's notice. I wished her the best and she thanked me unenthusiastically. Lillian disappeared soon after, before we'd had the chance to take an affidavit from her. She'd refused at first. Because Mrs Hartley died on her watch, Lillian was convinced she was the reason. There had been no calls for work references, and I worried she'd fallen back into her old profession.

I advertised for temporary replacements. Only untrained juniors applied.

⌒ ⌒ ⌒

He was at his desk, head in hands, mulling over my file. I sat beside his cabinet filled with dog-eared rolls of paper.

'Have you talked to Rupert about my matter?'

'Why do you ask?'

'Two heads…?'

'I'm handling this.' His voice was terse.

'You seem to be having trouble with it.'

'Trouble?'

'I'm not saying you can't handle my matter, Tom. Of course not. But…'

'I know exactly what you're saying, Anna. Thanks for your faith in me.' He shook his head, still focussed on the affidavit.

Maybe if I hadn't made that visit to Jamieson, I wouldn't now be seeing how fragile he really was. I'd not found the right time to bring up my discovery of his poems; there had always been an excuse. Tom would have a difficult matter on his hands or seemed at that moment to be vulnerable.

'It's just that you said you've never run a case like this before, have you? I mean, don't you need help with it? Aren't there any barristers you know who'd take it on? What about your uncle?'

'There's no such thing as a free lunch, Anna. We have to do this without counsel.'

'Even though Hartley has one.'

'You have me. Is that not enough?'

'Of course! It's just that…'

'Damn this, Anna!' He slammed his fist on the table and I jumped.

I heard an office door shut.

'That's Rupert,' Tom said. 'He has clients.' He reached over and squeezed my hand gently. 'I'm sorry,' he whispered. The sun caught his hair, cropped close at the sides, so that his head glinted gold.

I wanted to kiss him. 'Let's talk about this, Tom. Tonight.'

'I'll be working late.'

'Soon, then?'

He sighed then pushed himself back in his chair. 'This is our last chance to get your material in. I've organised expert witnesses to address Hartley's claims, and on that count, we are as ready as we could ever be. But your statement is not fully answering his allegations about the lack of proper care for mother and baby. This is important. The law says that surgeons have a duty of carefulness to their patients, and we have to show there's been no *mala praxis*. At least Sarah Hartley's post-mortem showed no evidence of inappropriate levels of medication. That's why they're taking this more indirect approach.'

'But I'm just a nurse, not a surgeon. I don't know what else I can say. I wrote everything down, *every* medicine, *every* treatment. But yes, there were times when the nurses might not have recorded them. Now Hazel has left and I've no idea where Lillian or my contract staff have gone. I can only state what I instructed my nurses to do and what Albert Clarke advised me to do. But now I'm thinking maybe Hartley is right. Maybe we did something wrong and I missed it. Maybe we weren't alert enough. That is possible. We were all so exhausted. Perhaps I should just throw my hands up in the air and give up.'

Tom shook his head. 'They're going to cross-examine you about your experience, your qualifications, about your past. They'll go digging. Thank Goodness you're squeaky clean. What's worse, is that Hartley's gone to the police to press murder charges against you. I was told this morning. If they run with it, expect a knock on our door soon.'

Words stuck in my throat.

'With luck they'll press for manslaughter only. But still…'

'I'd better go. I'll try and dig up more records.' I went to kiss his cheek but had to hold onto the chair as the sickness grew in my gut.

'You're as good as your evidence, Anna.' He sounded strangely quiet, as if only part of him was in the room.

That sleepless night in bed, when the door opened and let in a slit of light, I saw Tom's silhouette standing over me. He reached down on hands and knees under the bed. Too irritated with him to say anything, I pretended to sleep, hoping for him to make the first move. He hovered beside me for a few more seconds before leaving, I assumed to sleep on the sofa. During the calm of the next day, I would sit him down and suggest we go to Roy Jamieson together.

But Tom was gone in the morning. And he didn't come home that evening. After a night of worry and telling myself that he'd be back soon, I went to his office, assuming he'd slept there. Rupert Foster said he hadn't been in. He thought Tom might be ill and had taken the day off, he seemed off-kilter lately. Hadn't I noticed? The last he'd seen of Tom was yesterday, after my appointment there, when he told Foster he'd be working late. He noticed an empty bottle of whisky on Tom's desk in the morning, which must have been left after the cleaner finished up.

I rang everyone I knew and visited those who didn't have telephones. I went to the police station and registered him as missing. I rang Broughton Hall. I scrabbled through all his possessions, looking for clues. I searched under the bed and discovered his gun holster. The army revolver was missing.

A week later the police came to tell me that a naked body, or what was left of it after the crocodiles had started to feed, had been found. It was lodged in the roots of a mangrove and spotted by a crabber checking his pots.

Before shock sets in, you function at a basic level. In the cadaverous rot of the mortuary, I saw a butchered torso, with the head and most of the limbs and feet, missing. The mottled purplish-green of the flesh obscured any freckle or mark. Tom had such even-toned skin, there would have been little to identify him apart from his scars and the tattoo on an arm now missing. The vital evidence, the bullet, would probably now be in a crocodile's stomach. Quickly performed, the autopsy found nothing to indicate the cause of death other than by 'misadventure'. The police statement said that the person could have been taken in the early hours while walking along the shore. The initial position was that this person, identifiable only as a European male, had not deliberately caused his own death, nor was it at the hands of a third party, but this was subject to coronial enquiry.

Indignant about the 'awful accident', the town assumed it was Tom, and I had nothing to contradict them with. Someone hunted down a crocodile they saw near where the body was found and riddled it with shot, then posed beside the reptile with a stick forcing its mouth open. *Vanquished*, is what the newspaper headline said. Nature defeated. Of course, this attitude was widespread, you could see it in the new houses that edged closer to the eucalypts in the rainforest mountains, stripping the bark, shaving the trunks.

The police took statements from me, Rupert Foster, and everyone who'd had contact with Tom in the days before his disappearance. The officer took down my statement with sympathetic nods but my anxiety in the interview was not just about Tom. They still hadn't approached me about Hartley's allegations. They interviewed Jamieson, who claimed patient confidentiality – until such time as it could be ascertained the body was Tom's. Out of respect for Tom, I didn't mention the revolver. But that night when he'd stood by the bed, I was sure he'd pointed it at me, and that made no sense either.

I couldn't have a funeral because there was no proof it was him, and the coronial enquiry had not begun yet. But a letter of blame came from Ilsa Austen: 'What was he doing to go out so early? Why didn't you keep an eye on him?'

I put off writing to Evie for a while, glad that her aunt would not be interested in country newspapers. Flowers came, people came. Foster visited with condolences and offered to take on my case without fee. I admitted and discharged my dwindling swathe of patients, performed daily rituals – dressed, ate, tried to sleep. When Sybil hugged me with tears in her eyes, I told her not to be upset, even though I was dying inside. What she didn't hear was my weeping; The *Where are you, Tom?* replaying constantly in my mind. I was tired of holding myself together, mustering a stiff-upper-lip.

In war, poets write about animals slaughtered incidentally on the battlefield, where small things don't matter, the bird, the mole, the hedgehog, the worm – little consequences, like the accumulation of little things that should have been said. That burden of silence.

PART FOUR

1924

34

It was midnight on New Year's Eve, the new moon feeble, and I was standing at the numbered wooden cross.

'The birds have taken him away.'

I jumped with fright. Amid the distant bangs and shouts of revellers' parties I had not heard Jean arrive.

She lifted her lamp, highlighting the grave. 'My granny was taken by the birds too.'

'What d'you mean?'

'When I was a little girl, we were walkin' down to the village and two magpies chasin' each other crashed and fell in front of our eyes. My granny got such a fright she dropped down on the dirt. Just like that. The magpies got up and took her along with them, to heaven. People say I'm silly, but it's true, I saw her dust go up with them, clear as anythin'.'

'I reckon you're right, Jean. The magpies took Tom away from me.' I was slurring, my earlier consultation with his whisky was having its effect. 'You shouldn't feed the wildlife, you know.' I found myself telling her that I was a criminal, that the world should be told what I had done.

She looked at me quizzically.

'You been drinkin', Matron?'

'Maybe not enough,' I said. 'Y'know, they've stopped taking people into this graveyard. All five acres are full. I told them *if* it was Tom, he wouldn't mind being in any of the sections – Roman Catholic, Protestant or even the section for so-called Aliens. *Hell*, he wouldn't either!'

Jean crossed herself. 'Maybe they're all fightin' with each other in there.'

'Tom would hold his own.'

'We'll just have to stop being so good at our jobs, ma'am. Fillin' up this town with so many people, fillin' up the world, fillin' up *this* place.'

I found myself pointing at the grave. 'This Pagan section where they put him… I reckon he'd approve. Especially now.'

I swayed, almost rocking, as we stood meditatively for a while. An impulse came to lie on the grave and maybe talk to Tom, but I realised, almost soberly, that a *Wuthering Heights* scenario wouldn't help my pain, and would probably make Jean faint.

'Come, Matron,' she said, taking my hand.

'Yes. *Matron*. That's who I am. *Matron*.'

She led me back across the road to the hospital where I flopped into bed in my cap and uniform. I woke through the night, vomiting.

⌒⌒⌒

Rupert Foster casually clasped his hands on the desk. 'I suggest you make an offer to Hartley. I'm sorry, but that's my advice.'

'I don't understand.'

'We've done our research and examined all the evidence that's in.' He nodded in the direction of Tom's office, already occupied by a locum. 'And we're of the view that there's some chance Hartley might win, based on our shortfall in evidence and the contractual grounds.'

'But I have nothing to offer.'

'There's not much time left. Your trial is listed as one of the first in the year's court calendar. It's only a week away. If you don't sort this out now, your likelihood of having to pay an even higher amount if you lose, including the cost of Hartley's legal advisers, is high.'

'That's impossible…'

'If you don't like this advice, Anna, I suggest you get a second opinion.'

'That's out of the question. No one else would be as kind as you and not charge fees. Besides, who would take it on at such short notice?'

'You're right. But, as I've explained, you still have to pay for our outlays, the out-of-pocket expenses in mailing, serving documents, and so on.' He looked at me over the rim of his spectacles with the satisfied expression of someone who feels he has granted an enormous favour to the hapless and ignorant.

'What about Tom's interest in this practice. Is there anything I can access?'

'It's true that you're the beneficiary and trustee of Tom's estate. And he's built up some equity in Foster and Austen. Once his death is actually confirmed by the coroner, then of course his share can be sorted. But that won't happen until the inquest and his death certificate is issued. That could take a couple of years. It certainly won't be finalised in time for the trial.'

This was the formidable side of Foster, the unblinking stare from behind the wall of law.

'What if it wasn't Tom who was taken by that crocodile?'

'It's hard letting go, Anna. I understand. But you *do* have a hospital. The only way out is for you to get a loan or sell up. You don't have much time to decide.'

'I've already tried various banks. They told me lending money for my case would be like betting on a lottery. And I'll not sell my hospital, I'll not lose it.'

'I have to tell you also that I've been contacted by the local inspector of police. He's a friend and I've put them off taking a statement from you for now due to your current circumstances, but I understand they've talked to some of your other patients and also are checking staff.'

'Is this about Hartley's murder allegations?'

He nodded. 'If it comes to it, you have no prior criminal history,' he gave an exaggerated laugh, 'I *assume*… So that would alleviate any outcome. But let's concentrate on the civil claim for the moment. If you agree to settle, we could request that Hartley withdraw his police statement.'

I stumbled home. The bedroom was stuffy and hot from being closed up all day. I sat on the bed and pulled off my jacket, stockings, and shoes. Maybe Hartley was right in calling me to account. In exposing me. Maybe the letter-writer was right, too. I thought I could control my own fate. I thought I could escape. But I would always be trapped in myself. Just like Tom. I remembered him in the rainforest that morning. It was me who needed him now.

I went to the kitchen drawer, took out the third letter, and without opening the envelope, burnt it over the gas hob. Then I opened the oven door.

35

I didn't hear the knocking at first. It was drowned out by the temporary night nurse's footsteps drumming a tattoo across the floor above, but also by the noise of my thoughts.

Leon's face, torch-lit from below, peered in through my window and I got up to let him in.

'What were you doing on the floor in the dark? Checking out the cockroaches?'

'Sometimes you've got to get down to get up again.' I closed the oven door.

He looked at me curiously.

'I think better down there, with the locals.'

He laughed. 'How about some coffee?'

'I've only got tea.'

'You Colonials of the Empire. Okay.'

As I turned on the stove for the kettle, the rush of gas was sickly. 'Where's Sybil?'

'Don't know. I wanted to talk to you, alone.'

'Our discussions never end very well, Leon.' I hoisted the kettle onto the hob.

'You might like what I have to say.'

'You're marrying Sybil?'

'Don't go there. No, it's about Hartley.'

'What about him?'

'How do you think he got his money?'

'Shipping? Fishing? I don't really care.'

'I'm saying this to you in complete confidence. Can I have your word?'

'Of course.'

'You've kept a secret before. Sybil would have dumped me if she'd found out back then.' He was not talking about our night together. 'You're a good sort, Anna.'

'Good sort? You don't know me at all.'

'Well, if I don't that's not my fault. Anyway, what I'm saying is that I need you to keep what I'm gonna tell you completely to yourself, for now.'

'What *are* you saying, Leon?'

'Hartley was behind all of it. It was his business. It's how he got started. It's how I got started too, in a smaller way. He'd use his fishing boats to transport the stuff and he'd offload it in the wee hours onto buyer's vessels. I was only small fry, just a minion in his conglomerate. I only did it for a while, but I've stopped. I've heard he's still at it.'

'Why are you telling me this?'

'You could use that information.'

'And if I go to the police, to Customs? It would implicate you.'

'Yup. But now I've worked you out, I don't think you have the heart. Not after everything you've been through with Tom, and, well…'

'Us?' I could admit it now. Something about him made it seem easy.

He glanced away. 'I've given this a lot of thought. Use it. Use it to threaten him. He knows it could kill his business – including his legit one.'

'But if I do that, he'll work out my source and come for you. And I can't keep something like that from Sybs. I can't lose her trust again.'

'I think it's best if we keep her out of this – for her own protection. So just think. What would Tom tell you to do right now?'

'He'd tell me to do what is right.'

'I guess he would. But what is right is always an arguable point, damn hard to pin down. Look, I'm handing this to you on a plate. Take it.'

'It's not my style, Leon.'

'What is your *style*? Hmm? Your style hasn't worked very well for you, so far.'

A stab of pain.

'Christ, I'm sorry, Anna.' He looked at me as if he wanted to hug me. 'Jesus. Me and my goddamn mouth.'

I took a breath. 'I can't just front up to him and say, "Hello Mr Hartley. You are involved in the illegal opium trade. So, stop suing me".'

'Very funny.'

'And as my lawyer would point out, we need evidence.'

'I can get evidence. But it won't be easy. We were always very discreet. When's the trial?'

'In a few days. I've been told to settle. Even if I wanted to, I'm not sure I can afford to.'

'I'll lend you some cash. Sybil has been on to me about it.'

'No. It's far too much. I went to the bank for a loan but now I haven't got enough collateral for security. The hospital is very quiet these days. Would you believe that some patients travel to Townsville rather than come to the Huntly?'

'Even if you sell your hospital and pay him out, how are you going to support Evie?'

'I think about that all the time.' Not only Evie, but all my staff whose livelihoods depended on mine.

'Take my advice.' He emphasized each word as if I were hard of hearing.

⌒⌒⌒

When I arrived at Hartley Shipping Company's brick premises, I was told he was not in his office. But his car was parked outside, so I waited across the road under a fig tree covered in flying-fox droppings, and thought about the bag lady, who often sat in vigil outside my hospital waiting for her long-dead mother to appear from the graveyard. I'd tried to talk to her a couple of times, asked her in for a cup of tea, but she always politely declined and said that her mother would be joining her soon.

I sat for two and a half hours, feeling the familiar nausea, the rising adrenaline before a raid, before I recognised the dashing Homburg and rounded frame of Hartley emerge from the building.

I approached him as fast as I could, half-running. 'Mr Hartley.'

When I caught him, he was already at the door of his car, hunched like a pot-gutted question mark.

'Excuse me.'

He turned.

'Mr Hartley, will you give me a few minutes, please?'

He straightened; his bull neck fleshy as he towered stolidly before me. 'Matron Austen. I can't talk to you – lawyer's orders. But more to the point, I *won't* talk to you. Now, be off.'

'Mr Hartley, please.'

A well-dressed woman in shiny shoes walked past.

He raised his hat to her. 'Afternoon, Eunice.'

'Hello Stanley!' A breezy smile. 'See you in church this Sunday?'

'I'll go just to hear you play.'

As he turned to get into the car his elbow caught on my shoulder and knocked me backwards. No apology. He adjusted the levers, put the key in the ignition and started the engine. There was only one option left. I ran around to the passenger door and climbed in beside him.

'Are you mad?'

'I'm entirely sane, Mr Hartley. But I do wonder about you.'

'Get out of my car!'

'You must want to know what really happened.'

'Oh?' A thick eyebrow raised. He was expecting a confession. 'I'll give you one minute.' He ostentatiously raised his wrist to look at his watch and turned the ignition off.

'I'll be quick. First of all, I have to say how sorry I am for your tragic loss. I understand how you must feel. I've lost two husbands.' The words tumbled out.

'Get on with it.'

'Yes. Put simply, it was not my fault.' I did not feel as certain as I sounded, but this was my only chance.

'*That's* your position?'

'Will you please let me finish?'

He clenched the steering wheel with both hands. 'Just hurry. I have a meeting to get to.'

'Thank you.' I leaned over my handbag to catch his eye, but he looked away. 'I have to ask you: do you have any idea of the size of the geographical area and number of patients that my hospital and the Cairns District cater for?' It was a rhetorical question. 'The

District sends me theirs when they are overbooked. On top of my own load, there are times when I've had so many patients, I've had to bed them down on the veranda.'

He looked at his watch again.

'If you win, if the court decides to accept your point of view, decides your lawyer's arguments are better than mine, then you will ruin my hospital.'

A stiffening of the shoulders.

'You will be doing this town a great disservice.'

'I'll be doing it a great favour, judging by *your* standard of care,' he said coldly.

'We can't always win against nature. It's so extremely sad that your wife and son lost their battle.'

'Don't you mention them!' His eyes reddened, spittle at the corner of his mouth, as if he had just swallowed a teaspoon of bicarbonate of soda.

I felt my own eyes water, his reaction triggering mine. I pretended to cough. 'Mr Hartley, with respect, even if you pursue this to the end you can never bring them back.'

He cleared his throat loudly and swallowed, the tough trawlerman turned business entrepreneur.

'Please. You will ruin not only me, but my daughter as well.'

He turned to me with a hateful frown. 'You have a child?'

'Yes.' No sooner had I said this than I realised my gaff.

'Well, good for you,' he said with effective sarcasm. 'I don't.'

'Look, can't you see how this lawsuit will never make things better? For this town, for everyone. And I'm sure you don't need the money, the damages you claim.'

'Impertinent, aren't you. Are you done?' I'd seen the expression before, on the faces of police officers, and of crowds hurling abuse. To him, I was the typical hysteric.

'All I ask is that you consider what I've said. That you take a step back from the hurt and vengeance and look at this matter for what it is. That pursuing it is destructive for you – and many others.'

He turned on the ignition and reached for the throttle.

I stepped out of the car as it moved away so abruptly that my ankle buckled and sent me sprawling on the dirt road.

36

The next morning, in a sleep-deprived fug, I washed and changed into a skirt suit. The bird melodies and warming light on the forested mountains didn't bring me the usual joy. Light shimmered ominously at the periphery of my eyes, and I had to sit down to quell the commotion in my chest. I ate, but almost immediately brought up my breakfast. Eventually, after four cups of black tea, I drove to Foster and Austen with my hospital treatment records.

'Trial starts in an hour. It's not too late to try settling. You'd get something for the equity in your hospital. You may even be able to negotiate him down.' Rupert Foster was still adamant about what he thought was the only sane decision.

'I need to look Hartley in the eye, under oath, and tell him I did not kill his family.'

'Principles. They belong in textbooks, in philosophy, not in the world where real people live.' He flicked his Woodbine into the ashtray.

'He's already ruined my reputation, my hospital.'

'I wouldn't take it that far, Anna. By the way, I've been pressured into arranging that police interview. We're expected down the station at the end of the week. If the case is decided against you that'll be extra incentive for them to pursue this.'

'Is this what Tom would have done? Told me to settle?'

He looked steadily at me. 'If he'd seen the evidence I'm looking at, he'd have given you the same advice, though grudgingly, I'll admit.'

'I'd rather get skinned alive than back down now.' This time, I decided, I wouldn't run.

'As you know, Hartley's briefed a silk from Brisbane – something we can't afford to do. So, you're left with just me versus his lawyer and one of the best barristers in the state.'

We walked over to the new courthouse, an attractive structure with shaded columns, moulded ceilings and arched Corinthian casements. A number of my veteran patients had used their skilled labour to help build it. We sat to the left on a seat smelling of wood oil. The judge, who had not yet arrived, would preside a good few feet above and in front of us, on what could be best described as a carved wooden throne.

Foster looked at his watch. 'No sign of them,' he said, looking at the vacant bench to the right. 'Dickson, that's the circuit judge, won't tolerate lateness.'

'That's one up for us,' I said with a self-deprecatory smile.

He cleared his throat and took out a volume from his briefcase. 'We've subpoenaed the only staff we could track down, but your main witnesses can't be located. It's a pity you had to…'

'Yes, I know,' I interrupted, not wanting him to remind me yet again about Lillian and the contract nurses and how I'd allowed an unregistered nurse to look after a seriously ill patient.

'Five minutes to go.' He was checking his watch again.

The court orderly was outside calling our matter when two men, one in a suit, the other in barrister's robes, blustered in, followed imperiously by Hartley.

'All rise!' the orderly called from a door beyond the judge's chair.

Foster whipped to attention and Hartley and his lawyers slid quickly behind the table to the right. The barrister leant over towards Foster, but the judge entered. Everyone bowed, except for me, caught unawares, so I bowed as the rest straightened. The judge flicked his robes out and sat down. His coarse grey wig, slanted on his head like a badly-fitting toupee, foreshortened his hairline in a simian way. But his voice carried across the court in a refined bass tone.

I needed to sense the wards' smells and sounds, to hear the timber frame of the building creak among snores, whistles and groans, to turn patients, and give the restless ones water or a bedpan. I went to the empty delivery theatre and gripped the firm steel of the trolley, feeling warmth transfer from my hand. *You should be getting your rest, you'll need it.* This was Tom's imaginary voice in my head. But I was avoiding sleep; avoiding the man on the mountain who'd returned, screaming *murderer* at me.

I was kidding myself, thinking I could come here and get on, thinking that this new life would stand firm and eradicate the last; thinking that if I signed a paper, registered it with a seal, and secured myself to a person or to property, that they could not be as easily bowled over as houses during monsoon storms.

The day had not gone well. Hartley's barrister outlined his case in detail, not failing to emphasise the tender relationship between Hartley and his wife, how excited she had been about the birth of her first child, how the Hartleys had placed so much trust in my ability to provide natal services, and my professional representations that my hospital specialised in births. These were the terms of the unwritten contract they had entered into with me when they paid fees in advance, or so he alleged. Having trusted me, how could they possibly have predicted that my deleterious actions would lead to the death of a wife and her newborn son and destroy a family?

I found it hard to see how the judge could not be emotionally swayed by the death of a beautiful young wife and her baby. I barely listened to Foster's reply. After the first few sentences, his monotone seemed to bore even the judge. It was clear he had no enthusiasm for my matter, no faith in its prospects of success, that he was representing me wholly out of duty to his former partner.

'Settle,' was all he said at the end of the day.

If I did lose the case, there might be enough from the sale of the hospital building and payout of debts to return home. *Home?* Why did I still call it that? Evie knew nothing of the place. She never asked about her grandparents, hardly knew such a thing existed. Her longing was for her father. She'd accepted without question her aunt who hovered over her like a proud hawk, and used only her full name, 'Evelyn'. She seemed satisfied with the intense friendships she'd made in the city, and the fact of a lost stepfather, who now would become just one more person to miss. I suppose that was why Leon featured so strongly in her affections. She'd seen only his kindness, his 'happy adventures'. I couldn't risk taking her – my barefoot ten-year-old who'd hop with joy on the hot earth like a skittering dragonfly – away from this country she belonged to. Especially if I were to end up in an Edinburgh gaol.

The only person who knew what I'd done that night was Andy. My secret had died with him – or so I thought. Checking his khaki reflection in the mirror, polished boots still untouched by soil, he'd said, 'Don't be silly. You're being overdramatic.' A favourite saying of his. 'You were with a group. How can they pin it on just you?'

'Because I was the one who ground up and processed the chemicals – saltpetre, sulphur, charcoal – filled a jar with them and lit the damn thing! Thought I was a heroine, didn't I? Saving all womankind. At least my chemistry wasn't wasted.'

'Was it your idea?'

'The WSPU came to the decision together. Our goal was only to target property. Never lives.'

'I think you need to speak to a lawyer about this.'

'Can't. I wouldn't betray my colleagues and they wouldn't betray me.'

'Are you sure about that?'

That was long ago now, before the three letters. I'd lost contact with the group. Friendships and family necessarily abandoned.

37

On the second day of trial, a cryptic letter from Georgia Kennedy, an RN at the Townsville District Hospital, arrived in the morning mail. I might not remember her from Edinburgh, she said. She would be travelling up to Cairns soon, and 'it is imperative that you receive me,' she wrote.

I reread the letter a number of times, trying to place a 'Georgia' from Edinburgh. She didn't suggest that she was looking for employment, which puzzled me, as this would surely be the only reason for making the choppy boat trip north. I wondered if she was Andy's 'Georgia', and author of the biblically-inspired threatening letters. Dread sluiced in as I realised that if Georgia from Edinburgh could find me so easily, then so could others.

I was distracted by this as I sat in court listening to Hartley's witnesses. His experts – doctors carefully selected from down south – gave statements about the most current procedures applied in birth clinics. They made sure to criticise the evidence outlined in my defence, and disguised the fact that their methods were similar to mine simply by translating them into different terminology. I wondered how Clarke's and Jamieson's witness statements would stack up against these slickly confident southerners.

⌒ ⌒ ⌒

Later that night I peeled away my sheets and clammy nightgown. I was lying there, watching the familiar shadows of trees outside when I heard the door to my parlour open. It was a slow, creeping sound. A hollow step on the wooden floor. My first thought was that a patient had gone wandering in their confusion, so I grabbed my gown off the floor and went through.

Someone was sitting in my chair, an outline just visible in the dark. 'Hello?' I said tentatively.

The figure rose and I cried out as the man from the mountain materialised. Jean crashed into the parlour, armed with a washing paddle. She set upon the apparition until it wrenched the paddle from her.

We both stood transfixed by this doppelgänger. It took Jean a few minutes before she accepted that Tom's restless spirit had not returned to violate our peace. But something about his appearance had changed. It wasn't obvious at first, but the lines on his face were deeper.

We didn't embrace, more comfortable in the space between us. He'd wanted to be lost, he told me. At first, he drifted around. When he got as far as Melbourne he came to his senses and admitted himself as a voluntary boarder at Kew Asylum. He'd registered in his natural birth name, surprised at how easy it had been to disguise his identity and disappear.

'It was an instant decision. I was disgusted with myself, and for how I'd treated you. Had to get away. I was too mixed up to try to explain anything to anyone, not to you, not even Jamieson. I took my revolver and walked to the Barron River. After a while I just threw the gun in. I got pretty scruffy, didn't care – there's some freedom in not shaving or washing – and people *did* give me a wide berth on the boat down south. They must have wondered why a dero had such a thick wallet.' He smiled. 'I knew I'd be gone a long time. Wasn't even sure I'd ever return.' He said this matter-of-factly, without any hint of regret in his voice.

'Well, you've got some explaining to do. To the police. To the coroner. To your doctors. To Rupert. Talking of which…'

'I know I left you in the lurch, Anna. Completely irrational. It was all I could think about down there. That wasn't me back then.'

'I don't know what to believe anymore.'

The next hour seemed only minutes as he poured out his life, his covert attempt at suicide in the trenches, his sense of disgust with himself. 'It's taken a lot to get me to where I am now. I'll never do anything like that again. I swear I won't,' he said.

'I'm glad the sniper was such a terrible shot,' was all I said, moving onto the sofa beside him.

We sat for a long while holding each other, listening to the small sounds of the night. He seemed so calmly rational. Would this version of himself triumph over the one capable of violence? I wanted to trust him again. I wanted to take him as he was. No fixing, no mending, just being. Let nature take its course.

Later, with Tom drifting off on my shoulder and me wide awake, watching the window fill with cobalt blue, I said, 'Tom, I have something to tell you.'

He sat up drowsily.

'I'm a murderer.'

'What?'

'Before I left Edinburgh, before I came here…' I scratched an imperceptible itch under my sleeve. 'I… killed a man.'

His face drained.

'I was a medical student at the time…'

'A what?'

'I was a member of the suffragette league in Edinburgh.'

'Slow down for goodness' sake.'

And so, it all tumbled out.

He sat through my confession, his gaze averting to the wall where his painting hung.

'Do you want a glass of water, or something?' I said, not knowing what else to do.

He shook his head. I searched his eyes for a glimpse of recognition that we had found each other again, the whole of each other, the gaps between us, joined. If he could not accept this, or if the trial forced a criminal confession out of me, I was about to lose him, perhaps forever.

38

It was the third day of trial. Hartley's barrister gathered some papers and slammed their edges on the bar table as if to neaten them, while Foster repeatedly cleared his throat and looked at his watch. There was no sign of Hartley yet. His testimony and cross-examination were due to begin today.

Through the courtroom window I focussed on a garden bed where roses had been planted, thriving among the palms. An emblematic boast, British justice in the tropics. Later, it would be my witnesses' turn – Jamieson, Clarke, and Hazel. Hazel had filed a self-serving affidavit stating that all the treatments she'd provided were under my strict direction.

Lastly, I would take the stand, with all my life secrets. It was possible my name had shown up on some register of villains from my arrest in Brisbane at the rally. I anticipated my cross-examination: *Your lawyer says you have an exemplary background. Can you confirm this – for the record? What did you do in Scotland before arriving in Australia? Why did you leave your medical studies so suddenly? As it happens, we've received a wire from Edinburgh.*

The courtroom gleamed with polished wood, the lawyers sat poised with perfectly pressed suit and gown, the orderly glanced at me expectantly, and the spectre of Georgia loomed above me, brandishing her letters. I was hyper-vigilant with adrenaline. If I was exposed today, there was a good chance I would lose Evie. The mother of whom she was so proud would be yet another disappointment to carry. I was a stubborn fool, so blinded in protecting my hospital – my trophy for an 'exemplary' life – that I'd failed to protect my child, and her expectations, from shame.

Judge Dickson entered the courtroom, and after the compulsory bowing was over, he said, 'Yes?' to the barrister McManus.

'Good morning, Your Honour. Once again, McManus, D. Counsel for the applicant. I refer to the application before you of Mr Stanley Hartley filed on the second…'

'Where is your client and his solicitor, Mr McManus?'

'Ah… I was coming to that, Your Honour. Perhaps… if the court would indulge me a little… I…'

'Yes?' The judge was now peering over his spectacles at the silk.

'I would like to request an adjournment of this case. For a short period, if it pleases Your Honour.'

'I have a long list ahead this week, Mr McManus. What is the reason?'

He cleared his throat. 'As the court can see, neither my instructing solicitor nor his client has showed as yet. They…'

'Indeed, and how can you present to me without instructions? This is Mr Hartley's application, is it not? He's due to start his testimony today, is he not?'

'Yes, Your Honour but…'

'This court does not cater for those who do not have the manners to respect it, Mr McManus.'

Foster jumped up. 'Your Honour, I move to strike out the application.'

'You better introduce yourself today, Mr Foster – for the court record.'

'My name is Foster, Rupert, solicitor for the Respondent.'

'On what basis, Mr Foster?'

'Without instructions the counsel applicant has no application to pursue, Your Honour.'

'Don't be too hasty, Mr Foster,' the judge said. 'A fair hearing for all.'

'Yes, Your Honour.'

'We'll return in one hour.' Dickson stood, as did we, and left by his door.

'Bugger,' Foster said. 'I don't like this.'

'Isn't this good?' I asked.

'McManus – don't be fooled by his bumbling and stalling. He's a mate of the judge. Seems they're lodging at the same hotel. I heard they tied one on last night.'

'If Hartley doesn't appear, we should go ahead and strike out his application as you've suggested.'

'It was just a stab, really. I don't know if it will work. Depends. Wait here, I'll be back.'

He sauntered over to McManus who was beside the rose bushes, lighting a cigarette. They huddled together like two crows over their kill. As they talked, McManus squinted at me in a peculiar way.

Nausea bounded through my body and I started to shake. Then, a voice in my head told me not to forget the person I should be, the person I had run away to become. Despite his vitriol, Hartley had a point. I could in all honesty admit to him that I was negligent, if only to the extent that I did not supervise Lillian well enough, particularly the dispensing of medication during her watch. That was clear from the missing records. I'd congratulated myself for standing my ground this time, when in fact I was running away from the truth.

Hartley's solicitor arrived, puffing.

I stood mortified as the solicitor, McManus and Foster laughed together like intimate friends over the tragedy of my hospital.

It wasn't long before Foster came over to me. 'Something's going on with Hartley. They're asking for a day's adjournment on the basis of his health. Apparently, he's had an accident.'

⌒⌒ ⌒

Tom was there when I arrived home. I couldn't read his face. I didn't say anything about the trial, but simply stood by the door, waiting to see what he had to say.

He parted my hair to trace the zigzag scar with his finger. 'Just a pale shadow,' he said. 'I never noticed it before, and it's always been there to discover. From the beginning I sensed you were hiding something. But who would have thought?'

The next morning, as the sun brightened the bed, catching his perspiration, he said, 'How long have you been staring at me?'

'As long as you've been pretending to be asleep.'

'Waiting for me to *turn*?'

'Don't say that, not even as a joke. They do say that people never really change. Not their core, anyway.'

'It's not my core that's the problem.' He shifted to face me. 'I've been thinking… I'm going to sell my share in Foster and Austen. I'm sure Rupert'll be pleased to be rid of the *unreliable* component of the firm.'

'You sound relieved.'

'I will be, but only if you'll say you'll put up with me again, warts and all.'

'Maybe. But definitely on this one condition.'

'What's that?'

'That you give your Shakespeare quotes a rest.'

He studied my serious expression until we both burst into laughter.

'Seriously though, I can help out at your clinic if you like – you know, doing administrative work, talking to veterans' groups, and so forth.'

'Hmm. A man should never depend on his *wife's* income, should he?' I was testing him, our familiarity.

'Maybe we're more alike than you realise.' He kissed my nose. 'I don't want to be *beholden*, either.'

'But you shouldn't assume that after tomorrow I'll have a hospital.'

'I've thought this through, Anna. You aren't ultimately responsible for Sarah Hartley's death, or her baby's, are you? This sort of thing happens all the time. Too often, really. I think this is just another case of circumstance, of rotten luck. Like in Edinburgh. You are not a murderer. You are the best person I know.'

'I could have made another deadly mistake. Another death on my hands. It may be that I didn't supervise Lillian properly, but I don't want that poor woman to take the blame. I'm thinking of selling up, offering a settlement. But that's only out of self-interest – I don't want them digging into my background.'

'Or are you saving Evie from shame? I'll speak to Rupert…'

'No! You mustn't tell anyone. But you're right. It's not only for Evie. It's also for the women in WSPU. Once I'm exposed, then…'

He sighed. 'You can't save the world.'

'Well, I gave it a damn good try.'

He drew me to him. 'What am I to do with you?'

'Just accept me for what I am, as I do you. That's all.'

He kissed me on the forehead. 'When the time's right, my Anna, I'm going back to the law under my own steam, back to the bar. The gossip will find fresher and racier subjects soon enough, and the legal fraternity here is broad-minded enough to give me good briefs. I'll do occasional work down south as well. I'll look after you.'

'That's a very irritating thing to say. You know I don't want to be "looked after".'

'Someone has to,' he said.

△ ◠ △

As I got ready for court I changed into my suit, buttoned it over my blouse, buttoned myself tight as well. I took deep breaths against the day.

Foster was waiting for me outside the court building with McManus hovering a few paces behind him. His expression was unusually animated, and he beckoned me to hurry.

'I can't believe this,' Foster said. 'You hold all the cards.' He took me aside. 'For some strange reason, Hartley's offering to withdraw his application. He says this doesn't mean he doesn't still think you were at fault. But to avoid any backlash, he wants you to guarantee that you'll not try to sue him for defamation.' Foster shook his head. 'I'm completely baffled. Never seen this happen before. But, as they say, don't look a gift horse in the mouth.'

I was trembling. 'He's ruined the livelihood of all my staff, he sent my husband over the edge…'

'There's no room for indulging emotions in the law, Anna. This is great news. We've only got a few minutes before court goes in. The judge is already annoyed because of the delay.' He checked his watch.

I drew a deep breath. I'd judged the trawlerman too harshly. He'd listened to me, after all. 'All right… tell him this: I'm deeply sorry about the death of his wife and baby and I truly believe that no amount of my money will ever heal his grief. Importantly, I hope he realises now that me and my staff were not outrightly responsible for their deaths.'

'I suggest you remove the word "outrightly",' Foster said.

'Whatever you say. But tell him that if he withdraws his application and publishes a statement in the newspaper that his claims against my hospital were based on mistaken information, I won't sue him for defamation. That should be face-saving enough for him – you'll think of a way to put it. And I want him to pay your outlays. And I want him to withdraw his charges to the police.'

Foster smiled, despite himself. 'That may be asking too much. We don't know what's really behind all this. We can get him to withdraw his statement but, ultimately, it's up to the police whether or not they charge you. But we'll see.'

We were celebrating quietly in the parlour with sparkling ale when Leon arrived. His look of shock at seeing Tom was soon followed by a vigorous handshake and a continental kiss to each cheek. A reformed felon embracing a fallen lawyer, resurrected from the dead.

'How did your trial go?' Leon asked.

'My approach worked after all,' I said. I told him about my meeting with Hartley. How I thought this was why a man so set on revenge had come to a sudden change of heart.

Leon smiled and said, 'Oh, I see.'

'Today has been such a relief.'

'That's what I was hoping to hear. I'm glad it went well.' Then, looking at Tom then me, he said, 'Exceedingly well.'

'Thank God he withdrew his claim. And he's going to apologise in the newspaper,' I said.

Leon didn't look surprised. 'And you say it's because you spoke to him? What did he say, exactly?'

'Not everything has to be about threats and blackmail, Leon. I appealed to the decency in him. That's why he's prepared to apologise. The trouble is that you think the only way to get ahead is by doing things on the sly…'

'Hold on a minute. There's nothing sly about my business. It's perfectly legal.'

'I'll go get you one of these,' Tom said, lifting his glass to Leon.

'You and I both know how your shop was financed, Leon. But my point is that nasty tricks aren't needed to get what you want. I simply spoke to Hartley rationally, told him the facts, and he eventually saw sense.'

Leon let out a bellow of laughter.

'Everything all right in there?' Tom yelled.

'Leon is just laughing at the prospect of decency,' I said, rattled.

'Well, no. It's *you*, sitting there looking down your nose at me, your naïve delusion that Hartley responded to your appeal to his decency. The man hasn't got any.'

'Stop being a jerk,' I said. I liked that word. I'd learnt it from him.

'Actually, it was me who changed his mind.'

'How?'

'I saw him the other night. Scared the living daylights out of him.'

'I find it hard to believe that he would just listen to you like that,' I said.

'It's not so much what I said as what I showed him. I finally found a paper connection. Mr Lee, the shopkeeper who is such a stickler, his son had innocently receipted some deliveries… So, Hartley shows me his big trawlerman fists. But he came off second best. Did he front court with his bashed cheekbones?'

It was hard to take this in.

'You can't turn the world into a great big sugar ball, you know. Hartley had it all over you and I did what had to be done. That's the problem with you, you're always on your high horse. Too bloody proud to ask for help.' He had that look, the one he probably reserved for me, the one that said: *you're just another up-yourself middle class hypocrite.*

'You got it in one. Too bloody proud.' Tom was at the threshold with Leon's drink.

I threw my hands up in surrender. 'Okay, okay. I'm not the only one here guilty of that. But…'

'But what?' Leon asked.

'Since Hartley's still at it, you should report him. You're out of the picture now.'

'Is your evidence current?' Tom asked him.

'I've been told he's moving everything further offshore, out of jurisdiction here. I'm just lucky he's twitchy about what I have on him.'

'Look, Leon, – thank you. You took a big risk for me. I owe you. I still don't believe brutality is the way to solve things, but you've taught me something about my high horse.' I was smiling, but I meant it sincerely. I reached out my hand to shake his, but he just took my fingertips.

'Yup, it was a risk. He'll send his wharfies after me for sure. But I'll be ready. My old commie mates are always itching for a punch-up.'

'What if he tries something worse?'

'I ain't stupid. Getting rid of me won't get rid of the proof. He knows that. I've given it to someone I can trust, just in case.'

'Who?'

'I've told Sybil everything. And the strange thing is, she still wants me.'

'But I thought you weren't going to bring her into this?'

'She's happy to be in the know. She's tougher than I thought.'

39

The Huntly became busy in a matter of weeks. The area was inundated with southerners arriving to work in the various expanding industries, particularly agriculture, where sugar farms at the foot of the Great Dividing Range attracted the government's close attention. Entomologists erected research laboratories and insectariums in their war against the cane beetle. Scientifically created sugar plants flourished, and the estate where Tom had first lived in the cane barracks was producing bumper crops. Even more workers arrived to boost the townships around the new mills, bringing their pregnant wives. New rail lines, the expansion of the port, wharves and jetties, land reclaimed with dredge spoil – all this fed the post-war fecundity, the need for sweetness.

With some resistance from the board, we allowed the mostly homeless ex-servicemen to do odd jobs in payment of fees. There was always plenty for them to do. The hospital's sun-flaked exterior needed constant scraping and painting, there were shelves to fix and doors to plumb. Not being a greedy man, and making enough from his private practice, Jamieson was generous with his time. He used his cases as research, and his findings had started to be taken seriously in the medical world. I believe he truly enjoyed his work, helping lost men to find themselves, or as much of themselves as would let them function in society once again.

The soldiers didn't always return to clinic. I hoped it was due to our success rate, but in some cases, it was because they disappeared into the bush or took themselves to wherever they could engineer a discreet and dignified release. We suspected that the 'Crocodile Man' – as the torso in the mangroves was now known – may have been one of them. He may even have been Harry Barnes, the miner who almost throttled Roy Jamieson during a session. There was no warning. Barnes simply rose from the wicker chair and threw himself at the doctor. It took three of us to pull them apart. Barnes ran down the stairs, knocking a patient against the wall, as he left for good.

To my surprise, Sybil had grown placid. I guessed it must be about her promotion to Deputy Matron, or more likely, about Leon. For Sybs, everything seemed to be about him. Evie hadn't forgotten him either. In one of her regular letters came a declaration that a Box Brownie camera for her birthday would be very useful, and Leon would be the best ever person to teach her how to use it, when she next 'visited' Cairns. From the graceful heights of her bedroom overlooking the Brisbane River, my girl had lost sight of frugality.

When I tried to divert Sybil's focus away from Leon to her own achievements – the nurses' union, her promotion – she insisted these things had not brought her complete happiness. She hinted that relative bliss could not be achieved until she'd secured the compulsory husband and produced at least two children. Just like most other young women around. But that was until our trip to the beach at Fitzroy Island during our girls' day out, a celebration of sorts, for life being better than it might so easily have been.

After a dip in the diamond water, we planted our striped umbrella on the beach – a composition of tiny skeletal pieces of coral, shaped into white Ls, and stars, not yet sand. The sun was high and from behind our sunglasses everything glared.

'You're wasting your time, Sybs,' I said, as she sucked on a black cigarette. 'If it's marriage you want from Leon you'll be waiting forever. He's already made that clear.'

'Yeah. His parents never married, you know. Well, I think there was some sort of traditional ceremony. But he reckons they were madly in love. Sometimes I wonder if I'm the marrying kind, after all. I've realised it's not so much marriage I want, as what comes with it.'

'And what's that?'

'Apart from the kisses? I want someone who's there for me. All the time. But the more I think about it, I realise that a piece of paper from the Registry Office won't guarantee any of that.'

'Nothing is ever guaranteed. Marriage fits nicely into our ideals – husband, champion of the family, bringer of income; wife, bringer of slippers and pipe. But anyone'd be crazy to think that it's a guaranteed shelter from the world.'

'True. But I have this thing – I just want to be with Leon every day. In all his big, brawny badness.' She pulled off her wide straw hat. 'Look at me,' she said, gesturing with her smouldering Sobranie, 'look at what he sees. Flat chest, hair totally out of control, rough as guts. I'm as attractive as a bandicoot on heat.'

'Don't be ridiculous,' I said. 'What happened to that sassy girl, the one who didn't give a…?'

'… a rat's arse? That girl was never there, love. It's just my smokescreen. I'm as silly and weak as the next sheila. I've absolutely no idea what he sees in me.'

'He's proud of you – I can tell by those photos he took of you. He obviously thinks you're something. And you are. Anyway, real love, real affection doesn't depend on how smooth your hair is, the size of your breasts, or how clipped your diction is.'

'You just described yourself, y'know – you've got all that. I should be jealous.'

'Ugh, well there you go. Just look at me as proof – I'm hopeless at holding on to husbands, and I'm living in exile.' I immediately regretted the last slip, but she didn't notice. 'I think the question you should be asking yourself now, is: Is he good enough for *me*?'

'I think so.' She flicked the cigarette ash onto the coral.

'You just think so?'

'It's not just *that* about Leon. He's told me a few things, things he's kept from me all this time. I've been a fool with him. He must've thought I came down in the last shower.'

'What things?'

'I think you have a clue. He's said as much.'

'His *herbal remedies*, you mean?' I said, fanning the heat from my face.

'That's one of them.'

'Yes. I recognised it that day when I caught you… when you were posing for him. I didn't tell you because you were the happiest I'd seen in a long time.'

'Yes – he told me about the bollocking you gave him. He's stopped now, you know. It's like he's gone all confessional. The things he's told me…'

'Yes?'

'Well, there are things I know, that you don't know I know.' She looked at me, meaningfully, I thought.

'I'm not going to ask you to interpret that.' I gave an embarrassed laugh. 'I presume these things that Leon has told you are about others?'

'Yes. Others pretty close to me.' She stubbed out the half-smoked cigarette in a lacquered snuff box, taking her time, then snapped the lid closed. 'So now I have my secrets too.'

'Are we even now? Secret wise?' I said.

'Maybe. Maybe not.' She smiled mysteriously.

'What's done is done, Sybs. You'll always mean more to me than I can say. I'm sorry, I…'

'Don't say it. Don't say anything more. Some secrets between friends should stay in their box.' Contemplating the horizon, she said, 'I've never told you about my mother, have I? She was always on the grog. That's the real reason I went out nursing. To escape her. My brothers left pretty early, too, leaving my little sister to look after her.'

'When did you last see her?'

'Never been back. I haven't told Leon about her, yet.'

'Oh, Sybs. I think I know just how you feel.'

She stretched out on the towel. 'You know that to-do with your trawling guy – what's his name – Heartless somebody? Head like a drover's dog.'

'Hartley,' I said.

'Leon told me what he did. He said he went over to your place to tell you about it but, in his words,' – she lowered her voice, mimicking an American accent: "It didn't go that well, gal. Got the superior treatment, as usual." That Heartless guy, he's a bad 'un.'

'Leon admitted his connection with him just before my court case. He made me promise not to tell you. You've no idea how that ate me up. I was relieved when he said you knew.'

'He was involved in a lot more than that. Heartless, I mean, not Leon. One night of your trial, Leon went over to see him. Told him a few things, like: "If you don't withdraw your case, I'm going to expose you". The guy didn't believe him at first because that would mean Leon would be exposed, too. Leon said he had proof.

Heartless gets bêche-de-mer, you know – those disgusting sea slugs – from the Thursday Island luggers, and sells them to the Chinese boats. Easy to hide your contraband in that slimy lot. No paper exchanged hands between them when Leon was his go-between, but he tracked down old crew from the fishing boat. Leon found out that one Chinaman had written a note in English receipting opium from Heartless's company. Leon got hold of it, somehow. Was fuzzy on the details there – I doubt the Chinaman would have given it to him voluntarily – but anyway… Leon shows it to Heartless. Heartless says: "No one will believe you. Not against *my* word. I mean something in this town." Leon says: "Maybe. But you also have far more to lose than I do. I'm prepared to take that risk." And the guy buckled.'

'Yes – he and his broken face. I wish it hadn't come to that. Despite everything, I feel sorry for what happened to him. But why would Leon take a gamble like that for me?'

'He admires you, believe it or not. But mostly he was worried for Evie. He adores her, you know. Considers himself a kind of Hawaiian hānai father.'

'Tom says it may not be over. Says he knows Hartley's type. Says he'll find a way to get me somehow. He may be right. You should have seen the hate puffing up in him, Sybs.'

'If ever that happens, just call Leon.'

'You know, Leon laughed at me for sanctimoniously taking all the credit for Hartley withdrawing his claim. It makes me cringe to think about it now. He has a way of cutting to the truth. He's a one-off, your man. I have a lot to thank him for.' I could admit to myself now that he'd captured a small part of my heart.

I lay back in the shade of the parasol and propped a towel under my head, wriggling into the softer coral, letting it form around my body. Distant white sails glided past the blue hills of the mainland, above unseen sea forests.

40

It was midday. We were standing on the verge beside the grave of the Crocodile Man, for whom I still felt both sadness and a superstitious gratitude for not being Tom.

Here for the holidays, Evie laid a frangipani on its headstone. She put other flowers from her clutch onto the graves of little Maude, and Bill, who'd failed to survive his polio. Their suffering was now reduced to uniform stone inscriptions: *remembered, missed, loved*. This spot close to home was where I found a kind of peace and a resolve to make the most of my days. I rarely saw other visitors in the cemetery. Most gravestones, even recent ones, were tufted in weeds, making you wonder at how quickly they'd been forgotten. But probably it was just too painful for the living to be reminded of finality. No comfort of loitering ghosts or promises of heavenly reunion, just red loam and dandelions.

A woman shaded by a flimsy umbrella walked towards us wearing a broad-brimmed straw boater and an old-fashioned blouse with pinch-waisted skirt. I nodded at her, expecting her to pass by. But she stopped beside me.

'Good day,' I said.

'Hannah? Hannah Huntly? Or should I say Mrs Sinclair?' she said.

A chill swept through me.

'They told me you were over the road.' She was holding out her hand. 'Oh! This must be Evie!' She beamed down at my daughter.

'Hello, I'm Evelyn,' Evie replied, getting up from her knees and politely taking the woman's hand that had been meant for me.

'Oh, she looks so like Andrew!'

'Do I know you?'

'I'm Georgia Kennedy. I wrote to you.'

'Evelyn, go back to the hospital, please.'

Evie was off, running across the dirt road, past our canvas-hooded Ford, towards the Huntly. A barefooted boy in a knocked-together billycart, complete with goat and a cargo of cans, careered past her.

'Watch out!' I shouted after her. 'And lookout for cars!' There still weren't that many in Cairns, but enough of them had truculent drivers and sluggish brakes.

'You ignored my letter,' the woman exclaimed in her cultivated Edinburgh accent.

Something tight inside me grew tighter. 'Letter? Or letters?'

'Don't you remember me at all?'

'Sorry, I have things to do right now,' I said, turning to leave.

She grabbed my arm. 'I remember *you*. At the WSPU meetings.'

I looked more closely at her face. It was pink, the colour of someone new to the tropics. I tried to keep my voice calm. 'From Edinburgh you say?'

'Yes, eleven years is a long time, I agree. I became a V.A.D and was stationed at the First British Red Cross Hospital in Montazah. That's what got me started in nursing. That's where I met your husband, Andrew.'

'Yes. He told me they sent his battalion to Egypt for training.'

'Andy's camp was about to go to Gallipoli. He'd been given permission to visit a mate who was convalescing in our hospital.'

'Is that what this is about? Andy?'

'He told me I sounded like you. That's how we met.'

I took a step away. 'Look, I'm not really interested…' I was still shaken and did not want to hear a confession about their affair.

'No, wait. Please. I have something important to say. Something I couldn't put in my letter.' There was sincerity in her voice.

I exhaled, a kind of resignation.

'As I was saying, we got talking and I realised that his wife was *you*. You'd disappeared after the… you know… *explosion*.' She whispered the last word.

I turned and faced her squarely.

'It wasn't until I mentioned how I knew you, that Andrew told me you'd told him about it. I'd no idea where you'd gone! He made me promise not to tell anyone where you were. Did he not ever mention me?' Her face was open, expectant.

'A letter came with his effects, half-finished, addressed to "Georgia", who I presume is you. He must have been killed before he had the chance to send it.'

'He was a good man, Hannah. He said how war changed his perspective. Even told me he'd not been the most attentive husband but that would change when he got back home. He mentioned that I should write to you. To explain what I knew. He was probably sending me your address. He forgot to tell me after we got chatting. When I found out he was one of the casualties of the Dardanelles, I thought that chance had gone.'

'So, you and he were simply friends?' In the presence of this artless woman, it seemed silly even to be saying it.

'What? Good Gracious, yes!' She started to colour even more. 'Is that what you've been thinking?'

Poor Andy, I'd misjudged him.

But something felt unresolved. 'Look, I've been rude, please come inside. I have cold lemonade and fans.'

'It was a terrible business. I don't know why they call it the *Great War*. There was nothing great about it.' Georgia was now a more natural colour. Sitting on my breezy veranda not far from the day beds, she had unbuttoned her blouse and rolled up her sleeves, but only at my urging. She'd dosed herself with lavender water to smother the body odour that humidity extracts from unprepared new arrivals.

'You might have to learn to wear a little less clothing if you are to survive out here,' I said.

'I've been hearing all these theories about white women in the tropics, how we should dispense with the corset and other such uncivilised surrender. I've met many who are still wearing their good woollen ones from the Old Country.' She said this with the deprecation used by new arrivals before they encountered their first real monsoon.

'I'm surprised you say that. Given the views we shared on female constriction and immobility. Even a health bodice would be preferable.' She must have been around my age, but already there was a sunken chest, rounded belly and a sloping back, common deformities wrought by the corset.

She caught my expression. 'Oh, I don't wear it tight. Besides, it helped disguise my politics. And it keeps my mother happy, not that she would see me out here. But still.'

'We've become quieter, haven't we. Almost silenced.'

'Yes, I'm a very different animal now. Not quite so splendid. Had all my ideals knocked out of me in service. Besides, what's the point? It's nineteen twenty-four already and we still haven't got the vote in Britain, well, not unless you're an old girl of thirty like me, *and* you've married into property. Our crusade didn't bring much change, really – the war stopped us in our tracks. We might as well have been bashing our heads against a brick wall.'

'It did get the message across. We not only have the vote in Australia, but we can stand for Parliament, too. I'm sure you're aware of this. But... you say you know me from the Union?'

'Really, I should be hurt that you don't remember me. Admittedly I wasn't a regular at the meetings, or perhaps not as passionate as our other sisters. It was all so exciting though. Showing up the old guard.'

'I'm sure I noticed you at the time. You do seem familiar.'

'You were close to that doctor – Jane Landy. We all idolised her.'

'I haven't heard from her in years.'

'We all lost track, didn't we? What about your family? Do they not keep in touch?'

'I haven't heard from my family in a long while.'

'Oh...'

'No, I'm fine with that now. But Jane, how is she?'

'Very well. At least when I last heard a few years back.'

'What I meant was – did she end up in gaol?'

'For what?'

'For the explosion, of course. That's why you're here, isn't it? You've been sent to find me?'

Georgia looked at me with amazement. 'Only a few were caught, including me, the coward of the bunch. Ironic isn't it. They waited until our next meeting. They knew it was done by one of us because of the note they found at the scene. The one about votes for women.'

'It was meant to be found.'

'But most of us managed to disappear into our families, who didn't have a clue what we'd been up to. Still don't, or if they do, they don't want it to become public knowledge. But the police did know your name. It wasn't me who mentioned it, even though they had some inventive ways to try to get us to talk. I thought you were so brave climbing up Blackford Hill that night on your own, staking out the observatory with a bomb in your handbag.'

'I obviously didn't stake it out well enough, did I?'

'No, but…'

'I watched and waited until it got dark, and I was sure no one was there. I didn't see him, I swear. That poor man.'

'Andrew said you were beating yourself up about it. He said I should write to you. He said he would too, but I guess…'

'Look, I killed an innocent man. Was he a guard? Do they know? When I broke in and threw the jar inside, I never saw him. If I had I wouldn't have gone ahead with it.'

'He was homeless. A drunkard. But Hannah, the thing is, he'd been lying dead in the bushes for at least a day before the explosion. This is what I've come to tell you.'

I sat in shock, processing her words.

'How he wasn't noticed I don't know. But it was the autopsy that gave it away. The police kept this quiet.'

'Why?'

'Perhaps they were trying to flush out the perpetrator, you know, with guilt or something… sorry… You know how much we were hated. They took ages to drop the charges. Kept us in the cells as long as they could. But couldn't tie any of us personally to the blast. I was in real trouble with my family. Had to get away. That's the main reason I joined the Red Cross at the Front. They still haven't forgiven me and that's really why I'm out here in the colonies. That way they get to pretend I'm rather a hero. An adventurer. Doing good works and all the rest.'

'I'm so sorry you had to go through that, Georgia. But, you know, we were the lucky ones. The girls from the factories had a lot more to lose than us. They were the brave ones. We were just hobbyists, targeting those damned male bastions which excluded women. The Royal Observatory stood for all of that.'

'And the factory girls had a lot more to gain, too. But you were one of the bravest in our lot. And the smartest.'

'Not at all. I only volunteered because I lived close to the hill. It was within walking distance of home. But when it was done, Georgia, I bolted like a coward. You stayed.'

'But you were injured. They found your blood – though they thought it was from the dead man, at first.'

'Glass fragments all over me, in my scalp. And my arm was torn from the window panels when I broke through the door with a brick. Went home first, but my father had been wakened by the explosion. He put two and two together. There might have been traces of black in our kitchen where I'd processed the chemicals and charcoal powder late that night. He threw me out in a rage, yet there I was dripping blood, and he did nothing to help. I didn't wait long enough for him to calm down. Jane Landy treated me, though it was a while before I got to her. She said I'd been lucky with my injuries.'

'Judging by the damage you did to the building – floors shattered, walls cracked – you certainly were!'

'I still get episodes – headaches and whatnot – from it.'

'You were a bit of a hero of mine. But I have to admit, when you escaped, I was disappointed. I'd go so far as to say that after my stint in the watch-house, discharged with gastritis, I disliked you for a while. I wasn't the only one. Do you remember Violet Stevenson? She used to go on and on about you in gaol. They thought it was her at first. She was probably the one who gave the police your name. We used to keep her on the outer in the WSPU because it was clear she wasn't quite right in the head.'

'Now you mention it, I think I remember. I didn't have anything to do with her, didn't even know her name, but yes, I think she's been sending me threatening letters. I've no idea how she found me. You didn't tell her where I was, did you.'

'Goodness, no. I didn't have a clue where you were until I arrived in North Queensland. But Violet used to go to church in Morningside – that's where your family live, isn't it?'

'Yes, that's their church. But I can't imagine anyone from my family telling her, or anyone for that matter. Unless…' I'd asked my father to make discreet enquiries about the dead man's family and that obviously led him nowhere. But if he'd read Violet's name in the papers, he would have connected her to me. He must have approached her.

Georgia rested her hand on mine, a wordless comfort. 'That makes sense. Violet has been admitted to a mental institution now. But it wasn't easy for any of us in the gaol. One particular nasty fellow, a corporal, when he was shoving me out of the cell, he said: "Pity no one knows the tramp was dead already". That's how I first found out about the autopsy. Now, I'm not so sure if your crime, or should I say, *our* crime of property damage, would be worth the expense in chasing you all the way here. If they find you, they have to find us, and we'd all be happy for you to keep lying low. I have to say, Hannah, they're still keen to be seen solving the mystery of Blackford Hill.'

'Call me *Anna*, please. Actually, I'm Mrs Anna Austen now.'

'Austen?'

'It's a long story. I've remarried.'

'Well, what's in a name, eh?'

'Nothing, I suppose. But for me, a lot.' Tom and I were closer than ever, now.

'So, that's what I've been trying to tell you. I couldn't work out where you lived until I came up here. How glad I am that I did.'

'That man on the hill. For years he's been haunting me in dreams. But he's not the only one.' I told her about Sarah Hartley and her baby; how I'd been on the brink of being criminally charged after Hartley's civil matter; how prosecution eventually dropped the case.

'That's the risk of our profession,' she said, as if understanding. She put her arm around me, and to her astonishment I started to sob. Her kindness had cut through. 'Remember, you're free now, Anna.'

I knew this was not completely true.

I resolved to write to Angus to tell him about Evie. He'd pass the news on to my parents, and I had to trust that they would write back. Evie would discover her family, and Malcolm could live again through her eyes.

'I just hope by the time Evie has a daughter *she* won't have to fight for equality,' I said.

'Listen to you! The rebel hasn't really left, has it?'

'I'm sorry – back on my soapbox. Maybe in thirty years' time I'll get my placards out and hit the streets again. I certainly don't want to grow old gracefully. Do you?'

She hugged me, and we laughed, and there was no need for words.

Leon and Sybil's celebration of their living-together-no-need-for-marriage relationship was flamboyant, boisterous, and happier than any formal wedding I'd attended. Sybil wore orange flowers from Leon's hibiscus bushes in her hair, and Dorrie mingled easily with the bohemian miscellany of Leon and Sybil's friends. There was a baked pig-in-the-ground, and the amateur opera group brought guitars and ukuleles.

The party rollicked through the night and as the moon rose over the esplanade, Leon carried Sybil into the ocean for a theatrical kiss. I could see the logic in their arrangement. This way she could keep her career, though her work at the District would never make her truly independent. She'd still have the draconian moral standards, and probably snide comments, to deal with.

I resolved that when Sybil had had enough, I'd ask her to join me. I needed a partner for my hospital, someone I could trust who had experience in the tropical frontier. And there would be no objection to her new living arrangements.

The past reaches out to the present, and you invite it in, though warily. I can hear the car engine that night, the only sound as we drove the few blocks home. The night carts had finished, and it was too early for the milk vans. Gas streetlamps lit the road in incandescent patches – electricity would arrive the next year. The mountain range had drawn mist down into the settlement, mingling with the salty dawn air. As we approached the Huntly with its white verandas, tongue and groove walls, and doors never quite meeting the frame, it floated in the gaslight, much like the one in Tom's painting, and as welcoming as a lover's arms.

ACKNOWLEDGEMENTS

A Hospital in the Clouds takes place in Cairns just after the First World War. Researching those times helped to open up the vibrant frontier world of my characters.

In the years creating this novel, there are many who have assisted in my research. I thank those historians, medical academics, scientists, and librarians, with specific gratitude to the staff of the State Library of Queensland, the Cairns Historical Society Research Centre, the Historic Village at Herberton, and Roderick Fletcher who provided scientific information about the cane industry.

For all those who have read and provided useful commentary on the manuscript, especially my first readers and editors, Nadine Davidoff and Philip Neilsen, I give you my heartfelt thanks.

My particular thanks and appreciation go to Les Zigomanis for his unfailingly generous support and professional assistance in this edition of *A Hospital in the Clouds*.

I respectfully acknowledge the Traditional Owners of the lands where this story takes place, including the Yirrganydji, Djabugay, Gunggandji and Yidinji nations. I pay respect to Elders past, present and emerging.

ABOUT THE AUTHOR

Mhairead MacLeod's writing is inspired by the lives of real historical figures – ordinary people who have found themselves in extraordinary circumstances – but also by her personal experience.

Like the main character in her novel, she made the journey from Scotland to Cairns when young, and built a career in the tropics.

A Hospital in the Clouds has received national and international screenwriting awards. Her previous historical novel, *The False Men*, has received and been shortlisted for two national manuscript awards.

Before becoming a novelist, Mhairead MacLeod was a lawyer and lecturer.

www.mhaireadmacleod.com

Outer Hebrides, Scotland, 1848

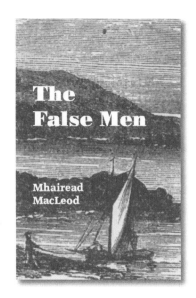

Jess MacKay has led a privileged life as the daughter of a local landowner, sheltered from the harsher aspects of life. Courted by the eligible Patrick Cooper, the Laird's new commissioner, Jess's future is mapped out, until Lachlan Macdonald arrives on her island amid rumours of forced evictions just to the south. As the uncompromising brutality of the Clearances reaches her community and Jess sees her friends ripped from their homes, she must decide where her heart, and her loyalties, truly lie.

Set against the evocative backdrop of the Hebrides and inspired by a true story, *The False Men* is a compelling tale of love in a turbulent past that resonates with the upheavals of the modern world.

> *"Mhairead MacLeod passionately and evocatively tells a story of a community split by status, privilege and power, and the personal story of one woman's courageous struggle to resist social pressure and choose her own path, a struggle which will resonate with readers today."*
> — Stornoway Gazette

> *"The False Men shines a light on the personal stories of those impacted by the violence perpetrated on families by their landlords and neighbours in a period of Scottish history that devastated communities, split families and depopulated huge swathes of the country."*
> — The Scotsman

Printed in Great Britain
by Amazon

61568585R00190